HEMLOCK ISLAND

ALSO BY KELLEY ARMSTRONG

Rockton

The Deepest of Secrets	*Watcher in the Woods*
A Stranger in Town	*This Fallen Prey*
Alone in the Wild	*A Darkness Absolute*

Cainsville

Rituals	*Deceptions*
Betrayals	*Visions*
Omens	

Age of Legends

Forest of Ruin
Empire of Night
Sea of Shadows

The Blackwell Pages (co-written with Melissa Marr)

Thor's Serpents
Odin's Ravens
Loki's Wolves

Otherworld

Thirteen	*Living with the Dead*	*Industrial Magic*
Spell Bound	*Personal Demon*	*Dime Store Magic*
Waking the Witch	*No Humans Involved*	*Stolen*
Frostbitten	*Broken*	*Bitten*
	Haunted	

Darkest Powers & Darkness Rising

The Rising	*The Reckoning*
The Calling	*The Awakening*
The Gathering	*The Summoning*

Nadia Stafford

Wild Justice
Made to be Broken
Exit Strategy

Standalone novels

Wherever She Goes	*The Masked Truth*
Aftermath	*Missing*
The Life She Had	*Every Step She Takes*

Rip Through Time

A Rip Through Time
The Poisoner's Ring

HEMLOCK ISLAND

A NOVEL

KELLEY ARMSTRONG

ST. MARTIN'S PRESS
NEW YORK

First published in the United States by St. Martin's Press,
an imprint of St. Martin's Publishing Group

HEMLOCK ISLAND. Copyright © 2023 by KLA Fricke, Inc. All rights reserved.
Printed in the United States of America. For information, address
St. Martin's Publishing Group, 120 Broadway, New York, NY 10271.

www.stmartins.com

Library of Congress Cataloging-in-Publication Data

Names: Armstrong, Kelley, author.
Title: Hemlock Island / Kelley Armstrong.
Description: First edition. | New York: St. Martin's Press, 2023.
Identifiers: LCCN 2023019745 | ISBN 9781250284198 (hardcover) |
    ISBN 9781250322104 (Canadian edition) | ISBN 9781250284204 (ebook)
Subjects: LCGFT: Horror fiction. | Novels.
Classification: LCC PR9199.4.A8777 H46 2023 | DDC 813/.6—ddc23/
    eng/20230512
LC record available at https://lccn.loc.gov/2023019745

Our books may be purchased in bulk for promotional, educational, or business use.
Please contact your local bookseller or the Macmillan Corporate and Premium Sales
Department at 1-800-221-7945, extension 5442, or by email at
MacmillanSpecialMarkets@macmillan.com.

First Edition: 2023
First International Edition: 2023

10 9 8 7 6 5 4 3 2 1

For Jeff

HEMLOCK ISLAND

PROLOGUE

I never wanted to rent out the island house. Even after a year of doing exactly that, the very thought has me raiding my tiny stash of edibles before the panic attack hits. The island is my sanctuary. It's also the one thing in this world that is mine, all mine.

The island had been a wedding gift from Kit, and he insisted on signing it over after we split. The problem is that Hemlock House is not some tiny cottage perched on a sliver of land. It's a custom-built home on a five-acre private island in Lake Superior.

It's the sort of place that a guy like Christian "Kit" Hayes—CEO of his family's tech corporation—can afford as a getaway. It is *not* the kind of place his high school English teacher ex can afford to maintain . . . unless I rent it out. Unless I allow total strangers to invade my private domain. Allow them to move the chairs from my secret spots, to burn down my gazebo with a bonfire, to destroy my grandmother's coffee table with what are clearly canid teeth marks despite promising their dog would stay outside . . .

I told myself to stop being so sentimental. If I want this amazing place, I need to make concessions. Just keep my insurance paid up and be happy that the worst thing that can happen is a burned gazebo or a chewed table.

That is not the worst thing.

The worst thing is that someone now knows every inch of your private space, and they can do whatever they want to it—and, maybe, to you.

ONE

aney," a voice says in my ear. "Aunt Laney!"

The last one startles me, gasping, out of sleep. Some parents call their kids by their first and middle name when they're in trouble. My sixteen-year-old niece calls me "Aunt" when I'm doing something to piss her off, and right now what I'm apparently doing is sleeping when she wants to talk to me.

My mumbled "What?" comes out as a groan.

"Your phone?" The offending object appears, waggling back and forth as I struggle to focus on blurred text.

Four missed calls.

I thump back onto the pillow. "It's the middle of the night," I mutter. Then I bolt upright in my narrow bed. Four missed calls in the middle of the night. I snatch the phone from Madison.

"It's not Gran or Gramps," she says. "It's the campground at Fox Bay."

It takes a moment for my sleepy brain to process that. I blink, seeing only Madison's face hovering in front of me, spiky auburn hair framing a pale oval face so much like my sister's it makes my heart clench with grief.

"Laney?"

What was she saying? Right. The call came from a campground at—

"Shit!" I blink fast. "Hemlock House."

I fumble to retrieve my messages. "Please don't tell me it's a fire. I told the renters the area's under a no-open-flame order, and it's always 'Oh, but it was just a little fire.' If they—"

The phone vibrates. FOXY LADY CAMPGROUND flashes on the screen, and I jab the Accept button.

"Hello?" I blurt.

I'm quivering, rocked by visions of Hemlock House in flames. Does insurance cover it if renters light a fire after I warned them? Did I warn them by text? If it was a phone conversation, they can deny—

"What is going on in that house of yours?" The woman's voice is loud enough that I think I have it on speaker, and when I hit the button to turn it off, I actually switch *into* speaker mode. I go to flip it back, but Madison swats my hand and leans in to listen.

"I'm sorry," I say. "Is there a problem? I'm not there right now. I've rented out the house—"

"I know that," the woman snaps. "Because you rented it to me."

"Ms. . . ." I struggle for the name. "Teller?"

"Abbas. Mrs. Abbas."

Right. The Tellers were the last renters. Or maybe the ones before that . . .

"Mrs. Abbas," I say. "Is there a problem?"

"No, I'm calling to ask how to use the shower . . . in the middle of the night, after driving that leaky boat five *miles* to town, and then hunting everywhere for a pay phone because our cell phones won't work even when we're *not* on the island."

My first impulse is to say that the boat is in better shape than my damn car because I need to keep it that way for guests. Any "leak" was water sloshing over the sides.

But that's not her point, and so I say, as calmly as I can, "What's the problem, Mrs. Abbas?"

"There is blood in the green bedroom."

Madison's brows shoot up.

"So there seems to be blood—" I begin.

"Not seems to be. *Is.* My husband is a doctor." Her voice goes distant, as if she's moved the pay phone receiver away from her mouth. "Tell her it's blood."

"It is blood," a man says, his accented voice sounding weary.

"Okay, so there *is* blood in the green bedroom. The last guests weren't planning on using it, but I presume they did, and the caretaker didn't realize that and didn't change the sheets. I'm very sor—"

"The blood isn't on the sheets. It's in the closet."

"In the *closet*?" That's Madison. I dimly realize I should shush her, but my gut is clenching too hard for me to follow through.

Not again.

Please, not again.

"Yes, the closet," Mrs. Abbas says. "I woke up cold. You said not to light any fires, so we couldn't start the woodstove."

"I didn't mean the—" I stop myself. "You woke up cold and . . ."

"I'd already used the blanket from our closet. I was checking the second bedroom. I opened the closet door, and it was right there."

"The blan—? The blood?"

"Yes. On the door. All *over* the door. And scratches, as if someone tried to claw their way out."

"Holy shit!" Madison whispers as I clap my hand to her mouth.

"Blood and scratches?" I say. "*Inside* the bedroom closet door?"

There's a shuffling sound, interspersed with angry words. Then the man's voice comes on.

"We do not actually believe anyone was confined in that closet, Ms. Kilpatrick. There is no lock, obviously. We believe the last person who rented your house played a practical joke. Your cleaning woman must not have needed to access that closet, and so she did not see the damage. My wife is understandably distraught."

"Understandably, yes. I am so sorry. I'll refund the rest of your booking, of course, though you're welcome to stay for the whole thing. Monday was your check-out day, wasn't it?"

"You're refunding *all* of our booking," Mrs. Abbas says in the background. "And I'm not spending another minute on that island. There's no cell service. No telephone. No internet."

All of which they knew when they rented it. That's a selling point for most renters, and just in case they miss that heavily bolded part in my listing, I make sure they understand before they rent it.

Still, I get what she's saying. Yes, she knew Hemlock Island was remote and unreachable, but she'd only been thinking of how nice it'd be not to get work messages on her vacation. She hadn't considered what that would be like when *she* needed to contact someone.

"I understand—" I begin.

"No, I don't think you do," she says, still in the background. "You're lucky we don't contact the police. We *will* contact the rental agency—"

"No, Charlotte," her husband says. "This is not Ms. Kilpatrick's fault. It is the previous guest playing a prank. You will need to file a report on them with the agency, Ms. Kilpatrick. You might also, if I am not being too bold, suggest that your cleaning woman do a more thorough examination of the house after each rental. I can imagine it is not easy when you have such a popular property and a narrow window in which to clean."

He's right about that. How many times has Nate—our cleaner—told me that he's shown up to find the previous guests still in bed? Or had the next guests arrive hours early and grumble when he politely suggests they explore the island while he finishes cleaning?

"I'll do a thorough examination myself," I say. "Again, I am so sorry. I'm refunding your money right now." I open my app. "Then I'll head out there and see what's going on."

I bet it was a raccoon," Madison says when I hang up. "Hopefully not a rat. We haven't seen rats on the island, right?"

I stare at her as I try to connect her words to what just happened.

"Blood and scratches in the closet?" she says. "Obviously, some poor critter got trapped in there. Maybe a bat. That would make the most sense, right? A bat?"

I squeeze my eyes shut, struggling to collect my thoughts. Then I swing my legs out of bed. I head to the kitchen and flip on the coffee machine.

Madison's footfalls pad from my room, which is about ten paces from the kitchen. Yes, it's a tiny house, but it's all I could afford in Madison's school district. After my sister died, I couldn't bear to up-end my niece's life any further. I'd paid Anna's remaining medical bills with the sale of her heavily mortgaged house and rented the one place I could kinda-sorta afford on the edge of her upscale suburban neighborhood.

"It's four in the morning, Laney," Madison says when she comes in the kitchen. "Why are you making coffee?"

"I need to head to Hemlock Island and resolve this before they register a complaint, which Mrs. Abbas absolutely will."

"Yeah, she's really freaked."

"I don't blame her. I'm sorry, Mads, but I might not be back until late. We'll need to find you a place to stay the night."

I brace for her to say she'll stay here, which will inevitably lead to a fight. She'll argue she's old enough to stay alone, and I'll remind her about what happened last month when some guy peeped at her while I was out late.

I start to put my coffee cup under the brewer, but she gets her travel mug in there first.

"I'm going with you," she says.

"Uh-uh. I'm *not* taking you to the island after that."

"After what? A bat got trapped in the closet?" She peers at me. "There's more to the story, isn't there?"

I concentrate on pouring exactly the right amount of cream into my empty cup. "More to what story?"

"You never even thought it might be an animal," she says. "That guy said it was a prank, and you rolled with it. Now you're rushing out to investigate."

"I'm not rushing out." I fill my mug and settle onto a wobbly kitchen chair. "See?"

"What else has happened?"

Here's where I always get stuck in this new role as Madison's legal guardian. I need to be the parent, not the fun aunt, and I'm grappling with that shift. Which is worse? Lying to her? Or sharing something potentially disturbing? Knowing my niece, I cross my fingers and make what I hope is the right choice.

"There have been other things," I say. "Other . . . incidents."

"Incidents?"

I set my mug down on the thrift-shop table. "Nate found charred animal bones in the boathouse. I found a hex circle under the crawl-space rug and then feathers and bones hanging from the gazebo."

"Ah, Halloween came early this year. Some renter's kids got bored and staged a house of horrors for the next guests." She takes a bag of Oreos from the cupboard. "Part of me wants to high-five them for their creativity and part wants to give them shit for scaring innocent people. I blame Mom for the finger-wagging. The high-fives are totally on you."

"Me?"

"Uh, remember the stories you told me when I was a kid? The haunted houses we set up? The Halloween parties that had parents telling you off for giving their kids nightmares? I always said you're missing your calling. Mysteries are fine, but you really should be writing horror." She flips me an Oreo. "So some kids staged . . ."

She stops, cookie halfway to her mouth. "Wait. How long has this been going on?"

"Nate found the bones in mid-August."

"And no one has used the green bedroom since? Nate hasn't opened that closet door since? That's not possible."

"The room has been used twice since, and Nate and I thoroughly searched the house after I found the hex circle."

"Meaning it's repeated violations. Not a one-time staging."

"Yes."

"Local kids sneaking in between guests?"

"The security system says no unexpected access. The house hasn't been empty since spring."

"Then it must be the renters." She frowns in thought. "Any repeat customers?"

"Nope, which means it can't be renters, and it wouldn't be Nate."

"So we have a mystery to solve?" She grabs the bag of cookies and her travel mug. "Excellent. When do we leave?"

TWO

It takes four hours to get to Fox Bay, and I don't leave right away. I insist on having breakfast while waiting until the sun's fully up. Once we leave the city, it's a gorgeous drive along winding roads through trees painted red and gold. It's peak fall foliage season, and while I complain about the slow-driving gawkers, I'm mostly irked because I can't be one of them. It's a perfect autumn day, sunny enough to have the windows down, breezy enough for fallen leaves to dance and swirl before us.

How many times had I made this drive with Kit, my feet out the window or my nose pressed to it looking for wildlife? He'd rip over the hills and zoom around the curves in a roller-coaster ride that always made me grin. We'd stop to buy in-season fruit along the way and pull into our favorite roadside bakery to stock up on cinnamon rolls.

Kit and I always joked that we'd had a surprise wedding—a surprise to everyone including us. Growing up, he'd been my best friend's little brother. Then, when my sister got her cancer diagnosis, I'd taken a job back in our home city. Kit reached out and a catch-up dinner blossomed into friendship. When I sold my first book, he whisked me off to Vegas to celebrate, and we ended up in bed. Two days later, we were exchanging vows in a wedding chapel. There may have been alcohol involved.

We made it work for a while. Hell, there hadn't been much *work* involved. We slid into marriage as we'd slid into friendship, so easily and naturally that I'd wake up, see Kit beside me, and grin like I'd won the lottery without buying a ticket. Then the pandemic hit, and we survived but our marriage didn't, and I'm not quite sure why. My surprise marriage ended in a surprise divorce, and I'm still reeling.

When I see the sign for Fox Bay, I turn left. I don't need to pass through the town itself, which can be a relief. If anyone spotted me, I'd catch shit for not stopping, and stopping means chatting and then coffee and more chatting . . . I love that about Fox Bay, but today is all about expediency. Get to Hemlock Island. See what's going on. Fix it. Get Madison back home.

We round a corner to see Lake Superior stretching out to the horizon, and I motion as if pulling a conductor's bell. "Last call for internet connectivity."

Madison flips through her phone, getting and returning messages before we'll be offline until we return from the island. I barely drive another half mile before the cell phone signal indicator on my dashboard vanishes.

"We are officially disconnected," I say. "No email, no texts, no voice mail, no social media, no way to summon help if a masked killer leaps from the bushes."

"'Tis the season," she says. "Though, up here, if some guy in a goalie mask leaps out, he's probably looking for his lost road-hockey ball."

"Truth."

To my left is the local campground with the pay phone my renters had used. I slow and peer into the visitors' lot. I'll notice their vehicle if it's there. The people who rent Hemlock House do not stay in a place like Foxy Lady Campground, where the facilities can best be described as "rustic."

I turn in to the boat launch. There's a giant willow in the middle of the lot, and I'm steering around it when Madison says, "Is that Kit's car?"

I hit the brakes so fast that Madison jolts forward, and for a split second, my heart stops as I imagine her flying through the windshield.

"Oww . . ." she says as she plucks at her still-fastened seat belt.

That heart-stopping moment also makes me forget *why* I jammed on the brakes. Then I see the back end of a silver car. Yes, it looks like Kit's, but I don't even know what model of car *I* drive—it's my sister's, and I took over payments that I can barely afford, as another part of ensuring a stable transition for Madison. I couldn't exactly teach her to drive on my motorcycle. Well, I could, and she'd have loved that, but no. Responsible Parenting 101.

I presume the high-end silver sedan belongs to the Abbases, and I cringe. They've stayed behind to give me shit in person. Great.

Behind the car, a woman stands with her back to me. She adjusts one sleeve of her chic jacket with a dark-skinned hand. Mrs. Abbas, I presume.

The woman turns, and my insides clench. It's not Mrs. Abbas. It's a woman my age, with a flawless profile and intricate braids.

Jayla.

Oh, shit.

Jayla Hayes. Kit's older sister.

In high school, Jayla and I had been best friends. In college, we'd danced around the possibility of more. Jayla had been figuring out her sexuality as she realized that guys didn't do it for her. I'd dated both boys and girls in high school, having discovered that for me it was about being attracted to a person rather than a gender.

In the end, Jayla and I didn't do more than flirt with the idea. One awkward date, a few kisses, and we realized we didn't click on that level.

After that, we should have gone back to being friends, right? It didn't work out that way. She went off to law school and drifted, and there's been a Jayla-sized hole in my life ever since.

That *is* Kit's car, then. Jayla must have borrowed it—

"Kit!" Madison shouts as she gets out, slamming the car door.

I dimly hear Madison greet Jayla, too, and there's more said, but I don't catch it. I'm frozen in the driver's seat as Kit appears. He looks toward my car and shades his eyes against the sun. Then he lifts a hand in a tentative wave.

If Madison were still in the car, I might have hit reverse, peeling from the lane. That's silly, of course. Our split was amicable. *Hey, we tried, and it didn't work, no hard feelings.*

That's the story.

That's the lie.

Still, I've put on my happy face for Madison. She adores Kit—has since she was a baby—and I'm not about to take him out of her life. Neither of them deserves that.

I steel myself and open the car door. In three long-legged strides, Kit's there and holding it for me. I look up to feel my heart twist as I see the Kit I know—dressed in a hoodie, faded jeans, and hiking boots. It's so much easier to see him in an expensive suit, all corporate CEO, a far cry from the little kid with a skateboard, the teen with dreadlocks and a guitar, the husband who'd come to Hemlock Island every weekend, looking exactly like this.

"Hey, you," he says.

"Hey, yourself." I wave at his face. "Check out the new look."

He rubs a hand over the short and perfectly trimmed beard. "You hate it."

"No, it makes you look very distinguished."

He crosses his eyes and sticks his tongue out the side of his mouth, and I laugh, the tension slipping away, as hard as I try to gather it back in.

"*So* distinguished," I say, and his dark eyes light up in a grin.

The moment lingers two heartbeats and then fades. He clears his throat. "I, uh, heard what happened. With the renters."

Tension snaps back as my gaze shoots to Madison.

"Nah, it wasn't Mads," he says. "Bill at the campground called me this morning. I decided to come up and check it out for you."

He glances at Jayla, who's walking toward us with one arm looped over Madison's shoulders.

"Yep," Jayla says. "That's exactly how it happened."

I narrow my eyes at her. She meets my look with one that warns me if I call out Kit on this particular lie, I'll be dealing with her.

"So," Jayla says. "We hitting the high seas? Or hanging out awkwardly until nightfall?"

"Ooh, we *should* wait until night," Madison says. "Get the full-creep effect."

They riff on that, but I don't hear it. I don't hear anything. Don't see anything either, until Kit's face is lowered right in front of mine.

"Laney?" he murmurs.

I snap out of it, and pull my jacket tighter. "I've got this. You guys go into town for an early lunch. The fish-and-chips place is open."

"What?" Madison says. "We're all going out—"

"I've got it." I head toward the dockside lockbox.

Jayla jangles the keys. "Not without these." She walks toward the boat. "Someone put blood in your closet, Laney. From what we heard, it isn't the first disturbing thing that's happened out there. You are not going alone."

Without waiting for a reply, she starts the boat. "Pile in. Last one on board is swimming."

I tell Kit and Jayla what's been happening on Hemlock Island. They say little, and I struggle not to hear judgment in that.

Kit is at the wheel. He's the expert, having grown up with boats. No yachts. The Hayeses might be that kind of rich, but they aren't that kind of family. No country clubs. No yacht clubs. No dinner clubs. Not his scene, and definitely not Jayla's.

I look over at him, piloting the boat, and the sight is so familiar that I need to lock my knees to keep from walking up beside him, leaning against his shoulder, feeling his arm go around my waist . . .

I shake off the thought and glance over at Jayla. Her stylish jacket looks out of place here, but otherwise, she's dressed for Hemlock Island, in sneakers, tights, and a baggy men's shirt. She's comparing sneakers with Madison, who's wearing her "October specials"—a pair of horror-themed Vans. Then they're trading shoes, and I'm watching them, remembering when Jayla and I used to do that. I'm imagining I can hear her laugh over the motor and the surf and—

"What happened to the boat?" Kit calls.

I give a start and glance over at him. He waves me up to the helm. I hesitate, and then make my way there.

"The engine sounds different," he says.

"It needed some work."

"Seems like a total overhaul."

I shrug. "Renters. Insurance covered it."

Not true. The engine blew right after the warranty ran out. I'd tried going through insurance—I pay a small fortune to allow renters with boating experience to use it—but they called it normal wear and tear, and it cost me another small fortune to fix.

"You should have an old beater for the renters," he says. "Save this one for you."

"I'm fine."

He takes out his phone with one hand and brings up his notes. "I'll have a boat here by next—"

I put my hand over his phone screen. "No, Kit. Please."

He looks away, his jaw working. Does he think I'm punishing him by not taking his money? Making him look bad?

I already seem like "that woman"—the one who marries a rich guy in Vegas, sticks around for a few years, and then puts out her hand for a divorce settlement. I won't be her. I won't even risk being mistaken for her.

"I'm good," I say. "Really. Have I told you how much people pay to rent Hemlock Island?"

"You don't need to rent it out, Laney."

"I want to."

"Bull. Shit." He meets my gaze. "Look me in the eye and tell me that you honestly don't mind having total strangers living in your house. And now this? I know you've been up here writing, alone, at least once while all this has been going on. It isn't safe."

"I'm thinking of getting a dog."

His eyes narrow. "Really? Or are you blowing me off? If you actually want a dog—" He stops, and I tense for him to say he'll buy me one. Instead, he rolls his shoulders back and says, "That's a good idea. I know Mads would like one."

"She would."

"Maybe a poodle? I remember the one you had growing up. Ginger, right?"

I relax. "I've been thinking of a standard poodle, too. They're good stealth watch dogs."

He grins. "They are. Remember the time you tried to sneak out to meet Jayla, and Ginger woke up the neighborhood, barking like you were being abducted by aliens?" He snaps his fingers. "Wait. Isn't that what you told your parents? That you'd seen what looked like an alien ship, gone out into the yard and that's what Ginger was barking about?"

"Hey, it worked. Mom and Dad didn't think I actually saw aliens, but they bought that I'd go outside for a closer look if I thought I did."

He laughs, and I am caught in the tractor beam of that laugh. This is how I want things to be between us. The happy version, where we can still laugh together and pretend he didn't walk away during the worst time of my life, pretend he isn't desperate to buy his way out of that guilt.

I want the lie.

We move to the bow, where I lean out, catching the spray as I focus on the distant green and gray mass that slowly takes form as Hemlock Island. When I see it, my heart speeds up, and I find myself leaning forward until I can just make out the solar panels atop the house.

People talk about their "happy place," and I thought that was sentimental nonsense until Kit brought me to Hemlock Island. It wasn't just that he'd bought me a damn island as a wedding gift. He somehow figured out exactly the sort of place my soul longed for, even when I didn't know it myself.

And now someone is fucking with that. I've stomached renters' intrusions and incivility. I've chirped "Accidents happen!" when my things are destroyed. I've weathered the screaming when I politely inform renters that I can't get someone out until morning to fix something *they* broke. I've endured the bad reviews complaining because I lock up my personal boathouse . . . and I've endured those locks being broken, my kayak and paddleboard used. But this? Staging weird ritualistic shit as a prank? Scaring off the guests I desperately need?

This I will not endure. I'm going to find who the hell is behind—

I freeze. I've been gazing up at the wooded bluff where I like to sit and write, my legs dangling over the rocky edge, surf crashing below. Now I'm gazing at that spot . . . and someone is gazing back.

My foot slides as I reel backward. Kit is there in a heartbeat, catching me. For a second, I let myself stay there, secure in his embrace. Then I grip the railing, straighten, and stare up at the bluff, searching for what I'd seen.

"Laney?"

I snatch the binoculars and fumble to get them up to my eyes. My gaze sweeps the top of the bluff. I stop at a tall tree stump, scorched by a lightning strike. Through the binoculars, it is clearly a stump, but when I lower them, it looks like a human figure.

"Laney?"

Madison's there with Jayla, joining Kit in frowning at me.

"I thought I saw a . . ."

I see their faces, and I anticipate their reactions, Jayla thinking I'm just spooked, Kit worried, in case I really did see a person.

I did *not* see a person. I have an overactive imagination—that's why I'm a writer. When I'm stressed, it's an explosive combination.

"A moose," I blurt. "I thought I saw a moose."

"On the island?" Jayla says.

"Hey, they can swim," I say, forcing my voice light.

"They can also dive," Kit says. "They eat along the lake bottom."

"Mmm, unproven," Madison says. "That's one of those weird facts that gets passed around, but it may not actually be true."

"Ugh," Jayla says. "Can you please stop educating this child, Laney? She was so much more fun when I could tell her that vegetables would make her hair curly, and she'd believe me."

"I never believed you," Madison says. "I just humored you."

As they keep bantering, I turn to look at the bluff again. There's just that blackened stump. That's what I saw.

It must be.

THREE

Hemlock Island. The name refers to water hemlock, the deadliest plant in North America. It's not supposed to grow this far east, and certainly not on an island in the middle of Lake Superior. We suspect someone planted it here long ago. Kit bought the vacant island from a holding company that didn't even know about the hemlock. It was the locals who warned Kit about it, and he'd used that detail to lower the price, claiming the island was fairly teeming with a highly toxic plant and that's why no one ever built there.

Not true. There's a single patch of hemlock in a marshy area. Before the holding company bought the island, it'd been owned by our cleaner Nate's family, having been passed along through the generations, who only used it for tent camping. Then the holding company made Nate's great-grandparents an offer they couldn't refuse, put the land up for sale at double that price, and anyone who could afford it was turned off by the remoteness.

"It never sold because it was waiting for you." That's what Kit said the first time he brought me here, and . . . is it weird that even while I laughed, part of me felt as if he was right?

While Kit docks the boat, Jayla and Madison hang back, chatting, and I stride toward Hemlock House. She is a thing of beauty, in a way I never imagined a mere building could be. Scandinavian in design, sleek and minimal, blending into the scenery with thick wood beams and walls of windows that give amazing views from all sides.

I climb onto the massive front deck and punch in my door code. Once the whir sounds, I zip through to disarm the alarm. I stop myself at the last second and confirm the red light is on. Yes, the alarm was engaged. Everything is fine. The house is empty.

Why wouldn't it be?

I tell myself that I'm just thinking of the Abbases, in case they chartered another boat and returned to gather any forgotten belongings, but it's more than that. I'm unsettled, and it pisses me off because this is the one place where I can truly relax. Now I'm checking the lock and the alarm and then fighting the urge to go around to the other doors.

It's fine, Laney. Everything is fine.

No, it's not, and it hasn't been fine since Kit walked out and Anna died and—

Breathe, just breathe.

It *will* be fine, and part of that is becoming the parent Madison needs, which means getting my ass up these stairs to check that closet before she sees it.

I zoom up the sweeping open staircase, only to have the railing wiggle under my hand. I pause and give it a shake. It's loose, which means someone decided it'd be fun to slide down the curved banister again and that someone probably wasn't even a child and—

Stop.

I continue my flight up. The house has four bedrooms: a huge main and three smaller chambers. When Kit first showed me the architect's plans, he'd stumbled over himself to explain why there were so many bedrooms. One for Madison, when she came to visit, and one for Anna, if she visited with Madison, and if my parents came, too . . . See? We need four bedrooms. Same as if Jayla came and their parents came or any other combination of guests. It was a vacation house; you couldn't have too many bedrooms.

What he hadn't said was "children." It was too early in our marriage, which had happened so fast that we never had that conversation, and so he wasn't comfortable even joking that we needed rooms for future kids.

Good thing he hadn't, or it would be just one more thing for me to regret. Another shimmering dream of the future to mourn.

The green room—where the Abbases saw the blood—is right beside ours and also the smallest. I stop in the doorway and look at the closet. The door is shut but light shines around the edges.

I rub down the hairs on my neck. The closet lights come on automatically when the door is opened. They're also supposed to shut off automatically after five minutes, in case the closet door isn't closed properly. Our solar and battery array is amazing, but we still can't afford to waste electricity.

The automatic sensor must be broken. It's not the first time that's happened. Kit wanted the house to be state-of-the-art, and I love all the little touches, but each one is also another thing that can break.

I reach the closet and yank open the door. Something swoops from inside. I fall back with a yelp . . . as a thick woolen blanket crumples at my feet. I curse under my breath. Mrs. Abbas must have pulled it partly out.

I kick the blanket aside and open the door all the way to see the inside. When I do, my breath catches.

There's blood smeared down the inside of the door.

I fight a shudder as I make out fingerprints in the blood, whorls and ridges. I push the door open farther, and the light illuminates gouges. I lift my hand, and my fingers fit in the marks.

"Bat or rat?" a voice says, and I jump as Madison and Jayla walk in.

"Holy shit," Madison says, stopping with a squeak of her sneakers.

"Those are *not* from a trapped animal," Jayla says as she walks over.

Madison joins her and examines the blood smears. "The marks are human. I mean, staged, obviously." She glances at me. "Right?"

"Yes," I say as firmly as I can. I glance at Jayla, who nods, and I relax.

Madison does the same thing I did, placing her hand a half inch over the gouges. They fit her fingers, too. It really does look as if someone had been trapped in there, trying to claw her way out, someone like Madison—

No. That's my writer's imagination. No one was locked in my closet. For one thing, there's no lock.

What if someone braced a chair under the handle. What if—?

"That is one sick prank," Jayla says. "We'll find the bastard who did this, and I'll sue their ass for you . . . and strongly suggest court-ordered psychiatric counseling."

Madison nods, and they file from the room, the situation dismissed. I stand there, staring at the gouges. I put my own hand up to them again and imagine—

"Laney?" Madison says, peeking back around the hall door.

"Coming," I say, and hurry after them.

I've shown the others the site of the charred bones in the boathouse and the hex circle under the rug, along with photos from before Nate and I cleaned up. The last stop is the gazebo.

Jayla looks around. "This is new. Why did you put the gazebo *here*?"

The gazebo sits atop a windswept hill looking out over endless water, the distant land hidden by a light mist. The hill is topped with sparse trees, all stunted from the lack of soil and gnarled from the wind exposure.

"Uh, 'cause it's awesome," Madison says, lifting her face to the wind.

"It's dead-ass creepy, that's what it is."

"Like I said, awesome."

Jayla looks between me and Madison, and her eyes pop wide. "Wait! Are you two, like, related or something?"

I lift my middle finger.

"It's atmospheric," Kit says. "Very Laney."

"Dead-ass creepy?" Jayla says.

Kit's right. It's atmospheric. Jayla is also right. It's dead-ass creepy, which might be why I love it. I'm loving it a whole lot less right now, remembering what I'd found here. Two macabre wind chimes—raven feathers threaded through hollow bones, with human hair tied at the ends.

Jayla says something, and I'm turning to her when a whisper floats up from below. I follow the sound. The others don't notice when I step away from the group. They're busy discussing the grotesque wind chimes.

The wind has picked up in the last hour, rustling the trees and whipping Jayla's braids. The forest is below, and I shouldn't be able to hear anyone in it, but I swear I catch whispers on the wind.

I'm about to turn away when another sound slithers up, and this time, there is no mistaking what I hear. A single word.

Laney . . .

I wheel toward it.

"Do you hear that, too?" Madison says, and I audibly exhale in relief. I'm not losing it. Someone *is* out there.

"Oh, yeah," Jayla says. "That's a boat motor." She shades her eyes and squints toward the dock as I pick up the distant sound of a motor. "We are about to have visitors."

FOUR

By the time we reach the dock, it's clear that the boat is heading in the other direction. I start to relax. My first thought had been that the Abbases were returning to finish out their stay, which could turn ugly. But obviously the boat wasn't coming to the island . . .

No, wait. Two figures stand on the dock. A man and a woman . . . with luggage. Shit! The boat dropped them off. The Abbases—

"Sadie?" Jayla says. "What the hell are you doing here?"

I slow, and the seconds seem to drag into minutes as dread settles into my gut.

Jayla must be wrong. That can't possibly be Sadie Emerson. Then the woman moves out of the shadows, revealing a willowy strawberry blonde with upswept hair and a model's grace, tugging a bright pink carry-on after her.

Sadie Emerson.

Sadie and I had been friends in elementary school. Then I met Jayla, and the three of us formed our own little clique until . . .

My breathing quickens. I choke back the panic and slowly pivot to Kit. "What is going on?"

Kit blinks in surprise. "Why are you asking me?"

"Because she knows it's your fault, Kit dear." Sadie passes Kit, her fingers brushing along his arm.

"My—?" Kit says. "What?"

He looks genuinely baffled, and I want to seize on that. See? Ignore the scuttlebutt I read on our high school chat forum.

Did you hear Sadie Emerson is with Kit Hayes?
Again? Weren't they a thing in college?
After college, I think. Before he married Laney Kilpatrick.
Are we sure it ended after that? Wink-wink.

Yes, Kit and Sadie had a "thing" before we got together. According to Kit, it was one night. According to Sadie, it was a whole lotta hot and heavy nights. Either way, being before we married, it's none of my business. It's also none of my business if they're seeing each other now that we're divorced.

"Sadie." Jayla strides over. "What bullshit are you up to now?"

"Bullshit?" Sadie says. "I came to help Laney. Is that okay with you? Kit and I were supposed to have drinks tonight, and he texted to explain why he couldn't make it. Laney has a harassment problem, so I brought a professional to investigate."

She waves, and for the first time, I pull my gaze away enough to see who's with her. When I do, I go still.

"What the *fuck*?" Jayla says.

"Uh . . ." Garrett Emerson's brows rise. "Nice to see you, too, Jayla."

"As I'm sure you all know, my brother is a cop," Sadie says. "A detective now. He was promoted last month."

"No, Sadie," Kit says, his voice a near growl. "Tell me you did not bring—"

"Madison!" Sadie says, and we turn to see Madison looking

at us all, her expression wary confusion. "Oh my God, you have *grown*."

Garrett's gaze travels over Madison, making my hackles rise.

"Been a while, kiddo," he says. "What's with the short hair and the baggy clothes? You decide you're a boy now?"

"*Garrett,*" Sadie says.

"No," Madison says, with exaggerated patience. "This is how I choose to dress today. Tomorrow, I might wear a skirt. The next day, I might wear work boots and flannel. It depends on what I feel like when I wake up, which is none of your business, dude whose name I barely remember."

"Ignore him," Sadie says. "He was just surprised. Your hair looks *amazing,* by the way." She looks at her brother. "Doesn't it suit her face?"

"*Her* face? Or his?" Garrett snarks.

Sadie looks stricken. "I'm so sorry, Madison. Ignore him, please. May I ask your pronouns?"

Kit slides over to block Garrett's reaction, but Madison's not looking Garrett's way and misses his eye roll.

"Still she/her," Madison says. "But thank you for asking."

"It's been forever since I've seen you," Sadie says. "Let's take these bags to the house and talk. You're a high school junior, right?"

Madison glances uncertainly at me. An empathetic kid, she must feel the tension pulsing. I force a smile and wave for her to go along with Sadie.

When they're out of earshot, I turn to Garrett. "Speak to her like that again, and you will be dealing with *me*. Understand?"

His eyes narrow. "I came to help you out, Laney. Don't make me regret it."

"Is that a dare?" Jayla says. "Please tell me it's a dare, because I will happily make you regret it. There are *so* many things I'd like to make you regret. Give me an excuse, please."

When he opens his mouth, I cut him off by saying, "If you're really here to help, then let me explain what's going on."

This is a nightmare. Oh, I don't mean the ritual-staging shit. That I can deal with. It's the company that makes me want to run, screaming, with Madison in tow.

Having Kit here was bad enough. Yes, before Sadie arrived, we'd managed to settle into something that felt like old times, and somehow that made it worse. The three people I love most, chattering and laughing, happy to be in each other's company. It's like a glimmer of a dream that will evaporate in the light of day, leaving your soul aching.

Throw Sadie and Garrett into the mix, and it's turned into one of those horror stories where you wish for something and get it in the worst possible way.

I wish things were normal again. I wish I had Kit back as my husband and Jayla back as my best friend, and even Sadie back as a friend, everything as it used to be, once upon a time.

I might long for that, but having all of them on my island—with Garrett tagging along—is the most evil wish-fulfillment imaginable. I can't even insist we don't need Sadie and Garrett and send them on their way. They chartered a boat to get here, and it's long gone.

Naturally, being both a cop and an asshole, Garrett tries to take over the investigation. Naturally, being a tough-as-nails Garrett-hating defense attorney, Jayla isn't putting up with that shit. She means well, but it splashes kerosene on an already roaring fire.

We searched the house and island and found nothing. Now it's evening, the sun falling, and we're cooking sausages over a bonfire. Sure, there's a no-open-flame edict, but a fire here won't catch anywhere else, and it's a small blaze contained in a pit, which has no vegetation within ten feet.

We're ringed around the bonfire, cooking sausages that Sadie brought. I've added beer, coolers, and s'more fixings from my personal food stash.

"You need security cameras," Garrett says, his mouth full. "You blow a million bucks on a vacation house and don't spring for cameras?"

"We have them," I say. "We shut them down while guests are here because they're considered an invasion of renter privacy and a violation of the contract. There's an indoor security system linking all doors and windows. That's on whenever no one's home, and renters who aren't comfortable with the isolation use it at all times."

"You need the type of system that keeps a log so you can track unauthorized use."

"It has that. I can show you the logs. Each guest receives a unique door code."

Garrett stops, beer bottle to his lips. "How does that work when you don't have remote access?"

"I send renters their code, which Nate sets while he's cleaning."

"Meaning this kid has owner-level access."

"The *kid* is twenty-one."

"Still a kid. And what's he doing in a shit job like this? Cleaning houses isn't exactly normal for a twenty-one-year-old guy."

"Nate takes what he can get."

"You mean he's desperate."

"Eager for work," I say evenly. "He went off to college before the pandemic. When it hit, he came back to live with his dad, who has liver disease. He's still here looking after him."

"So dad's an alcoholic. How about the kid?"

"His father has liver disease," I repeat. *Yes, he's also an alcoholic, but I'm not giving Garrett that.* "Nate dumps all booze that renters leave behind."

"Are you sure?" Garrett raises his hands. "All I'm saying is that this kid obviously needs money, and he's going to feel stuck in a shit town doing shit jobs."

"How would scaring Laney fix that?" Madison asks.

I tense, ready for Garrett's reply, but when he turns to her, his tone softens, belligerence fading. "Good question, kiddo. Maybe it's a diversion. Has anything gone missing? He could be stealing while staging the Satanic stuff to distract you from the thefts."

"I haven't seen anything missing. But, yes, while I completely trust Nate, I understand that having access to the island and the security system makes him a suspect."

"Also," Garrett says, "when we were searching, Kit mentioned that his family used to own this island. How did he feel about that?"

I try not to squirm. Nate was fine with it—or he'd let on that he was fine with it, for my sake. I'm the one who'd been uncomfortable with that. His family once owned the island where he was now employed as caretaker.

"It didn't bother him," Madison says firmly. "We talked about it. I know it made Laney uncomfortable, so Nate and I talked. He said the money his great-grandparents made selling the island meant his grandma could get treatments for her leukemia. Without that, he wouldn't be here. He's fine with it."

"Or so he says," Garrett murmurs.

Madison bristles. "He *is* fine with it. Laney lets him stay out here anytime it's empty."

"So he uses the house? Has full access to it?"

"He already did as the caretaker," I say. "We just discussed that. When he stayed, he usually camped. The point is that I understand Nate's a potential suspect, even if I disagree."

"I'll need to talk to him when we go back tomorrow."

I wait for someone to state the obvious.

We're not staying the night, right?

But no one says that. Garrett and Jayla and Madison keep throwing around theories while Kit tries to steer the conversation to solutions for making sure this doesn't *keep* happening. Sadie only listens. And I sit there, casting anxious glances into the forest, remembering what I saw, what I heard.

Nothing. I saw and heard nothing that couldn't be explained.

It doesn't matter. My gut says we should pile into the boat, and get the hell off this island. It isn't that I'm afraid to be here. I'm afraid to let Kit and Jayla stay here if there's a chance something is wrong, and I'm utterly terrified of having Madison here.

Maybe Sadie and Garrett can stay, take one for the team.

I might joke about that, but in spite of everything, I still care about Sadie. I don't give a shit about Garrett, but I wouldn't do that to his wife and kids.

I glance toward the forest, the hairs on my neck rising as the falling sun twists the semi-dark into a web of shadows. Anything could be out there. Any*one*.

"Laney?" Madison whispers.

I lower my voice so only she can hear me. "We didn't bring overnight bags."

"We have clothing here."

"I just think . . ." I glance at the forest again.

"It's too dark to take the boat," she says. "We can go back in the morning and talk to Nate. It's too late to do that, and he should be in on this conversation, right?"

Kit slides along the log and leans in to whisper, "Everything okay?"

"Laney is fine, Kit," Sadie calls from across the fire.

"Laney is not fine," he calls back. "Laney has some sick bastard putting ritual magic trappings all over her island."

I straighten. "I was just telling Madison that I'll need her help making up the beds."

"I can help with that," Sadie says. "No rush, though. It's a gorgeous night."

"The wind's picking up," Garrett says.

"Not over here," she says. "Now, if someone can pass me a marshmallow, I will demonstrate the proper way to char it to coal."

I have to smile at that, and I relax, too. When I half close my eyes, I'm transported back in time to dozens of bonfires like this. We're twelve again, and I see Jayla shifting seats constantly to avoid the smoke—*it's following me, don't you see that?* I see Kit and his friends, wrestling on the lawn and swooping in to steal marshmallows, sometimes right off the end of our sticks. Mostly, though, I see Sadie and me, huddled together, giggling and chattering, her face lit in flame and shadow as she whispers secrets she only trusts me to hear.

I look at her now, taking the marshmallow bag from Madison, her face once again lit in flame and shadow, and I can't help smiling, in spite of everything she's done.

"Toss one my way," I say. "I challenge you to a charring contest. Winner is the first one to roast a guaranteed carcinogen."

FIVE

It's nearly ten by the time Sadie and I go inside. Kit offers to help, but she blocks him with a fresh beer and insists he enjoy the fire. After a furtive glance at me, he obliges. It's only then that I realize why Sadie might want me alone: to tell me about her and Kit. Because this day could not possibly get any more awkward, could it?

To my relief, she doesn't mention Kit. We remake the main bed and freshen up the other rooms, and she asks how I'm doing, what it's like being back in the classroom post-pandemic, how exciting is it to be a published author?

"I read your book," she says as we're putting on fresh pillowcases, and I stiffen.

"It's really good," she continues. "No surprise there. You always were the one with the wild imagination."

Now I'm tensing enough that I'm frozen there, pillow in hand.

"Are you writing the next one yet?" she asks.

"It's done and at the publisher."

"Same characters?"

I nod, still wary, still stiff.

She smiles. "Good. That's what I was hoping. It really was good, Laney. I'm not just saying that to be nice. You're an amazing writer, and I'm thrilled for you." She meets my gaze. "Honestly thrilled. I know we've had our . . . issues, but I remember when we were kids and you used to write stories, and I always pestered you to let me read them. It felt like that. Like getting to read your stories again."

Again, I only nod, not sure what to say to that. After a moment, I say, "You're doing really well, too. Running your own company."

She makes a face. "Sounds more impressive than it is. I wasn't getting anywhere with my last employer, so I struck out on my own to build up my portfolio. Then I'll probably duck back into another company where I can count on steady paychecks and benefits."

"I hear you," I say. "People keep asking when I'll quit teaching to write full-time. Not anytime soon. As much as I love writing, I love steady paychecks and benefits more."

We keep chatting about work and life, and we're finishing when I realize we're short on towels. We head down to the main-level laundry and find a basket of dirty towels with a note on top.

These were not washed! We found them piled on the floor!

I presume the note is from Mrs. Abbas. Does she mean that Nate forgot to finish the laundry? More likely the Abbases showed up early. He may have even mentioned that he hadn't finished the towels, and they promised to do it themselves.

That's happened before, and it doesn't keep guests from complaining in hopes of getting a discount. One might think that anyone able to afford this place wouldn't lie to get a hundred bucks back. That would only mean one does not truly understand the rich. Having grown up with Jayla and Kit, I thought I did. I did not.

I'm shoving the towels into the washer when the back door slaps shut, and Madison calls something I don't catch.

"Time to assign bedrooms," I say to Sadie as I turn toward the door.

She steps into my path. "Before we do, there's something we need to discuss."

Every muscle in me tenses. Here it comes. She's going to tell me that she'll be sharing a room with my ex-husband, and she hopes that's okay, no hard feelings, right?

Except that's not what she says. Not at all. As she talks, I almost wish that *were* what she says. This is worse. She wants me to heal an old wound, and I understand her point, but if healing Sadie means hurting someone I love more, then I will not.

I tell her it's not the time—obviously.

"Make it the time, Laney. Either you handle this, or I will."

I turn to face her, slow and deliberate. "If you so much as *hint* to—"

The squeak of sneakers in the hall has us both going still.

"Later," I say. "Don't push me. You know better."

Sadie marches off. I retreat into the laundry area to collect myself. I'm not sure how long I'm there before Madison wheels in.

"What are you doing in *here*?" she says.

"Washing towels. Everyone's waiting for room assignments, right?"

"Nope, we did that. You and I share your room." She lowers her voice. "Did you talk to Kit?"

"About what?"

"He was looking for you. He came in while you were with Sadie. Then I saw him poking around, trying to find you. It seemed important."

I'm still looking for Kit when I hear Sadie's voice inside a bedroom. She's talking to someone, and she's angry. I can't make out what she's saying, just the tone. I hesitate. If she's speaking to Garrett, I don't want to hear it. If it's Jayla, and there's trouble brewing—

Another voice answers hers, this one calm and instantly recognizable. Kit.

Well, I guess it wasn't me he was looking for after all. I start to turn away.

"Don't do this," Kit is saying, his voice low. "Not now. Laney doesn't deserve it."

"*Laney* doesn't deserve it? What about what *I* deserve?"

I turn away quickly and hurry down the stairs.

I take half a sleeping pill before I go to bed. I still spend an hour staring up at the ceiling, the second half of the pill whispering in my ear. Tempting, yes, but if I take it, then my sedated brain will insist there's someone lurking around and what the hell was I thinking taking a full pill and how am I going to protect Madison like that?

When Madison shakes my shoulder, I startle. My fuzzy brain whispers that I'm dreaming, replaying my day on a loop, starting with Madison waking me.

"Laney?" she says. "There's someone outside."

That has me flailing up. When she doesn't say anything else, I hover there, heart hammering, and I expect to look over and see her still asleep. I went to bed worrying about someone lurking about, and now I've dreamed it.

Madison isn't asleep. She's not even in bed.

I scramble up, heart jammed in my throat now, only to see her by the window, the drapes clenched in one hand.

"I thought I heard something," she says.

I relax and start rolling out of bed.

"Then I came to the window," she continues. "And saw someone down there."

I freeze.

Do not freak out. For Madison's sake, do not freak out.

I compose myself and walk to the window.

"You think I dreamed it," she says.

"I—"

"You think I'm traumatized by that asshole peeper and dreaming of him."

"Can I finish, Mads? No, I don't think that at all. I . . ." I clear my throat. "Earlier today I was sure I saw someone on the bluff. I lied because I decided it was just the blackened tree stump."

"You think I'm seeing things, too."

"No," I say firmly. "I mean that I should have said something because I'm still not sure what I saw."

I peer out the window and give a start, only to realize I'm looking at a bird feeder, its pale top and wooden pole vaguely humanlike in the darkness.

"It wasn't the bird feeder," she says.

"I never said—"

"It wasn't. The person was in the woods. Over there. I saw a person." She shifts. "Or I saw what looked like a person. Something definitely moved. It seemed bigger than any of the animals here and . . ." She trails off to a mumble. "Maybe I'm wrong. The other night, I *did* wake up after dreaming there was another peeper at my bedroom window."

"We should wake the others."

When I turn to go, she grabs my arm. "No. *Please.*"

I hesitate.

She looks me in the eye. "Earlier, you didn't admit you saw someone because you were sure it was a stump. You didn't want to look scared and silly. Same here, only it's worse, 'cause I'm a kid, and everyone expects me to be silly and get spooked. Especially that Garrett guy."

I want to tell her not to give a damn what Garrett Emerson thinks of her, but I realize he's only the excuse. She doesn't want to look bad in front of Kit and Jayla, even if they'd never judge her for it.

I glance toward the window. "I'll go check it out."

"What? I mean, yes, someone should, to see if there are footprints or whatever, but I'll go with you. We'll take the gun. Is it up here?"

"No, I left it in the office safe."

We head into the hall. We're halfway down the stairs when the door nearest ours creaks open. I turn to see Jayla, yawning and peering at us.

"Just checking something out," I whisper.

"Coming with," she whispers back, and pads barefoot into the hall. I glance at Madison, who hesitates, and then nods.

When Jayla catches up to us, Madison says, "I heard a noise and thought I saw something. I'm sure I was imagining it, but we're checking it out after we get the gun."

Jayla gives us the thumbs-up.

I have two gun safes. One is in my room, and the other in my office. As I open the office one, Madison tells Jayla that she had a peeper a few weeks ago, which means she could just be paranoid.

"Don't make excuses," Jayla says. "Trust your gut, carry a knife, and don't worry about what anyone thinks."

"You carry a knife?" Madison says.

"Always."

The safe beeps as I finish entering the code. The door pops open and . . .

It's empty.

The others peer in.

"Let me check the bedroom one," I say. "Hold on."

I slip upstairs and into my room, where the safe is behind a hidden panel. Pop the panel. Enter the code. Door pops open . . .

No gun.

I go back downstairs, shaking my head. "Kit must have taken it out earlier. He's the only one with the code."

"Get him then," Jayla says.

I turn toward the stairs. Then I remember hearing Sadie in Kit's room.

"Uh, that . . . could be weird," I say, trying for a smile. "His ex waking him in the middle of the night. Might freak him out."

"Pretty sure Kit wouldn't mind," Jayla says.

I'm about to mention hearing Sadie in there. Then I notice Madison listening intently. I can't say anything that might turn her against Kit. She still hopes we'll reunite, and her parents split because her dad was fooling around, which could make this extra awkward.

"Let's just go," I say. "You have a knife. I'll get a knife. Madison can take a fork. We'll all be fine."

SIX

It's not until I'm outside, armed with my knife, that I realize what we're doing. Madison thinks she saw a shadowy figure on my private island, after someone left blood and scratches in the closet. Now we're venturing outside to investigate?

Coming out here had seemed sensible. Hell, I'd wondered if I was overreacting by getting a knife first. Now we're making our way through the darkness, the whistling wind drowning out all sound.

This is stupid. Really stupid. Go inside, get Kit and the gun—

Light floods the yard, and we all jump.

"Motion detector," I say with a half laugh.

The others nod, and we continue on.

"Wait," I say as I slow. "There's a motion-detecting light around the side, too. Under my window."

"Shit," Madison says. "I forgot about that. So if the light didn't activate, no one could have been there."

"Unless the bulb burned out."

"No, it came on earlier, when that Garrett guy wandered off to take a piss. Kit told him to go inside, but he pretended not to hear and went around the corner and yelped when the light flicked on." She glances over. "It was kind of funny."

"Well," Jayla says. "While this does seem to be a false alarm, at least we weren't idiots walking out of a security-armed house to confront an intruder."

"You realized that, too?" I say.

"Yep, about five seconds ago, when I wondered why this felt so familiar, and then I remembered I've seen this scene in every damn slasher movie you made me watch."

"Made you?" I say as we resume walking to the corner of the house. "That is not how I remember it."

"Totally how I remember it. You—"

Pain stabs through my foot, my gasp cutting her short. "And I just stepped on broken glass. Fucking renters."

"Ooh," Madison says. "You aren't supposed to use that word, Auntie Laney. They can revoke your guardian license."

"You okay?" Jayla asks me.

"I'm fine. Remind me to clean up the glass tomorrow."

I take a step, and the sharp jab tells me a sliver is embedded in my sole. I pause as Madison continues on, Jayla following.

"It better have been the renters," I mutter. "If Garrett dropped his beer bottle when the light came on—"

I stop as I pluck a shard from my foot. It's too fine to be bottle glass. I squint down at it, and then I *realize* I'm squinting. We've rounded the back corner, away from the first motion-detector light, and second one hasn't come on. It hasn't come on because . . .

I look up to see the empty socket and jagged remains of the bulb.

"In the house!" I shout. "Everyone in the house *now!*"

Jayla backs up fast. Madison is frozen there, her back to me as she stares down. I run to grab her. How did I let her get so far from me? Why the hell did I bring her out here? What was I *thinking*?

"Laney?" Her voice quavers, but she doesn't move.

"Get in the house. We—"

"That's fake, right? It's a decoration, right? Tell me that's—"

I grab her T-shirt and then stop as I see what she's looking at. It's a hand.

There is a *hand*. Coming out of the *ground*.

"It's fake," I blurt. "Halloween bullshit. Now get in the—"

She drops to her knees, shirt breaking from my hold. As I scramble to pull her up, I see the hand better. The white skin. The square shape. The garish high school ring. The chipped blue nail polish.

It's the nail polish that makes me freeze.

Nate.

I drop to my knees and claw at the ground around the hand. My fingers touch skin, and I know this is no prop, no decoration. I dig faster, praying I'm not too late to save him. I scoop out earth, my nails tearing, and then . . .

Then the hand falls over. It drops onto the dirt, ragged flesh and jutting bone where it's been cut—been cut—been cut—

That's where my brain stops. And that's when Madison starts to scream.

In the house," I say, when I can find words. "We need to get in the house."

I gather up Madison. She collapses against me, shaking and gasping. Jayla helps get her inside, and then she slams and locks the door. I stammer out the security code, and she activates it.

"The motion detector," I whisper when Jayla comes back. "Someone smashed it. Smashed it and left that . . . left *his* . . ."

I double over, gagging, but only bile comes. Jayla reaches for me. I brush her off.

"Get the others. Please. We're leaving. Now."

She's gone before I can finish. As I hold Madison, I dimly hear Jayla's feet on the stairs, then her shouts and bangs on doors. Other voices join in, but they sound a mile away, muffled and indistinct.

"That—that was Nate, wasn't it?" Madison manages between sobs. "His . . . His . . ."

"I-I don't know."

Everything in me throws up ridiculous alternate explanations. Ridiculous yet somehow more reasonable than the truth, that someone has killed Nate and cut off his hand and put it in the ground like some kind of fucking Halloween decoration.

They murdered a kid, a good and sweet kid, and they mutilated his body and staged it, and in that moment, I'm no longer lost in shock and grief. I am enraged.

When arms close around me, I almost whip around with my knife. Then I see Kit's face. He hugs me and Madison together. His embrace feels so damn good, and right now I will allow myself that comfort.

"I don't know what's going on," he says, "but I'm getting you both the hell off this island."

"The gun," Madison whispers. "You have the gun?"

"The what?" Kit says.

I tell him, and he swears he didn't even open the gun safe. That makes no sense, but it doesn't matter now. We just need to leave.

Still gripping Madison's hand, I slip from Kit's grasp and stand as Jayla walks in.

"Ready to go?" I say, and there's an odd croak to my voice, as if I'm fighting to sound calm when I'm anything but.

"We can't find Sadie," she says.

"What?" I glance at Kit. "Wasn't she with you?"

"Why would Sadie . . . ?" He trails off and then his eyes widen as they meet mine. "No, Laney. Absolutely not."

"I heard her in your room."

"Believe me, she didn't stay long. She was upset about—" He shakes his head. "It doesn't matter. Sadie and I aren't—"

"Where the hell is my sister?" Garrett storms in and bears down on Kit.

"Why is everyone asking *me*?" Kit says.

Jayla marches off, shouting Sadie's name at the top of her lungs. No answer comes.

"Check for her shoes," I say. "In case she went outside for a walk."

"At three in the morning?" Garrett says.

"We need to go," Kit says. "Laney? Where's your laptop bag?"

Garrett spins on him. "My sister is missing, and some kid has been *murdered*. No one gives a shit about Laney's precious laptop."

Jayla runs back in. "Sadie's not in the house."

"Okay," Kit says. "Can you go with Laney and Madison to the boathouse—"

"We are not abandoning my sister," Garrett says.

"We won't," Kit continues. "I'll help you look outside. Laney? Jayla? Take Madison to the boat and get it running. We'll be there soon."

"No one is leaving this island until I say so," Garrett snaps. "I'm a fucking cop, and this is a fucking murder scene."

"And the fucking killer is still fucking here!" Jayla snarls at him.

"So is my *sister*!"

"Someone needs to get Madison off the island," I say. "I'll stay and help search but—"

"I've got this," Jayla says. "Kit, go with Laney and Madison. Garrett and I will find Sadie."

We go. The longer we argue, the worse things will be, and I absolutely must get Madison off this island. What the hell was I thinking, bringing her here?

I barely process leaving the house or running to the boathouse. I dimly feel pain throbbing through my injured foot, dimly hear the slap of our bare feet on the rocks and feel the bite of the rising wind. We run. We just run.

When Kit pulls the boathouse door, it stays closed.

Did I lock it earlier? Did *he*? I can't remember. I can't care. I only care that it takes five precious seconds for Kit to get the code in. His fingers are shaking, and he mumbles "Sorry, sorry" when he fails the first time. Then he's yanking open the door and shining the flashlight on—

On the empty berth.

"Where's the boat?" Madison says. Her voice rises. "Where the hell is the boat?"

The exit door is wide open, and the boat is gone.

"Kit!" a voice shouts outside. It's Jayla, and I run to the doorway, knife gripped in my hand. She's running, Garrett behind her.

"Sadie's gone." She stops, heaving to catch her breath. "Her shoes are gone. Her purse is gone. Her bag is gone. I don't know where—" Her gaze moves to the empty berth. "What the—? Shit!"

Sadie is gone. She argued with me. She argued with Kit and god knows who else, and she stormed off in a snit, stranding us on the island . . . with a killer.

SEVEN

Back inside!" Kit shouts, herding Madison toward the boathouse door. "Everyone inside."

Garrett jumps into our path. "My sister is out here."

"No, your sister is out *there*." Jayla jabs a finger at the lake. "She stole our only fucking way off this island."

"She wouldn't do that," Garrett says. "The boy was murdered, and whoever did it is on the island, but when Sadie disappears, you decide she's fine—she just stole your damn boat."

"Because her things are gone," Kit says, his voice even. "She didn't mean to strand us with a killer. She was upset, and she left. She'll calm down, and in the morning, she'll come back or send a charter. Now we need to get in—"

Garrett crosses his arms. "Prove she took your boat."

"We will," Kit snaps. "Once we're safely in the house. Now move!"

When Garrett stays firm, blocking the doorway, Kit swings past me, but Madison is faster. She charges Garrett and slams both open palms into his stomach.

"Get the hell out of our way," she snarls.

He lifts his hands, backing up. She mistakes the gesture for another block and swings at him, but I catch her arm.

"Okay, okay," Garrett says, looking genuinely chagrined. "I'm sorry, kiddo. Of course, let's get you to the house."

"We *will* look for Sadie," I say as I prod Madison past him. "We aren't going to presume she left until we're sure she did."

"Even if we *are* sure," Jayla mutters behind me.

I get Madison out of the boathouse. Kit darts in front of us, and I'm about to barrel past him when I realize why he's taken the lead. Because I'm striding into the dark night, while Nate's killer is on the island and we've been making enough noise arguing to let a marching band sneak up on us.

Nate's killer.

His image flashes, and the memory of his hand.

I squeeze my eyes shut.

"Everyone stay together," Kit whispers. "Jayla, eyes right. Laney, eyes left. Garrett, bring up the rear, please."

"No one put you in charge. I'm the—"

"—asshole who doesn't know when to shut up," Madison snaps. "Kit even added a 'please,' just for you. Stop swinging your dick."

Garrett blinks. I brace, but he gives a curt nod, falls in behind, and we start forward. Kit told me to keep my eyes left. It's open rock, with forest behind. It's also the same side of the house with the broken lights. The same side where Nate's hand—

Stop. Focus.

The world seems to end after the rocky shore, the forest beyond a black hole. Ten people could be poised at the edge, and I wouldn't see them. I concentrate on the rocks instead, the lichen-dappled stone that stretches for fifty feet before reaching that forest's edge.

I strain to listen for unusual sounds, but the slap of water on rock would drown them out. We continue, step by step, until we reach the front door. I slide forward to punch in the code as the others stand watch.

I lift my finger to the first button. Then I stop and turn the knob. The door opens.

I fall back, shielding Madison.

"It's unlocked," I blurt. "Someone's in . . ." I trail off and turn to Jayla. "Did you come out the front?"

"Yeah," Jayla says. "And we didn't lock it behind us."

"Because we don't have the damn code," Garrett says.

"You don't need it," Kit says. "Just hit the lock button and turn the knob."

Garrett ignores him and pushes past us.

I catch his arm. "If the door was unlocked, someone could be in there."

He starts to snap something and then stops as he realizes I'm right. He might be the cop in this group, but I'm the mystery writer—I know all the tricks.

Being a cop means Garrett does, apparently, know how to enter an unsecured area. He motions for Kit to cover him, earning an eye roll from Jayla, who takes the task instead, her knife in hand. Garrett swings through and smacks on the lights.

They both enter as Kit and I keep watch on the open landscape behind us.

"Clear," Garrett says.

We cluster in the front hall as he heads into the massive great room with Jayla covering him.

I lock the door and set the alarm. When it doesn't work, I look up to see a red light flashing. Below it, in my handwriting, a tag reads MAIN BEDROOM.

"Something's open in our—your bedroom," Kit says. "The balcony door or a window."

I shake my head. "The balcony sensor is wonky." I hit the code again, and that warning light disappears. "See?"

"I'll get that fixed," he says.

I open my mouth, the argument reflexive, before Madison's elbow reminds me this is not the time. I glance at Kit. His expression says his brain is whirring to process the current situation, and he probably didn't even register what he said, the reassurance being equally reflexive.

"Clear in here," Jayla calls back.

"Secure," I call when the system switches on.

"I wouldn't say that," Garrett mutters. "We might as well be standing on the damn lawn."

I see what he means. That glorious wall of windows completely exposes us to the outside. There's also the winding staircase with the second-floor hallway overlooking the great room, which attaches to the kitchen and dining area.

I love the openness of Hemlock House, so airy and spacious, with its sweeping views, but now, the open concept means an attack could come from any direction. Having a security system made me feel safe. Now it's almost laughable.

"We should check the rooms with doors," I say. "Close them as we go."

"And this?" Garrett waves at the bank of windows. "Please tell me this fancy house has electronic blinds."

It doesn't need them, and that's another thing I love. At home, with a front sidewalk within spitting distance, my blinds stay closed. Here, I can lounge in my underwear all day.

Right now, those windows are a fishbowl, where anyone out there can see us and we can see only darkness.

"No blinds," I say.

Garrett gapes at me in exaggerated disbelief.

"It's a private island," I say. "We don't have to worry about neighbors or passersby, and yes, weirdly, we never considered the possibility of having to hide from a killer."

"The fact that it's a private island is the very reason you need to worry about that. Aren't you an author now? What if one of your fans tracks you down?"

"I'm a debut novelist. I'll worry about that when I actually have fans. Speaking of my job, I'm going to start the search with my office."

"Kit can go with you," Madison says. "Jayla and I will secure the laundry room. Asshole Cop Dude can take the bathroom. He should be able to handle that alone."

"My name is Garrett, kiddo."

"And when you stop acting like an asshole cop, I'll use it."

"Search the rooms and shut the doors," I say. "We'll reconvene back here and then tackle the second level."

There's no one on the main level. We shut off all the rooms, and then head upstairs. Kit and I will take the room Sadie used. Jayla and Garrett already searched it. Time for fresh eyes.

I'd been distracted during the room assignments. Otherwise, I'd have realized there was no way Sadie snuck in with Kit . . . because he was sharing the twin-bed room with Garrett. Jayla had volunteered for the green room, which may prove that, like me, she can't help still caring a little about our former friend, however unwittingly. Putting Sadie in the green room—the site of the bloody-scratches closet—would be a shit move. Jayla took it instead.

That left Sadie with Madison's room. It's not just the room Madison uses while she's here. It's actually hers and has been since Hemlock House was lines on a sketch pad.

"Mads should have her pick of the guest rooms," Kit had said. "Let her choose it and get her input and make it really hers."

That may have been the moment when I realized I loved him. Yes, I suppose that should have come before I said "I do." When I stepped into the wedding chapel, I knew I was falling for him, but it wasn't until that moment that the feeling solidified into something that felt like forever.

At that time, Anna's prognosis had been good, and Madison was just my thirteen-year-old niece. That wasn't someone you typically give her own bedroom in your new vacation home. But Kit understood the role Madison played in my life. She would be a regular visitor at Hemlock House, and he acknowledged that as if it was never in question.

The bedrooms are arranged along a central corridor that overlooks the main level. The main bedroom takes up one corner, with the small green bedroom beside it, the slightly larger twin-bed room next, and then Madison's in the opposite corner. Yes, it's the farthest from ours, and that was Kit's doing, which I'd agreed with once I figured out why. Having Madison as a houseguest wouldn't cramp our style; having her bedroom right beside ours might.

Her room, like ours, has windows along both exterior walls, with a seat in one and a small balcony off the other. When she's here, the room is—as my mother puts it—an apocalyptic disaster zone. Of course, Mom first used those words to describe *my* teenage bedroom, so Madison comes by it honestly. Now, though, it's ready for renters and, when Kit and I step inside, a pang stabs through me.

This is supposed to be Madison's room. Her personal space where she had the freedom to slap up K-drama posters and hand-paint the furniture and make as much of a mess as she wanted because it was hers. Renting it changed all that. Take down the posters. Paint the walls neutral. Replace the furniture. Stuff all her clothing and belongings in a locked trunk to be shoved into the crawlspace between visits.

It wasn't supposed to be like this.

And whose fault is that? Blame me for being too sentimental—and stubborn—to sell the island. Blame Kit for giving me a glimpse of a dream I can't let go. Blame the pandemic for upending our lives, for incinerating my marriage and hurrying along Anna's death with delayed treatments, both events sending me spiraling into financial chaos when I could least afford it.

Blame everyone. Blame no one.

It's just a damn bedroom. At least it's still here, and it's still Madison's, and she's never once complained.

So why does it hurt so much? Because everything hurts these days, and now I'm standing in her doorway, imagining this room evaporating before my eyes, because it doesn't matter if we're safely in the house with a security system and nothing else goes wrong. How am I going to keep Hemlock House after what's happened? After finding Nate's . . . ?

When I shiver, Kit steps up behind me, his arms going around my waist, and I don't stop him. I close my eyes, and I picture Nate. I see him smiling, always smiling, no matter what new joker card life dealt him. His mom long gone, his dad an alcoholic, Nate working his ass off to go to college, only to be ripped back to this nowhere life by the pandemic.

"It's fine," he'd say. "I'll get out next year, and someday I'll come back and be able to rent this place myself. This is just a pothole in the road, and I've got a long way to go yet."

My stomach seizes.

"Why don't you sit down?" Kit whispers. "I've got this."

I shake my head and pull from his grip. Then I turn on the bedroom light and look around as he heads for the balcony door. He checks that as I pace around the room.

I can see why Jayla and Garrett came back so quickly. It's obvious that Sadie grabbed her things and left. Her overnight bag is gone. The tiny en suite bath shows signs of pre-bedtime use—a damp hand towel and a toothpaste streak in the sink, plus a grease mark from moisturizer or makeup remover. I open the cabinet and vanity drawers. Empty but for the unopened toothpaste and toothbrushes I leave for guests.

I head into the bedroom, where Kit is checking under the bed.

"She got ready for the night," I say. "Signs of brushing her teeth and washing up. She used the bed, too, and remade it." The bedspread is in place, but rumpled, as if pulled up over the sheets in a half-assed effort. "Everything points to her leaving on her own. Garrett complained about not having the door code, but I gave Sadie that and the security code to pass on to him."

At my words, I stop and turn to Kit.

"Check the access logs," we say, almost in unison.

"I'll go down and do that," Kit says. "You okay up here?"

"I am. Go on."

It's only after he leaves that I realize we failed to secure the room on entering. I'd been distracted, thinking about Nate, but it's still embarrassing after we told Garrett we could handle it. We should have entered, checked the bathroom and closet first, then under the bed, then the balcony. All the places an intruder could hide.

I eye the closet door.

Should I call Kit back? Or get Jayla?

The answer, obviously, is yes. That is the smart thing to do. But it seems silly, and I don't want to be that woman, even if I recognize, deep down, that not calling for backup makes me another stereotype—the woman so intent on being tough that she takes unnecessary risks.

And in the time it takes me to work that through, I find myself at the closet door, knob in one hand, kitchen knife in the other as I yank it open. A squeak in the closet has me staggering back, knife rising, until I realize that my yank set the empty hangers rocking.

There's a rack with a dozen hangers and two shelves with extra blankets and pillows. Nothing else.

I close the door . . . and a figure moves behind it. I manage to bite off a yelp as I realize the figure is me, reflected in the dresser mirror. I shake my head and glance at the door to be sure the others didn't hear my yelp. When no one comes running, I walk to the dresser. I reach for the first drawer and pause. There's dust on the top of it. I bend and squint. Yep, definitely dust, which is not at all like—

Tears prickle. Damn it, stop thinking about Nate. Yes, he deserves every tear, but I can't afford them yet. Later I will mourn. For now, I can pretend that hand could have belonged to someone else. Whatever gets me through this night.

I open the top drawer to find candy wrappers. Huh. Did Sadie develop a sweet tooth? I remember when Jayla and I would swoop down on the candy aisle like vultures spotting road kill, while Sadie would riffle through every bag of trail mix looking for one without chocolate.

I pick up the wrappers. Kid's candy, the cheap kind you can buy at the store in town.

The guests before the Abbases had two young sons. That would mean Nate didn't finish cleaning in here.

I remember the laundry note downstairs, and then I look at the dust on the dresser top.

Nate didn't finish cleaning between the Abbases and the guests before them.

Because that's when he was killed.

No, that isn't possible. The Abbases arrived two days ago and . . .

And what? Someone would have reported Nate missing? Who? His alcoholic father who—if I'm remembering right—recently went into hospice?

I look around the room. Does that mean the signs of habitation aren't from Sadie?

I walk back into the bathroom and touch the inside of the sink. No, the toothpaste smear hasn't set, and the towel is still damp.

I head into the bedroom. Was the bed left like this from the last guests, their son "making his bed" by pulling up the coverlet?

As I walk over, I remember the laundry room. The alternate bedding for this room had been folded on the counter, freshly laundered. That means Nate had started working on this room. He made the bed and cleaned the bathroom but hadn't gotten to the dresser.

I move to the top of the bed, looking for signs that Sadie had crawled in and slept part of the night. I tug back the coverlet—

I stumble back, hand slapping over my mouth.

There's blood on the pillow. Blood and a hank of hair . . . with a torn chunk of scalp still attached.

EIGHT

I wheel, ready to run, and I smack into Garrett. His hands go to my shoulders to steady me, and all I see is him looming and something inside me goes wild, and I smack him away as I backpedal.

"Hey!" he says. "It's me."

"Yeah, that'd be the problem," Jayla says as she runs in.

Madison is right behind her and whatever she sees on my face has her looking from me to Garrett, her brow furrowed.

"Bed," I say. "On the pillow. There's . . . ." I swallow, unable to get the rest out.

"There's what?" Garrett says.

I pivot and see the pillow. There's nothing on it.

"No," I whisper. "I saw—"

"Whoa!" Jayla is three strides past me, moving to the bed, Madison beside her, and her arms fly out to keep Madison back.

"Is that . . . ?" Madison says.

I hurry over. The hank of hair is still there. When I dropped the coverlet, it partly covered it, and I couldn't see it from the doorway.

My heart slows as I catch my breath.

Because an *actual* chunk of scalp is better than an *imaginary* chunk of scalp?

I move up to the bed. As I bend to examine the hair, Garrett moves in too close to me, and I instinctively want to move away, but force myself to stay firm and focus on the hair. It's strands of dark brown hair maybe four inches long.

Kit arrives then, coming up from the main level, where he'd been checking the access logs. Our eyes meet. Then he sees the pillow and gives a start.

"It's too long to be Nate's," Madison says. "And it can't be Sadie's. She's blond."

"Her hair's dyed," I say, feeling oddly guilty, as if I'm being catty when I'm only making an important point. "It could have come from underneath, at the roots, but her hair was never this dark. This is also shorter."

I force myself to turn to Garrett. "What's your take?"

Until now, he's been quick to play the cop card. That's why he's here, although after my talk with Sadie last night, I know that was just an excuse. The point, though, is that he *is* a detective and I only play one on the page. Yet when I ask his opinion, panic flits across his face.

Shit.

How long exactly have you been a detective, Garrett?

Not long. Not on cases that involve forensic evidence like this.

Forensic evidence.

Is that what this is? Is that what Nate's hand is? Clues in some murder-mystery-weekend crime?

I shiver, but I'm not really thinking of it like that. I'm distancing myself to analyze this hank of hair so I don't completely break down because there is chunk of hair and blood and scalp in Madison's bed.

In the bed where Sadie was.

Sadie, who is now missing.

"You're right," Garrett says gruffly. "It's not her natural hair color, and it's too short."

"But being short wouldn't matter," Madison says. "The hair could have been cut."

"Good point, kiddo," Garrett says, and I try not to bristle. At least he's being nice to her.

I bend closer to look for split ends, which would suggest the hair *hadn't* been cut. The smell hits me. The stink of blood but something else, too. The very first hints of decay, like at my family's ramshackle cottage when we didn't check a mousetrap fast enough.

I rise. "This was ripped out more than a few hours ago. The scalp part smells of decomp."

Garrett gives a derisive snort as he bends. Then he straightens fast. "Laney's right."

He backs up, runs his hands over his face and hisses an exhale through his teeth, shoulders relaxing.

"It's not Sadie," I say softly.

"Then who the hell is it?" Jayla says.

Garrett recovers and folds his arms. "It's a prank. The hand, too."

"If you are telling me that's not a real piece of someone's scalp," Jayla says, "or a real fucking *hand*—"

"Course it's real," Garrett says. "From a morgue or something."

"A morgue?" Jayla says. "Seriously?"

I step between them. "He's suggesting that someone took them from a dead body, maybe at a funeral parlor, someone due to be cremated or . . ." I throw up my hands. "I don't know the specifics, but Garrett means that someone could have gotten these parts from an already-dead body and staged them to look like Nate's hand and someone else's hair."

"Is that possible?" Kit says.

"For a writer, anything is possible." I look at Garrett. "In real life, though . . . ?"

"Last year, we got called to a scene where a guy's wife died during the pandemic, and he never notified anyone because he wanted to keep her body for—" His gaze falls on Madison, and he clears his throat. "For collecting her paychecks."

"Yeah, that isn't what you were going to say," Madison mutters.

"I'm not ten, and I don't think *anyone* needed that story, but we get the point." She turns to me. "So that might not have been Nate's hand? Just some guy's, and they added nail polish and a class ring so we'd think it's Nate?"

Her tone is matter-of-fact, but I don't miss the look in her eyes. The look that does make her, in this at least, ten years old, begging me to say this isn't Nate.

I want to say that. God, how I want to say it.

Absolutely. That makes total sense.

I look at the bloodied hair. Would it make *more* sense that someone murdered Nate?

I answer slowly, working up to what I hope will sound convincing. "If it was Nate, that means he had to be killed before the Abbases arrived two days ago. Someone would have reported him missing. They'd have notified me."

"See?" Garrett says.

I continue, "Someone *has* been staging things to scare guests. I don't know what the point of that is, but it didn't seem to be working. They could take things to the next level."

"The point would be to scare *you*," Kit says. "Yes, it's the guests who see it, but ultimately, the fallout is on you. On your ability to rent this place. Even, possibly, on your comfort with coming here, especially alone."

"Money," Jayla says. "Now *that's* a motive Kit and I understand."

"You think someone's trying to scare me into selling?" I say.

"I've had several people contact me directly," Kit says. "They find the last record of sale and get in touch with me. I refer them to you, with the warning that I don't think you're looking to sell. Have they contacted you?"

"I've had a half dozen offers in the last two years."

"For a place like this?" Garrett says. "Yeah, it's fancy as hell, but it's the middle of nowhere, without even cell signal."

"It's the pandemic," I say.

His face scrunches. "What?"

"The pandemic. That's the appeal." I wave around us. "Perfect isolation, in the event of a global catastrophe. People have started thinking more about that. They want to buy it for some kind of apocalyptic luxury shelter or develop it for those who'd like a vacation home in an isolated community. I'm a divorced schoolteacher—they're hoping I'm desperate and they can get it cheap. I even had someone who started by offering condolences on the death of my sister."

"Motherfucking vultures," Jayla says. "Why didn't you call and get me on their asses? Or even Kit?"

"Even Kit," Kit murmurs.

"You know what I mean. You're not a lawyer, but you're tough when you need to be, and you're used to dealing with assholes like this."

I glance back at that hank of hair to avoid an answer. Why didn't I reach out to my *ex*-husband? To the former friend who only called me once since my marriage to warn that if I broke Kit's heart, I'd regret it?

Wasn't his heart that got broken, Jayla, but you're right—I sure as hell regret it.

I straighten. "I think this could be our answer. Someone staged the hex circle and the creepy wind chimes hoping I'd freak out and sell. They didn't know they were dealing with a horror buff who blew it off. So they went hardcore. Scratches in the bedroom closet paired with a severed hand and bloody chunk of hair from an already dead body."

"Then Sadie saw the hair, flipped out, and ran," Madison says. "Taking the boat with her."

Jayla shakes her head. "More like she found the hair, knew it was a prank, and decided I was responsible. Or Laney and me in cahoots, as if we're all back in high school. She got pissed off, stormed out, and took the boat to teach us a lesson."

Madison looks at Garrett. "Would she do that? Leave you behind?"

Garrett hesitates. Then his shoulders sag. "Yeah. She lost her temper and wasn't thinking. Stormed off, like Jayla said. Then she'll realize she abandoned *me* and come back."

"I checked the door logs," Kit says. "Someone opened the back door two hours ago and then relocked it. So we agree Sadie left on her own. There is zero evidence to support any other theory, yes, Counselor?"

Jayla nods.

"Detective?" Kit says to Garrett.

Garrett hesitates, but nods.

"Mystery writer?" Kit says.

I nod.

Kit turns to Madison. "Kid who is probably smarter than all of us combined?"

Madison rolls her eyes but agrees. Sadie was in this bedroom tonight. She was settling in for sleep after arguing with both me and Kit. Already on edge, she finds the bloodied hair, presumes one of us is being schoolgirl nasty, decides she's had enough, and takes the boat to shore.

There's no evidence anyone hurt her. No evidence she was kidnapped from the house—that single entry on the log means no one came in and then took her out. Her belongings are gone. She's gone. The boat's gone. There's only one solution to that equation.

"She'll send a boat for us tomorrow," Kit says. "This was a lousy thing to do, but she didn't mean to scare us. She only wanted off the island."

"Whatever her story, she can cry it on your shoulder," Jayla says. "I'm not interested."

"I didn't say it was okay," Kit says, meeting his sister's gaze. "Yes, I don't have your history with her, so I cut her more slack. But I won't forget this."

I cut in before Garrett can comment, "We've established that Sadie left on her own, meaning we just need to wait for morning . . ." I trail off, as a realization hits.

"I don't know about you guys," Garrett says, "but I need a drink. Something harder than beer."

I shake my head. "There's still someone out there. On the island."

"Uh, no, Laney," he says. "We just decided that, remember? Someone is trying to spook you with fake staging, and I still don't understand why they'd want this place, but apparently, that's why Kit is the Fortune 500 guy and I'm the cop with a mortgage. Point is, no one killed your cleaning kid. We're fine."

"Was the light off when you went to take a piss?" Madison says.

"What?"

"You went around that side of the house when you had to pee. Was the light on?"

"I guess so."

"You'd know if it wasn't," Madison says. "It was cloudy and there's no light pollution out here. You wouldn't have gone far in the dark, so the light *was* on. Now it's broken, and there was a hand coming out of the ground that you would have seen. That means someone's out there."

He hesitates. His eyes glint. "The bastard who scared the shit out of us tonight?" He smiles. "Guess we need to form a little search party, bring that asshole in."

NINE

We complete our interior search and double-check that all windows and doors are locked. Then I set the alarm, and we go outside, armed with flashlights and makeshift weapons—a kitchen knife, a hammer, a baseball bat. I don't like the fact that the gun is missing. Okay, that's an understatement. I'm trying very hard not to jump to some scary conclusions about that. The simplest answer is that I got distracted on my last visit and left it out back after target practice and a guest tucked it into their luggage like a nice hotel towel.

We split up again. Garrett goes off on his own, and no one argues with that. Kit takes Madison, and I'm with Jayla. Before we go out, she insists I pause to clean my foot and put on shoes. I grumble, but I do it. The glass only left a small puncture, easily handled by a quick wash and a bandage. Then we head out.

The island is big enough for someone to hide on but small enough to conduct a decent search. Our section is the gazebo portion—the rocky cliff and patches of meadow that surround it. I asked Kit and Madison to take the beach, because it's the least likely spot for anyone to hide. Garrett chose the woods, clearly thinking that's the most likely place. I picked the gazebo region because I'm now certain I didn't mistake that tree trunk for a figure.

Someone was on that cliff. They saw us coming. Whoever is staging this occult bullshit knew the Abbases had fled, and they came out to add the next props. Then we arrived, and they didn't expect that.

They thought I'd get the frantic call from the Abbases and fret and worry and eventually send someone from town to check it out. Instead, I showed up with five others in tow and settled in to stay the night.

The sensible thing would be for the intruder to retreat. But whoever is doing this is bold and determined, and instead they used our arrival to crank the spook show up to eleven. Skip the slow progression. Just scare the ever-loving shit out of us. If they're hidden far enough back on the island, they might even think we all fled when Sadie took off in the boat.

Except we didn't flee. We figured out what they're up to, and now they're trapped on this island with us. At the very least, our search will scare them into taking off, and we'll hear their boat start up. We might not reach it in time to confront them, but we'll get them the hell off my island.

That's what's driving me right now. The overwhelming compulsion to get them off my island.

My island. Every rock, every tree, every wildflower and weed is mine. Yes, this is nature, and no one owns it, but I am the guardian of this particular speck of earth, and I'm not letting anyone push me off it.

Would it be different if they'd offered me a good price upfront? If they hadn't looked at me and seen some middle-class sucker who didn't know what she had? Worse, looked at me with my divorce and my new teenage ward and my dead sister's debt, and decided my desperation could bolster their investment portfolio.

Had they made me an offer I couldn't refuse, I *wouldn't* have refused it. I couldn't—in those zeros, I'd see Madison's dream college, and no matter how much I love this island, I would have put her first. So, in a way, I'm glad they lowballed me and pulled this bullshit to scare me off, because I don't care what they offer now. I'm not budging. I'd rather take on the debt to put Madison through school.

I don't expect to find the intruder at the gazebo cliff, but I do hope to find proof they were there. And I hope our about-face scares the shit out of *them*. They're the hunted ones now. They're the ones trapped on a remote island with *us*.

The first part of our walk is silent, Jayla beside me, her flashlight beam straight ahead as mine scans the darkness.

Then, when we're crossing the tiny bridge over the stream, she says, "Do you think it could be Sadie?"

"Hmm?" I say, still deep in my thoughts.

"The person behind this. I'm wondering if it's Sadie."

I frown over. "Sadie trying to buy Hemlock Island?"

Jayla rolls her dark eyes. "She doesn't have the cash for that. I mean, could she be the one doing the staging? Yes, I agree that, as motives go, money is the obvious one, but there are others. Like payback."

I flinch, and it takes a moment before I say, carefully, "For stealing Kit from her."

"What?" She looks over, face scrunching up. "Kit and Sadie hooked up once years ago. And yes, I know about that. The idiot confessed to me, because he knows how I feel about her."

"And wanted absolution?" I consider. "No, that's not Kit. He wanted you to know before you heard it on the grapevine. Like he said, he's always been more willing to give her the benefit of the doubt. Because we didn't tell him everything she'd done."

"Yep, we were decent about it, and look where it got us. What's this about stealing him?"

I shrug. "She phoned me after the wedding. It was . . ." The memory flashes. "Kind of awful."

"She got nasty."

"The opposite, actually. She was drunk, and yes, she was angry but she was crying, too. She said she'd had a crush on Kit for years, and they finally got together, but the timing was wrong. When she backed off, I swooped in. Payback for . . ." I shrug. "You know."

Jayla stops, boots squeaking on rock as she turns to face me. "She seriously thought you married Kit to . . ." She sputters and waves a hand. "I can't even find words, and you know I *always* have plenty to spare. You got together with Kit two *years* after their fling, yet you apparently married him to *spite* her?"

"She was drunk."

"Obviously." She resumes walking as we climb the hill. "If anything, though, that's one more point in favor of my argument. I had no idea she had a crush on Kit—"

"Neither did I," I cut in. "Just to be clear."

"Oh, that was already clear. I did suspect she'd set her sights on him, but in a far more calculating way. Hearing she drunk-called in tears . . ." She shakes her head. "I won't feel sorry for her. You can do that. I won't. But she feels as if you stole Kit from her, and she already had issues with you, so could this be payback?"

"She staged the occult stuff to scare me?"

"Hey, we all know you're a horror fan. Someone else might have seen a hex circle and mistaken it for a kid's drawing. You'd know what it is. Also, if she thinks you stole Kit, then maybe, in a twisted way, this is appropriate revenge. You took him from her, so she'll take his marriage gift from you."

I shrug as we reach the top of the cliff. Then I turn to look out, the breeze tickling my face and setting my hair aswirl.

"You never want to think the worst of her," Jayla says. "Even when she damn well deserves it. She showed up here to get between you and Kit. You know that, right? He ran to your rescue, and she came to block him. That's a dick move. Bringing Garrett?" She whistles, the sound echoing around us. "She's lucky we didn't drive them off the island with pitchforks."

"I don't think blocking Kit was her motivation."

Jayla sighs. "Of course you don't."

"No, I really don't."

I tell her what Sadie said in the laundry room.

"She—she what?" Jayla sputters. "She actually asked you . . . ?"

"More like demanded."

"She *threatened* you? About *that*?"

I shove my hands into my pockets. "It wasn't a threat. At least, not yet. The thing is, I see where she's coming from. In regards to her own situation, I mean."

"It's not about her."

"Right. That's the problem. It has nothing to do with her, and yet she's suffered more than anyone because of it."

"More than *you*?" Jayla says. "Please don't tell me you think that."

"She lost something, and she wants it back, and with Anna gone . . ." I shove my hands in deeper. "It's complicated."

"It is. Which means she should have called you to discuss it. Not waylaid you here."

I take three steps and bend. "Is this a footprint?"

Jayla doesn't move from her spot. "Yes, because we were up here earlier."

I touch the patch of soft ground where there's a clear shoe impression. "We weren't over here, and this is fresh."

"Maybe it's the Abbases?" She crosses her arms and then uncrosses them. "Fine, I'm being contrary. You can say that, you know."

"Nah, it's always better to let you figure it out for yourself."

She mutters under her breath, stalks over, and bends to shine her light on the footprint. She's close enough that I can smell her hair oil, and it's the same one she's always used, the scent stirring memories of all the times we'd fallen asleep, in the back of a car, watching a movie, our heads together, that smell lulling me into slumber. *Jayla is here,* it said. *Everything's safe, everything's fine.*

I blink back tears and clear my throat before I look over at her. "How're you doing, Jay? I haven't asked that."

She waves around us. "Because you're kinda busy with all this."

Her gaze shifts to the side. "Which is a fine excuse, because I didn't ask about you either."

"It's good to see you."

"Don't pull that shit."

Her scowl makes me laugh, and she shakes her head.

"Fine. You have thirty seconds to be all friendly and whatever." Her voice softens. "I'm doing okay. I think I might . . . No, I *know* I've found someone. We're talking about moving in, which is scary as hell, because I don't do that shit, and she's got a kid, and I suck with kids."

"Madison wouldn't say so."

"Because she inherited your shitty taste in friends." She settles on her haunches. "Mads seems to be doing well."

"She's doing okay."

"And you?"

Not doing okay. Not by a long shot.

I make some noncommittal noise under my breath and gesture at the footprint. "Looks like a guy's by the length and width. The tread suggests a boot."

"Nice dodge of my question, which *answers* my question."

"I'll be fine," I say. "Yesterday, I thought I saw someone up here when we were coming out. I pretended I saw a moose because I figured it was that stump." I point.

She eyes me for a moment, as if debating whether to pursue the earlier question. Then she mutters under her breath again and starts shining the light across the ground.

"More footprints over there," she says. "Looks like several people—Ugh, because that's where we were earlier."

I laugh softly. "Yep."

When my light catches moisture glinting off a broad leaf at ground level, I shine the beam on it and my breath seizes.

"Is that blood?"

TEN

Jayla twists and her flashlight beam joins mine. "Shit. That really looks like it."

I touch it, and my finger comes back red. The blood is dry around the edges with a dull glint where the middle is still damp.

"There's more over here," Jayla says.

We follow the droplets. They lead to a custom-made sign.

WARNING! DEEP ROCK CREVICE AHEAD! PLEASE DON'T WALK UP HERE!!!

Yep, far too many exclamation marks, with a garish font in lettering as red as the blood below. I've posted three of these signs, plus I include it on the "Hazards" page of my visitors' book *and* there's a clause in the contract requiring that renters *read* that hazards page and share it with all family members. I've still had one person fall—bumps and bruises only—and one tumble in and get stuck. The latter said I should "block off" the crevice, as if I could just nail boards into rock to cover a twenty-foot-long crack.

There's a drop of blood on the sign. I'm examining that when Jayla steps past me and then:

"Motherfuckers!"

I glance over to see what prompted the extra-special profanity.

She's looking at a flat pale rock just past the sign, the sort that invites graffiti, and I've had to scrub off initials more than once. What's on it right now is different. It's a circular design, drawn in blood.

I shine the light on it as I hunker down.

"Hex circle," Jayla mutters.

When I don't answer, she waves at it. "That's what it is, right?"

"I'm not exactly an expert."

"Compared to me you are. Don't tell me you didn't know that's what the thing on the crawlspace door was . . . and that you didn't look it up to see what exactly it meant."

I did, and it was a fairly standard hex, which made me even more certain it was fake staging. Do an internet search for "hex circle" images, and it's the first one that pops up.

This is different. It's not so much painted on as smeared. It also just . . . looks different. If it weren't drawn in blood, I'd think it was a renter's kid making a design on the rock. Finger painting—that's what it looks like. A rough circle with slashes and swirls.

"It's different from the other one," I say, "but I suspect they were in a hurry this time. They had some pig's blood or whatever and dashed something out." I start to rise. Then I pause and walk around to the other side of the circle. "From here it looks like stick figures. Two of them holding hands."

Jayla joins me. "Kind of?"

"Like seeing dragons in the clouds, right?" I shake my head. "If that's what they were going for, they did a shitty job of it. Strike all artists from the list of suspects."

"How fresh is the blood?" she says.

"Again, I'm the expert?"

"Tell me you don't have any idea."

I shake my head. "Fine. It's not wet, so it isn't fresh. There was rain two days ago, which would have damaged it. So maybe yesterday?"

She peers around. "This afternoon, we stood over there. We

wouldn't have seen it. Did anyone walk over here after that? When we were looking for clues?"

"We'll ask if anyone noticed the rock. If so, then it happened after that. Oh, check out the lichen over here. It's crushed."

As I take another step, following the crushed lichen, she says, "Watch out for the crevice."

"Yeah, yeah."

"Just reading the helpful sign. Could you have added more exclamation marks?"

"Oh, I'd add fifty if it'd actually make people read it."

I'm looking at the crushed lichen when movement on the dark water catches my eye. My head jerks up, and for a moment, I'm so certain I see a boat that I open my mouth to say so. *Hey, looks like Sadie's coming back.* But then it's gone, and I'm left squinting and searching.

"Laney?"

"I thought I saw—" I take two more steps. "There!"

There's definitely something out there. Something pale against the night. It's not boat-sized, though. It's an odd shape, floating on the water but low and long.

A lost paddleboard? A canoe that came loose from its moorings? Or *part* of a canoe? It happens. New cottagers put up docks that get ripped away by the first storm. It's Lake Superior, after all. Entire carrier ships lie beneath this inky water.

I notice smaller pale bits moving on the lake, including some close to shore. Whitecaps? As if in answer, the wind whips through my hair. I'd noticed it picking up earlier but had been too preoccupied to give it much thought.

I stare up at the overcast night sky. *Tell me that's not a storm approaching.* I always check the marine forecast before coming out but, again, I'd been preoccupied.

Had there been boats on the lake when we came out? Boats tied along the shore? Damn it, why hadn't I paid more attention?

Because I expected to be back by now. Also, how much does a storm matter when I don't have a damn boat. It would just mean Sadie won't be able to send anyone out in the morning, and we'll be stuck here. Now that we've determined that anyone on the island with us is an asshole rather than a killer, that's more annoying than terrifying.

I squint out again. While I do definitely see whitecaps, the object that first caught my attention isn't that. It's still there, along with several other smaller pale things floating in the water.

Wait, is that—?

I take another step.

"Laney!"

It's the warning shout that does it, ironically. I wheel, thinking Jayla's in trouble, and my foot slides on the lichen. I scramble, clawing at the air as if that will save me.

As I plummet into the crevice, my flailing hands catch a root. Then my foot slams down hard, ankle twisting. I find myself hugging roots and vegetation, one foot down, the other braced against the rock wall. I test the foot that touched down. It's on something solid. I look down to see a ledge below me. A very wide, very stable ledge.

Okay, situation noncritical.

"Laney!"

"I'm fine," I call back with a slight laugh. "I fell onto a ledge. And even if I'd missed that, it's only another five feet to the bottom."

Only five feet, but tight, with no easy way out if you get wedged in there. Still, it's not like toppling off a fifty-foot cliff. At worst, I'd have needed to be hauled out, which is why I avoid this spot when I'm alone on the island.

I look up into Jayla's face, five feet above me.

She shakes her head, braids swinging. "You get yourself into some real situations, girl."

"Hey, it's not just me." I wave around. "Does this look familiar? Outdoor education class and someone had to get a selfie on the edge of a bank? Slid over the edge, caught herself, and flipped out . . . when she was barely a few feet from the bottom."

"And her best friend videotaped it instead of helping?"

"Jayla Hayes freaked out of her mind. It was a once-in-a-lifetime opportunity. And the moment where you realized it you could just hop down? Priceless."

She lifts both middle fingers.

I laugh. "It was fun, though. That entire class was fun. Seeing you out of your element and trying oh-so-hard to play it cool."

"Some of us find this outdoor shit scarier than any dark alley, okay?"

"And then, you're down at the bottom, covered in dirt, and Zahra comes along, and you're trying to pretend you climbed down on purpose, checking out a fossil. How the hell could you not know you liked girls back then? You had such a crush on her."

"On Zahra? Pfft. I just didn't want to look silly in front of *anyone*."

"*Such* a crush. I thought you took the class to hang out with your best friend, but looking back now, it was all about Zahra."

"Keep it up, and I'll leave you down there."

"Oh no!" I flail my arms. "Help, I'm trapped in a shallow crevice! How ever will I escape?"

She stands up and steps away.

"Ahh!" I mock-scream. "Come back! Do not abandon me in my hour of need!"

"Walking away now," she calls. "Taking my light source with me."

"The dark? No, we are afraid of the dark, yes, precious? Afraid of the dark we are."

"This is why you and Kit make the perfect pair. You belong to-gether, if only to save the rest of us from having to deal with your nonsense."

"Dark, so dark, so cold. Mommy, are you there? I can't see any-thing, and it's so cold. Mommy?"

"Walking faster now."

She's not, of course. She's standing just out of sight, listening to me goof around, as she always did when we were kids. She'd grumble and roll her eyes, far too cool for my nonsense, but she still listened, and she was still amused.

She's right about Kit. We shared the same sense of humor, and when we were younger, the two of us would get going, riffing off movies and books, being silly in a way the others couldn't bring themselves to be.

"Dark . . . cold . . ." I whisper. "Don't leave me, dearest friend. Do not abandon me to the void."

She covers a laugh with a snort. "Still not coming back. You got yourself into that mess. You can get yourself out."

I could point out that it was her sudden warning that actually sent me over the edge, but that would be rude. At least she still cares enough to warn me.

I look around for the best climbing route. Wow, it really is dark, isn't it? I dropped my flashlight into the crevice when I fell. I'll want to get that later—it's my good flashlight.

If you'd asked me five years ago whether there was such a thing as a "good" flashlight, I'd have laughed. Then my new husband built me a luxury vacation home on a private, off-the-grid island, where if the power fails, it can get very dark. For that, he'd gotten "good" flashlights—meaning expensive—and I'm rather fond of mine. Too fond to leave it at the bottom of this crevice.

I could ask Jayla for some light, but what fun would that be? I just need to find the right route. I also need to find it without, you know, stepping off the ledge that I can no longer see.

I feel my way along the ledge.

"I could help you," Jayla says. "Just say the magic words. I know you remember them."

I shake my head. The magic words are "Jayla is the most amazing person ever, and I'm so lucky to be her friend." Seems I'm not the only one who hasn't quite left childhood behind.

I tap my toe down. Yep, that's the end of the ledge, but the wall above me slopes inward, which isn't climbing-friendly. I feel my way to the other end of the ledge. Ah, *there's* what I want—a nicely angled rock wall with footholds and handholds. The only problem is that those footholds and handholds aren't directly above my ledge.

"Fine," Jayla says. "Just ask nicely, and I'll help."

"I've got it."

"Of course you do. Story of your life. While you're in there, maybe we can discuss this bullshit about you not accepting alimony from Kit."

"He gave me a million-dollar house. I don't need alimony."

I put one foot onto a nub of rock and test it. Seems solid.

"Are you punishing him, Laney? I don't know what happened, but with the way he's been moping, I'm guessing it was his fault."

"It was no one's fault, and if you think I'd punish him, you've forgotten everything you ever knew about me."

Her voice drops. "What happened, Laney? He was so damned happy. You both were, right? I wasn't imagining that. I know I wasn't."

My hand slips from its hold, and rock scrapes my arm before I catch my balance. "Can we talk about this later?"

"I kind of like this. You can't run away."

"I don't know what happened, okay?" I slide my foot up to the next hold. "We hit some bumps during the pandemic. He was having a rough time with the business, and I was dealing with Anna's cancer, and . . . it fell apart, I guess. Now, seriously, can we talk about something else? Anything else?"

A smell wafts past. The wind has been blowing from the lake, and that's all I've been able to smell, but now I catch a whiff of something that reminds me of that hank of hair, and my hand slips. I catch myself, but my fingers immediately start to slide.

"Jayla? Can you—?"

"Why did you post that dating profile for me?" she says.

I stop moving. "What?"

"Don't 'what' me, Laney." Anger edges into her voice. "It was a shitty thing to do, and maybe you thought it was a joke, but it hurt." A crack in that anger. "It really hurt."

My fingers slip again, and I try to grab a jutting chunk of rock, but it's covered in lichen.

"Jay—"

"We were young," she says. "We tried dating, and it didn't work, and yeah, that was awkward. Maybe there were hurt feelings."

My fingers find another hold, and I exhale. Then I look up her way. "There were no hurt feelings, Jay."

She continues as if she didn't hear me, "Maybe you thought you were being funny, but putting up a straight profile for me, on *that* kind of site, with *those* pictures . . . You owe me an apology."

"I literally have no idea what you're—"

My hand and left foot slip at the same time. I plummet, scrambling, hands grabbing for something, anything. Yes, it's only a short drop, but it's *rock*. I can hit my head and—

"Laney!"

There! I catch something and grab on, but it comes loose and falls on top of me. Something *big* falling on top of me. A rock? A—

I strike down, my body falling as far as it'll fit as the crevice narrows. A smell washes over me. *That* smell. Decomposition. Something animal died in here, and I've pulled it on top of me.

I can't see anything. The dead thing is on top of me and blocking all light. When I move my leg, it won't budge. My foot is wedged down into the crack.

A diffuse light fills what little of the crevice I can see.

"Laney? Is that—" Jayla stops short with a little gasp.

"I'm stuck," I say. "My foot is wedged in. You're going to need to get the others."

"Laney?"

She must not be able to hear me. I lift a hand to push away whatever fell on top of me. As I do, I inwardly cringe, bracing for the touch of fur and decomposing flesh. Instead, I touch . . .

What *am* I touching? It's smooth and cold, but not like rock. Bone? It's softer than that.

Do I want to know what part of the poor dead critter I'm touching? No. Just get it off me.

I push, and my fingers touch something else, something slick and ragged with a hard nub. Oh God, what am I touching?

"Laney?"

I grit my teeth and push up on whatever is in my hands. It moves easily and then the light hits, and I see bone. Bone sticking out of bloodied flesh. My stomach lurches. It's a leg bone. It must be. A fox, maybe? It's thicker than I'd expect but I'm hardly an expert and—

The light shifts, and I see the whole of what I'm pushing at. I see pale skin and dark hairs. An arm. A human arm. I'm holding a human arm, the hand severed off.

The hand severed . . .

Bile fills my mouth. Whoever staged that hand didn't just bring *it*. They brought the whole corpse and then dumped it in here.

"Laney?"

"I know."

She says something else, but I don't hear it. I'm gritting my teeth and shoving aside the arm, which is attached to a body, that body lying over my pinned leg.

I'm sorry. Whoever you were, I'm sorry someone did this to your corpse, and I'm sorry I'm shoving you aside like this. We'll figure it out and make sure you get to your proper resting place.

I have my hands under the armpit of the poor guy, and I heave, but my hip slips and pain shoots through my side and I lose my grip. The body topples toward me. My hands fly up to ward it off, and it lands on top of my arms, crossed over my face. I don't see it. My eyes are squeezed shut. I inhale, only to gag, the smell making it feel as if I'm tasting—

Oh God.

I swallow bile. Somewhere overhead, Jayla is frantically trying to talk to me, but I'm completely focused on this macabre predicament.

I open my eyes and—

There is a face over mine, held back by my crossed arms, but I can see it. I see the dark hair with a lock of blue. I see brown eyes, wide with final shock. I see the scar across one pale cheekbone, an ugly slice of recent scar tissue. Then, in a heartbeat, I'm seeing that scar in my memory, when it was still a cut across his cheek.

"What the hell happened?" I say.

"Shaving accident."

"Did your dad—?"

"I'm fine, Ms. K. It was an accident."

Nate. Oh God. Nate.

ELEVEN

aney?" Jayla calls.

"It's—it's Nate," I manage to say.

Her voice drops. "I guessed that. I'm sorry. Just stay where you are. I'm coming down."

I squeeze back tears. "Bring the others. I don't want you getting stuck down here."

"I'm not leaving you—"

"I've got it."

"Goddamn you. Stop that."

Her voice cracks, but I'm already nudging Nate's body off mine. I move him, as best I can, to the side, propped against the wall. His arm hangs to his side, bone jutting—

Don't look at it.

Don't think about it.

"He's off me," I say. "Please go get the others."

"Stay right there."

I bite back a laugh, because if it escapes, I'll start sobbing hysterically. "Not going anywhere."

"I'm sorry, Laney. I never met Nate, but Kit said he was a good guy. Kit was glad you had him to take care of the place."

I nod, fresh tears welling.

"I'll get Kit."

Her footsteps start to recede, when I remember myself and call, "Garrett. Tell Kit to stay with Madison while you bring Garrett."

"Yeah, no. I'll stay with the kid."

She leaves the flashlight on the edge with the beam shining for me. Then her feet tap over the rock as she takes off.

I shift, adjusting as best I can. Rock jabs into my hip, and there's nothing I can do about that. I'll be fine.

Nate . . .

"I'm so sorry," I say. "If this happened because of me—" I inhale sharply. "It *did* happen because of me. I brushed off what someone was doing here . . ." My vision blurs with tears. "I am so sorry. So, so—"

Nate's arm twitches. I fall back, hitting the rock hard, my trapped leg shrieking at the sudden jolt.

Did his arm really just move?

He's not alive. There is absolutely no way he's alive.

What if he is? What if that smell is his arm, the torn flesh rotting. What if he's comatose—

With his eyes open?

Is that impossible? No, it's not.

I force myself to creep toward him, look past that arm and see Nate, the young man I knew. If there is any chance he's alive . . .

Are you listening to yourself, Laney? His hand has been sawed off. Sawed off. *If that happened, he'd bleed out. There is no way he's alive. You're crying, and it's night. Your vision is swimming—*

His arm twitches again. I stare at it, my heart slamming against my ribs. Then, very carefully, I reach out and press my fingers to his chest. The cold creeps through his T-shirt, and no heartbeat pulses.

Because he's dead, Laney.

I swallow hard. There's another explanation for what I saw. A mouse or bug burrowing through the dirt, making his arm move.

I find a stick that's blown in the crevice. Using it, I lift Nate's arm.

Holding his arm away from the wall, I peer under it. Rock. That's all I see. Solid rock. Nothing could have—

The stick vibrates in my hand, and I fall back with a yelp. Nate's arm drops, thumping against the rock wall. His body starts to slide my way, and I scramble back with a shriek as pain rips down my trapped leg.

"Laney!" a man's voice calls, shoes thumping overhead.

I want that to be Kit. God, how I want it to be Kit, even when I can tell it's not.

Garrett's face appears over the edge. He sees Nate and blanches.

"Shit," he whispers. Then his hands fly up. "Stay calm."

"I am calm," I snap. "I slipped, and my fucking leg felt like it was being ripped off, okay?"

"Can you move it?"

"No, because it's trapped."

I swallow. Don't do this. It won't help. Nate is dead, and whatever we thought was happening here, it is so much worse.

Focus on Madison and getting her into the house, where it's safe.

Safe? Trapped on an island in the middle of Lake Superior?

"It's Nate," I say, as calmly as I can. "Someone really did kill him, and they might still be on the island. Can you please make sure Kit or Jayla gets Madison into the house?"

"Jayla went to find them. Let me get you out, and we'll all head inside." His eyes meet mine. "If Madison comes here, I'll make sure she doesn't see him."

"Thank you."

"Now let me get you out of there."

He climbs down until he's looming over me, and all I see is him there, and I can't breathe. My chest seizes, panic filling me, raw animal panic. The sight of him. The smell of him.

Breathe. Remember Madison. Breathe.

Inside, I am whirling and gibbering in panic. Garrett doesn't notice anything amiss. Shocking, really. So shocking.

That thought calms me enough to catch my breath as he works on freeing my leg. It hurts like hell, but at least that's a distraction. When it's finally free, I push to my feet, balancing myself in the crevice. Garrett reaches to steady me, and it takes all my willpower not to shove him away.

"I've got it," I say.

"Laney?"

Kit's face appears over the edge. He sees Nate, and grief ripples across his face. Then he meets my gaze and reaches down. He doesn't leap into the crevice to rescue me. I know that's supposed to be the romantic move, but this is what has always done it for me. A helping hand extended, should I need it, while acknowledging that I might not.

I start to climb. Garrett's hands close over my hips. He's only bracing me, but the look on my face has Kit's eyes hardening, his mouth opening to say something.

"I'm okay," I say, and he understands what I mean and nods, though his expression stays hard.

As soon as I'm high enough, Kit hauls me out. He tries to get me to sit so he can check my leg, but I slip from his grasp.

"Nate," I say. "Please. If we can get him out . . ."

Garrett looks at Kit. Kit tenses, ready to argue that yes, we need to get Nate out.

I shake my head. "It's a crime scene, and I've messed it up enough. I wasn't thinking."

Kit takes my hand. I hesitate, and my brain issues the command to pull away, but not only doesn't my traitorous body follow through, it falls against him when he tugs me into a hug. I bury my face in his shirt.

In a heartbeat, two years disappear, and I'm here, in this spot, scouting it before building begins. Kit's hugging me as I break down in gibbering fear that I will lose my sister. A few months later, she'll be in remission, and he'll take me away for the weekend to celebrate, and we'll spend most of it in bed, ordering takeout and drinking champagne and making love as if we'd been the ones granted a hall pass by Death. Then the cancer will return, and he won't be there. I'll get a couple "I'm here if you need me" texts that feel obligatory.

I need you, Kit. I needed you then, and I need you now, but I can't fall into the trap of needing you again.

I pull away and wipe my eyes. Then I start toward the house. When my leg wobbles, Kit puts out his elbow and I pretend not to see it.

We walk in silence, with Garrett bringing up the rear. A sharp sound from the east makes me jump, but it's only the whistle of the wind. That prods a memory, sliding past, and I make a half-hearted attempt to catch it, but when it evaporates, I don't give chase.

We reach the fire pit, and I stop short. The house rises in front of us, a massive wall of unrelieved darkness.

"Madison and Jayla," I whisper. "Didn't they come—"

A light flickers deep inside the house, and I exhale. Kit opens the door, ushers us in, and locks it behind him. We continue on to find Jayla and Madison sitting on the floor, behind the couch, Madison leaning against Jayla. A lantern rests at their side.

Seeing me, Madison scrambles up, only to glance over her shoulder, as if she's revealed herself to a killer beyond that bank of windows. I lower myself to the floor and sit with my back against the sofa, as if it's a bunker of sandbags.

"I didn't tell her," Jayla says.

"I knew." Madison's voice cracks as she snuggles in beside me.

I put my arm around her shoulders and scoot closer.

"I know you all thought the hand wasn't his," Madison says.

"We wanted to think that," I say.

"I wanted to, too, but after a while, I couldn't. I kept thinking what if you guys were wrong, what if someone did really kill him, and that was his hand and—"

She gulps, and I hug her. Kit crouches in front of me and motions at my leg. I pull up the leg of my sweatpants. My calf is scraped, and it'll bruise, but it's fine.

Compared to Nate, I'm completely fine.

"Did you bring him back?" Madison asks.

"We can't," I say.

She twists. "What?"

"I'll be the asshole here," Garrett says, "since you already think I am, kiddo. It's a crime scene. We can't mess up the evidence more than we accidentally did."

Madison is quiet for a moment. Then she nods, her voice small when she says, "You're right."

"He is," Jayla says. "As soon as we're back on shore, Garrett will contact the police. They'll take it from there, and we'll make sure Nate is treated right. A proper investigation and a proper burial."

"So, do we wait for Sadie?" Madison says. "Stay here until she sends someone for us?"

"She *will* send someone," Garrett says. "But I'm not sure I want to wait for that. She'll be embarrassed that she took off with the boat, so she'll send someone else, which means waiting for business hours."

"She has no reason to think we need rescue," I say. "We'd spent the evening drinking beer and toasting marshmallows. There's no rush to come get us."

"It'll be dawn soon," Garrett says. "What are our options? You've got a canoe, right?"

I nod. "A canoe, kayak, and stand-up paddleboard."

"A double kayak? Or can two people fit on the paddleboard?"

I shake my head. "The paddleboard is for one, and it's not made for crossing Lake Superior. The kayak's a single, and I wouldn't cross on it either."

"I could handle it," Garrett says.

"It's Lake Superior," Madison says.

Garrett's brow furrows, as if that was a non sequitur.

"One of the construction guys fell in and got pulled under," she says. "He nearly drowned. It's nasty and it's deep. Over a *thousand feet* deep. There are hundred-year-old wrecks with preserved bodies still on board."

"Laney and Madison are right," Kit says. "No one is heading for shore on the kayak or paddleboard. Laney and I can take the canoe." He looks at me. "Is that okay?"

"I'll go with you," Garrett says.

"Kit and I have done it before," I say. "That wind's picking up, and the sooner we get out, the better. It's a tough enough trek in calm water."

"You'll wear life vests?" Jayla says.

"They always do," Madison says. "Even when I'm not here."

"Safety first," I quip.

"Have I mentioned how cold the lake is?" Madison says. "The only thing life vests are going to do is keep your body afloat for the rescuers."

I rumple her hair. "Well, that's good, because while it'd be cool to frighten the crap out of divers a century from now, proving me legally dead would be a real pain in the ass. You'd be forty before you got your college funds."

"Can we *not* talk about dying out there?" Jayla says, and when I glance over, her face is serious.

I check my watch. "Dawn is in an hour. There's no chance of getting sleep, but Kit and I should have something to eat. It's going to be a long paddle."

TWELVE

Whatever happens, at least we won't starve. Living on an island means learning to stockpile food, because if you run out of something, you're not hopping in the boat to get it. In my locked storeroom, I have canned food, dried food, and a rotating stock of nonperishables.

When I'm here writing, I don't want to leave for anything. That might explain the massive bags of coffee beans and chocolate bars. I keep the kitchen stocked with the basics for guests—everything from flour to tea to spices—though admittedly, I don't actually use the same stuff myself, being a paranoid bitch. I'd rather switch out the opened jar of cinnamon in the cupboard for the one in my storeroom.

Guests also leave food. If it's unopened, that's fine—the next guests can use it—but one of the problems with renting to rich people is that they leave *everything,* sometimes with little notes like "Help yourself!" on a bag with two broken Oreos at the bottom. Surely the cleaner will be happy for those broken Oreos and stale bread, right? Saves the renters from adding to the trash they need to take with them.

This time, there's a lot of unopened food, because the Abbases understandably didn't pause to empty the fridge before they fled. I feel terrible about that, but on the other hand, I'm glad they ran when they could. At least they didn't end up like Nate.

End up like Nate.

I'm trying to wrap my head around that. We jumped on Garrett's explanation earlier, and that's partly because that made more sense. If someone wants my island cheap, they might resort to desecrating a corpse. But murdering my cleaner?

"Could the kid have been in on it?" Garrett says as I cook bacon and eggs, and we all pretend it's just an early morning on the island, and there's no killer lurking in the forest beyond, no mutilated body stuffed in a crevice.

When we all turn to face him, he raises his hands. "I'm not trying to speak ill of the dead. I'm not even blaming him. If I really needed to escape a shithole town, no matter how much I liked my employer . . ." He shrugs. "He was still working for rich people, and that's gotta sting."

"He was working for Laney," Madison says. "Not Kit."

I shake my head. "I understand where you're coming from, Garrett, and I don't want to be the clueless boss convinced her employees all love and respect her, but I would like to think if Nate was in trouble, he'd come to me." I flip the bacon. "And maybe even saying that makes me a clueless boss."

"He wasn't like that," Madison says, her voice low. "He really wasn't."

"I don't know Nate either," Jayla says, "but that might make me a better judge of the situation. This doesn't sound like a kid who'd screw Laney over. What if he made a mistake? Agreed to something and regretted it? Or agreed to something without realizing what they were up to? He finds out the truth, they fight, he dies, and they use his body. That's horrifying, but is it possible?"

"Maybe?" I say.

I take the bacon out, leaving two slices that I keep cooking for Kit. I do it automatically, and then I find myself staring into the pan. Am

I ever going to forget how he likes his bacon? His eggs? Toast? How he takes his coffee?

As a newlywed, I'd made a point of remembering all that. We didn't have years of dating to fall back on, and I wanted to show him that remembering these things mattered to me. Now he's gone, and the memories stay, and I'm not sure what to do with that.

Well, for starters, I could not think about it right now, when we're trapped on an island with a killer.

Ah, but it's so much easier to dwell on bacon, isn't it? Not to think of what happened to Nate and whether he could have been desperate for money, not feeling like he could come to me, while knowing, even if he did, I might not have been able to help.

I crack eggs beside Kit's bacon.

"Could you, uh, tell what happened to him?" Jayla asks. "That might help us know what we're dealing with. Whether it was an accident or . . . Not that I expect you to have been examining his, uh, body. I just meant whether you saw something."

"I didn't," I say.

"I looked," Garrett says. "As best I could, while I was down there. The obvious damage was . . ." He coughs.

"His hand. But that didn't kill him," I add quickly, before inserting any horrific images in Madison's head. "It was removed postmortem."

"Which means, yes, his death could have been an accident," Jayla says. "That absolutely does not excuse what those bastards did, but if that's what happened, then while they might have stuck around to stage his hand, they're long gone now. Back to civilization, where they're waiting for Laney to decide she wants to sell."

Kit takes an unopened loaf of bread and feeds slices into the toaster.

Jayla's theory makes sense. It would mean there isn't a killer out there. Everything is fine.

Everything is sure as hell *not* fine. Nate is dead, his body desecrated, and we're on this island with a storm approaching. But if we're on this island alone, that's the important thing right now. I haven't brought Madison onto the island with a crazed killer. Kit and I will paddle to shore, and everything will be as fine as it possibly can be.

After breakfast, Kit and Jayla insist on cleaning up, which I suspect means they want to talk. Garrett goes on patrol, stalking through the house, checking doors and locks. Madison and I wander to the far end of the great room, where two chairs look out at the view. They don't quite fit with the rest of the layout—and the interior designer had been horrified—but this is my favorite and most-used spot, where I curl up and write when it's too chilly to work on the deck.

The other chair had been Kit's. Now it's Madison's, and she takes it, pulling her legs in under her.

"You okay?" she asks.

I choke on a small laugh. "That's supposed to be my line."

"You're the one who found . . . him."

I sober and nod.

She switches position, pulling her knees to her chest as she stares out at the rocky beach and water beyond, her gaze saying she sees none of that.

"I liked him," she whispers.

"So did I. I liked him a *lot*. He was . . ." My voice catches. "He was a great guy, and I admired the hell out of him."

"Same," she says, her voice still soft. "But I mean . . . I liked him."

I glance over. "Oh."

Her cheeks color, and she pulls her knees in tighter. "Remember when you and Kit brought me here at the beginning of the pandemic? When Nate came for a few visits? He was cute and nice and smart and . . ." She swallows. "I really liked him, Laney. He was the first guy I ever thought of that way."

She shifts again. "I think he knew, but he never did anything. He just kept on being nice to me, and it wasn't weird or awkward, and that just made me like him more. Lots of guys would have . . ." She shrugs. "Taken advantage. Or backed off. He didn't. I dreamed that maybe, someday, when I was a bit older . . ."

Her cheeks redden again, and I reach over and take her hand, and we sit there, staring out the window and thinking about a boy who'd deserved every good thing life had to offer . . . and got none of it.

By the time Kit and I head out, it's dawn. We leave the others to secure the house behind us.

"I keep wanting to say I'm sorry about all this," Kit says as we make our way over the rock. "I know it sounds trite, and I just . . ." He throws up his hands. "I don't know what else to say."

"It's okay."

"No, it's not okay. Someone targeted you. Hell, I might have sent them your way. They contacted me, and I passed them to you without a second thought."

"Uh, because you presumed they were normal people interested in a normal property purchase. This?" I wave back at the house. "This is a million miles beyond normal."

"Is it?" He stuffs his hands in his pockets. "I should know, right? This is my world. I grew up in it. I live in the center of it now."

Not by choice. Taking over the family business wasn't what Kit wanted. As a kid, he'd dreamed of starting a band. When he was older, he realized he'd only make a living in music if his parents bankrolled him, and he sure as hell wouldn't allow that. So his next "dream" was a whole lot like mine, oddly enough.

Or maybe not so oddly, but rather another thing that drew us together. I dreamed of being a writer and became an English teacher to earn a living. He dreamed of being a musician and planned to become a music teacher to earn a living. As undergrads, we even shared teaching-college information.

Neither Kit nor Jayla ever intended to go into the family business, and they had the kind of parents who were absolutely fine with that. His mom had a brother not much older than Jayla, and he'd been working for the corporation since he graduated college.

That uncle died in a car accident six years ago. Then their dad had two heart attacks in a row, the second one scary enough that both parents decided it was time to retire. Jayla was in law school, and that left Kit. Oh, no one expected him to take over the business, but his family needed him, so he said he'd decided he didn't want to teach, joking he didn't much like kids anyway—*such* a lie—and he threw himself into the job of CEO. That means he does know this cutthroat corporate world, better than he ever wanted to.

"People do shit like this," he says as we walk along the rocky beach. "I've seen them do things that should earn a one-way ticket to a locked ward for sociopathy, and instead, they're admired for their 'guts,' for their 'business savvy.'" He shakes his head. "I knew those things happen, but I didn't think twice about passing developers on to you."

I reach over to rub his back, the gesture automatic. Then I pull back, hands going into my pockets. "It's not the same. If I were selling a corporation, you'd have been wary. This is a summer house."

"I'm still sorry."

"I know."

"And I'll stop moaning about it now. That's the last thing you need." He glances over. "Hey, did I tell you I learned some new sea shanties?"

I sputter a laugh. "Everyone else moved on from that midpandemic, Kit."

"I am not everyone else. And I know how much you loved hearing me sing them. I wrote one, about a fair maiden who waves her beloved off to sea, promising she will count the moments to his return . . . and then runs inside, pulls on her yoga pants, and bingewatches true-crime shows. Want to hear it?"

"I kinda do."

"Good, because either way, you're going to hear it. Over and over, while we row for shore. To keep our spirits up." He lifts his hands. "Don't thank me. It's the least I can do."

"Torturing me with sea shanties?"

"Yep."

I won't mind. The thought comes in a very small, quiet voice. *I won't mind at all.*

I'd loved the sea-shanty phase, because it came at a time when Kit was overwhelmed with work, grinding through his days, the two of us barely exchanging five sentences between breakfast and a dinner that came so late I was often in bed before he ate.

I'd played a couple of sea shanties from the internet, alone in my office, struggling to get through my own days of online teaching, and he'd come in during one and asked me to replay it. Soon we were spending lunches together, Kit with his guitar, riffing on shanties, as silly as he could make them.

We found time, Kit. Even in the midst of all that, we found time to be together and have fun and push the world away for a little while. So what happened?

We continue along the beach until I veer inland. To get to the secondary boathouse, we need to pick our way through a thick barrier of trees, half of them dead and gnarled. The building appears ahead, tucked into that gloomy forest.

The best thing I can say about my private boathouse is that it's upright. Pretty much upright, anyway. I'd bought it from a Fox Bay local who was planning to haul it away to the dump, and I'd paid for him to bring it out here and put it back together. It's weathered, with peeling paint that I keep meaning to redo as a summer project with Madison, but when we're up here together, we're too busy paddling and exploring and reading and lazing the days away. Important stuff, for both of us.

I'm also not in a rush to paint the shed because I'm hoping it's a temporary structure. The watercraft should all be stored in the boat-house, which is modern and gorgeous and designed for, well, holding boats. There's plenty of room; Kit had the builder put in berths for our personal watercraft. Yet I'd quickly discovered that no amount of polite signs—or clauses in the rental agreement—kept people from taking them out on the water. It isn't a matter of "don't touch my stuff"—it's a matter of "I don't want you getting killed by touching my stuff." I only discovered renters were ignoring my request when anglers picked up a near-hypothermic guest stranded on my paddle-board.

This isn't a little forest pond. It's Lake fucking Superior. I'm tempted to have people sing "The Wreck of the *Edmund Fitzgerald*" before they get the keys to the boathouse. If a freaking carrier ship can go down, taking the entire crew with it, they shouldn't be trying out my damn paddleboard for kicks.

Seeing the boathouse, Kit frowns. "Not to be critical but . . ."

"It's a piece of shit that ruins the aesthetic of the island?"

"I'd never say that. Madison told me you had to slap something together fast to keep renters from using your stuff. Which is fine, and yes, it's not the prettiest thing, but if you decide to keep renting, and it bothers you, you'll replace it. Otherwise, none of my business. I'm just surprised by the location."

"Fifty feet from the actual shore? Near a crappy sliver of beach covered in sharp rock shards?" I waggle my brows. "Think of it as my piranha-filled moat."

He hesitates and then smiles. "Renters don't venture out here. Which means they don't find the shed."

That's the idea, but they've broken the lock twice. I don't say that—I just nod. We cross the last ten feet. Then we're at the doors, barn-style ones that should open onto the water, but if I had it on the shoreline, people would definitely try to get access.

I spin the combination on the first lock.

"Two locks?" Kit says. "Has someone broken in?"

"I'm just making sure they don't try," I lie.

I get both locks open, swing the doors wide and—

"What the hell?" Kit says.

He brushes past me as he strides into the boathouse. I can only stare, certain I'm seeing wrong, *wanting* to be seeing wrong. Kit grabs a battery-operated lantern and shines it around the gloom.

Destroyed.

My boats. *Our* boats. They're . . .

We aren't taking these to shore.

We aren't taking them anywhere.

THIRTEEN

I can't quite fathom what I'm seeing. I actually have two kayaks, both single-person, plus a canoe, and looking around, I'm not sure what's what. The boathouse is littered with pieces of fiberglass. Chunks of it. *Twisted* chunks.

"I . . . I don't understand," I say. "What would do this besides a bomb?"

Kit bends to examine a scrap of wreckage. It takes a moment to recognize what it is—part of a kayak seat, melted.

"Can any bomb do this without damaging the shed?" I say.

He picks up a shard and turns it over in his hands. He's not giving an answer because there isn't one.

Kit straightens and raises the lantern to look around.

"One door," I say. "I boarded up the windows, and they're still boarded." I stomp the ground, dirt flying up. "There's no floor, but unless someone dug their way in . . . ?"

They didn't. We can both see that. I'm looking around when I notice something overhead.

I take the lantern and lift it. My paddleboard sits in its spot in the rafters.

"Tell me that's not damaged," I say.

He walks to the front of the board and reaches up, then shimmies it down and out the door. I follow him as he sets the paddleboard onto the ground. It's in pristine shape. Not a scratch that I didn't put there myself by scraping against rocks.

I run back in. The paddles for the canoe and kayak are among the twisted pieces, along with tufts of stuffing and scraps of fabric from the life vests. I use another paddle for the board, though, and it's still in the rafters. I yank it down and carry it outside.

Kit looks from me to the board.

Say something, damn it. Say what you want to say, what you're holding back because you need to be "nice." I'm the former wife you walked out on during a pandemic, and now you're treading eggshells to be nice to me. Just say it, damn it. State the fucking obvious.

"Well?" I snap, when I can't hold back any longer. "Say it."

"I don't need to. You already know it."

The wind falls from my sails. Did I want him to say the words, as if he thought I was too dense to figure it out? Give me a reason to take offense?

"Fucking useless," I mutter.

His head shoots up, genuine shock on his face.

"Not you," I say. "The board. It's useless."

I drop the paddle onto it, and I don't even get a satisfying clank, the aluminum falling with a dull thump on the fiberglass.

"There's no way in hell we can get to shore on that." I glance up at him. "Right?"

"Right."

I slump. Did I want him to say I could do it? Not to overestimate my ability but tell me I'm exaggerating the danger.

Sure, you can do it, Laney. It's only five miles.

Five miles across the open water of Lake Superior, which might as well be the ocean.

I walk down to the water. While I did pick this spot to hide my private boathouse, it's also near the perfect launch spot for the smaller watercraft, in the shallow side of a cove. The main boathouse is on the other side of that cove, on deeper water better suited for the motorized boat. Here, though, once you get past that treacherous stretch of rock, there's a strip of actual beach.

I take off my shoes at the rock edge and walk onto the water-smoothed pebbles and tiny rocks that approximate something like sand. There's no tide on the Great Lakes, and the wind dictates how far the water reaches. Today, it comes all the way to the edge, and I'm sloshing in it as I walk along that beach strip, looking across the seemingly endless water.

The last time Kit and I were here, we sat on this beach gazing out over the water as I told him the plot for my second novel. With anyone else, that might have been a quiet, thoughtful conversation. That wasn't us. It was me waving my arms and gesticulating wildly while Kit scratched a stick in the sand, mapping out my scenes and brainstorming ideas for the plot holes.

Yesterday, my agent had called to ask about the third book. I told her it was almost done.

I lied.

I have fifty pages written, and they don't even form fifty pages of coherent plot. I haven't written for nearly a year. I want to. I desperately want to escape into my stories, but every time I try, real life intrudes. My sister is dead, my husband left me, I'm not sure I can be a good parent to my niece, I'm not sure I can be a good teacher to kids traumatized by the pandemic.

Rocks crunch as Kit walks up. He doesn't say anything. Doesn't fall in step beside me or behind me. Just finds his own path to wander in the same direction, and when I glance back, he has his sneakers tied and hanging from one hand, the other shading his eyes against the morning sun.

When I'm on the island alone, I often rise early to enjoy the sunrise with my morning coffee. Sunsets on the lake get all the attention. They are breathtaking, with reds and oranges that turn the sky into a screaming portent for the end of days. I prefer sunrise. So much subtler, with the sky suffused with soft layers of pink and purple. I picture sunrises as the day waking, slowly stretching, while sunsets are the day flaming out in a blaze of riotous glory.

This morning, sunrise has stolen the cloak from her sister. She's blood red, a fiery warning. Storm's coming. I can feel it in the wind, hear it in the slap of waves, even smell it, I swear, whipping over on the breeze.

Red sky in morning, sailors take warning.

I shiver, and Kit says, "That's not good," making me jump to find him so close.

"Hmm."

"If you're out here because you're even considering paddleboarding, I hope that sky is your answer."

I wrap my reply in a look that has him twisting a smile.

"Okay," he says. "Obviously."

"Yes, I was taking a look, but I already knew the answer." I cross my arms as a gust cuts through my sweatshirt. "I'm mostly concerned about whether Sadie can send anyone for us today. I'm afraid the answer is no."

"Not this morning, at least. It'll calm down later, and she's not going to leave us overnight again."

I tighten my arms. "What if she doesn't send anyone?"

"You really think she's going to strand us out here?"

I hesitate, and then shake my head. "Not Garrett. Not you. Not Madison."

"Not even you and Jayla. I know there's history there, and I know why, but everyone makes mistakes, and I really think she regrets hers."

He doesn't know the whole of it, and I'm not about to explain. Sometimes, I think I should, so he can make a fully informed decision about any relationship he might have with her. But then I don't because, deep down, I'm afraid he has a point. She did make a mistake. She does regret it. Or, at least, she regrets it enough that I can't write her off as an evil backstabber I don't want anywhere near my ex.

"I know you two have issues," he says. "But you're still in touch, which tells me you know she regrets it."

"I haven't talked to her in years, Kit." I glance over my shoulder as I continue walking. "Sure, she sent flowers when Anna died but—" I wave it off. "Yes, I think she'll send a boat for us. That's all that matters."

"When exactly did you last speak to her?"

After we got married. When she called to accuse me of stealing you from her.

Jayla said that's ridiculous—no one marries a guy to spite an old friend—but could Sadie have thought it started like that? I hooked up with Kit knowing she liked him, and then I fell for him?

Damn it, the last thing I want is to feel bad for Sadie. Especially now.

"She'll send someone," I say. "Eventually. But all this has made me think you were right. If I'm not going to get a ham radio license, then I need to invest in a satellite phone. Not for the renters, but for me."

"Thank you," he says, coming up beside me. "Can I get one for you? Please? I run a tech company. I might not be an expert myself, but I can have someone find the most reliable one. If you're going to do this, I'd like it to be done right. Let me get it."

I push back the instinctive denial. He's right. I need one that's reliable, which means it'll be more than I can afford. This is about safety—mine and Madison's.

I shade my eyes to look out at that blazing sun rising over the horizon. "Okay."

"And I know I shouldn't push my luck," he says. "But there have been some real advances in satellite internet. You like being offline to write. I get that. But as a backup emergency contact system?" He shoves his hands into his pockets. "I think it'd make everyone feel better."

If you plan to keep coming here.

Those are the unspoken words. I'm acting as if I'm not letting these assholes steal my island—steal my love of it—but that's half bravado and half stubbornness. I found my caretaker's severed hand. I found his *body*.

I cross my arms and gaze out over the choppy water. Something nudges the crook of my elbow, and I give a start, spinning to knock it away. A candy bar tumbles to the ground. Kit picks it up and squints into the sky.

"Damn seagulls," he says. "If they're not shitting on us, they're dropping chocolate."

I take the bar and read the label. "Microbatch single-origin chocolate, no less. Damn *foodie* seagulls."

"Right?"

I peel open the wrapper. I break off a square and hand it to him. He takes it, and we stand there.

"I love storms," I say.

"I know."

"Got a feeling I'll love this one a lot less."

"It'll pass," he says.

I shade my eyes, hoping to see a fishing boat, but the lake is—

"Kit?"

"Hmm?" He leans in to steal another piece of chocolate.

I point. He pops the chocolate in his mouth and shades his eyes.

"Those white things out there," I say.

"Huh, they're on every wave. Weird."

I sock him in the shoulder. "Not the whitecaps. The floating things. I noticed them earlier. That's actually why I fell into the crevice. I was getting a closer look, stepped too close to the edge and freaked out Jayla."

"Who startled you into falling?"

"Something like that. But with everything that happened, I forgot what I'd been looking at."

"Which was . . . ?"

"I had no idea. Things floating on the water. They're closer now."

I pocket the candy bar and take off jogging along the beach. When I first saw the white objects, they'd been east of the island. Now they've drifted west, and they're heading for shore.

The beach part soon ends, and I'm climbing on rock.

"I'm going to the point for a better look," I say, though he hasn't asked what I'm doing.

I need to fight my way past some treacherous boulders and twisted trees, but finally I'm at the tip. The debris is less than a hundred feet offshore. And it *is* debris. Pieces of something.

"Kit . . ." I say as my stomach twists.

"I see it."

"Is that . . . ?"

"I can't tell anything from here."

I run past him.

"Laney?"

"I'm getting the paddleboard," I call.

He says something, but I don't hear him. I keep running along the interior where it's mostly lichen and flat rock. I reach the boathouse and lift the board under my arm.

"You're not going out on that," Kit says.

I heft the board.

He crosses his arms. "Laney . . ."

"I want a closer look."

"Whatever's out there will come to shore."

"We don't know that. It's not far. If I get in trouble, the current will bring me in."

"What do you think it is?"

"Can I just take a look, please? I *will* be careful."

When he hesitates, I could say I'm doing it either way, but that's never been our style.

"May I run and grab you a life vest?" he says.

I nod, and he lopes off.

I carry the board to the beach. I'm not lugging it all the way to the tip, not when it'll be impossible to launch from the high rocks. Once at the beach, I roll up my pant legs and dip my toe in, yanking back as if scalded. More like frozen. Yep, feels like Lake Superior in October.

I wait until I see Kit. Then I wade in, braced against the icy water, and lay the paddle over the board.

Kit already has his feet bare from earlier. When I lean out to get the vest, he waves me off and steps into the water with a convulsive shiver.

"That's why I reached for it."

"Bracing," he says. "It's refreshingly bracing."

I snort and take the vest. As I slip it on, he holds the board. Then I settle onto it, kneeling. He gives me a push. Once I'm out, I don't rise to my feet. I stay on my knees and start paddling along the shore.

"Thank you!" he calls.

I give him a thumbs-up. Being on my knees is slower but more stable. I hug the shoreline, which will also keep Kit from worrying. Once I'm near the tip, I veer out.

Here's where I'm really glad I stayed kneeling and even wondering whether I should have just sat my ass on the board. Or lain down and doggie-paddled surfer style. I love my paddleboard, but it really is meant for calmer water. Even these small waves have my every muscle tensing as I find my balance. I don't have the ankle strap on. Yep, technically that's a safety no-no, but Kit didn't comment. He knows the strap is intended for calm water, where if you take a tumble, you don't want to lose your board. Out here, with the chop, I'd rather rely on the life vest and my swimming skills and buy myself a new board if I lose it.

It's been a while since I've paddled in rough water. I sure don't do it when I'm alone. But soon I remember the rhythms and fall into it, working with the waves instead of against them. Paddle, paddle, pause. Paddle, paddle, pause. Water hits the side and sloshes over me, and my sweatpants are soon soaked, along with the baggy sleeves on my sweatshirt. I take a moment to focus on staying in place as I reorient myself.

Kit shouts from shore, barely audible over the slap of surf on the board. I look to see him pointing to my left. I squint and notice that one of those debris chunks is only about ten feet away. I turn and make slow progress in that direction.

What the hell is that?

I thought I knew. I'd been terrified that I knew, and told myself I was overreacting, but seeing this, I relax. What I'd seen looked like pieces of a boat, and my mind automatically jumped to images of *my* boat, Sadie on my boat, some horrible accident . . .

Yeah, that doesn't make sense, does it? There's nothing to hit out here. Okay, yes, there are islands, but Hemlock Island is unique, in a way that has had locals scratching their heads for decades. Lake Superior has plenty of private islands—and some big enough to host communities. But the ones around here are all close to shore. The locals say there shouldn't *be* an island out here. But there is, and that's all that matters.

That means Sadie did not accidentally steer into a neighboring island and dash my boat on the rocks. Even if she'd somehow dashed it on the shores of Hemlock Island, it's not going to be in tiny pieces like this.

What I see isn't part of a boat. It's trash. I can't quite tell what it is yet, but it's obviously garbage bobbing along.

A paper cup? Yes. An oversized paper cup. As it rolls on a wave, a familiar logo appears. Where the hell did someone get that? The nearest Starbucks is a hundred miles . . .

I flash back to yesterday. Jayla climbing on the boat with a venti Starbucks cup in hand.

"Isn't that cold by now?" Madison said.

"I like it cold." Jayla slurped to demonstrate, and we all shuddered.

I reach out. The cup rolls away from my fingers, and the order section appears. It's a venti cinnamon latte . . . for "Kayla."

Hairs on my neck prickle, but I rub them down. Yes, it's Jayla's, but either it fell out when Sadie sped off or Sadie pitched it over the side in her annoyance.

I'd take the cup to shore if I could, but I'm not toppling off the paddleboard to retrieve garbage, as much as it bugs me. I'll get it if it washes to shore. As for the rest . . .

I shade my eyes and squint at the other floating objects. Now that I think I know what I'm looking at, I can tell that one is a white plastic bag . . . like the ones I keep on the boat. It floats, empty, on the waves, and I can make out what looks like a paper napkin and a takeout bag and whatever else recent guests decided they had to eat on the short boat ride and couldn't bother discarding at the marina like I ask.

Garbage. That's all it is. When I think back, I recall Jayla stuffing her empty cup into the trash bag, which hadn't been empty. Either the bag fell in or Sadie threw it overboard. I can't see her doing that, though. Whipping Jayla's cup into the waves? Yes. Dumping an entire bag of trash? No. That's the fine line where Sadie lives.

I eye the trash bag and consider whether I can scoop up the garbage. My neighbors in Fox Bay like me well enough. I shop locally, I hire locally, and I recommend that my renters do the same. Still, when renters are entitled assholes, I'm not the only one who has to deal with their shit, and if anything in that trash identifies it as coming from my rental, I'll hear about it—in person, via the local Facebook group, and even possibly in the community paper. Also, that's mostly an excuse for the fact that I hate seeing trash on the lake. It's disrespectful. We do enough to the environment.

I paddle out to the bag. That's easy enough to snag on my paddle. I bring it in and confirm that it's definitely mine because it has the damn bag tag I buy to pay for local disposal.

Kit shouts something. I glance over. He jabs a finger at the dark clouds.

There's a freaking storm coming, Laney. You can play anti-litterbug crusader later.

A wave hits the board, enough to make me drop onto all fours to steady myself. Okay, Kit has a point. I start turning the board in a wide circle. The waves are heading toward the island. I can trust that the rest of the garbage will wind up there.

I'm half turned when the crosswind catches the bag. As it flies off the board, I lunge for it, realizing at the last second just how stupid that is. I've shifted to one side of the board and the wind snatches hold of the other, tipping it up. I grab the edge and belly flop down. On the beach, Kit's yelling, but all I pick up is the faint sound of his voice.

I'm gripping the right edge with both hands, and the wind is coming from my left. I need to adjust before it flips me. I get my legs to the left. Then I swing my left arm—

A wave hits hard. The board teeters up, and I overcorrect, twisting to look over the right side. I pause there, holding tight as I adjust. I'm still looking over the right side when the damn bag appears. It's underwater, maybe five feet down, teasing me as it bobs along.

I grit my teeth, and I'm about to wriggle back to center when the bag flips over . . . and long pale hair floats out around it. My heart stops. I blink hard, and then it's gone, and I'm staring down at black water.

I know what I saw. A pale shape that I'd mistaken for the bag, which made no sense—an empty bag would float. Then whatever I saw had turned over, and there'd been hair. Unmistakably hair fanning around a pale face, the rest of the pale shape shrouded in the dark water.

I saw a body.

FOURTEEN

I stare into the water, but it remains inky black and empty.

There's nothing there, Laney.

I know what I saw.

More garbage. You saw more garbage. Just this morning, Madison was talking about the corpses down there. Pale corpses.

I lower my face to the paddleboard, eyes closed as I catch my breath. That inner voice is right. My mind is playing tricks on me.

One last look over the side, and I reorient myself and get the board turned around. As soon as I try rising to sit, I know why Kit is shouting. I've stayed out too long. A wave hits hard on the back end, grabbing the board and slamming it toward shore, leaving me scrambling for a hold. I'm not a surfer, and this isn't a board meant to ride the waves. The moment the first one subsides, another hits. The board zooms forward, and I'm skittering along it, trying to stay on.

That wave dies, and I see the shore less than a hundred feet away. I'm okay. I'm close. As alarming as this is, the swell is actually taking me in—

A whitecap slams into me, and the board must have turned slightly after the last, because the wave hits wrong. The paddleboard flies up sideways, and I scramble for the fingerholds, but then the board topples, and I'm plunged into the ice-cold water.

The shock hits me first. Wading to the board, I'd felt how cold that water is, but now I'm submerged, and it steals the breath from my lungs. Another wave smacks into me, lifting me out of the water and then dragging me under.

I am *under* the water, life vest and all, surrounded by jet black. Then there's something there. A flash of white. I claw for it with both hands. It turns in the current, and I'm staring into a face haloed with blond hair.

"Sadie!"

I say her name aloud, and water rushes in, choking me. The face disappears. I fight, clawing and writhing, trying to find Sadie again, but the jacket finally does its work, jettisoning me up. I surface, gasping and hacking. Then I thrash, struggling to get back under the water, to find her, to find *Sadie*.

There's a moment where, in my fear and desperation, I almost undo the life vest. It's keeping me from getting under the water. Keeping me from getting to Sadie. I get as far as finding the first latch with my numb fingers before my brain kicks in.

I float and catch my breath. There's a lull in the wind, the waves only nudging me toward shore. I have a moment to look around. I can see into the water, and nothing's there.

Am I sure I saw something?

If I did, I should still see it.

Should still see *her*.

I don't. I'm not sure what I saw, but I'd been in a panic from going under the water, and I imagined seeing Sadie.

I close my eyes and inhale. Kit's shouts are frantic now, and I try to lift a hand to tell him I'm okay, but I can't get it out of the water. My arm feels like lead. I'm cold. So cold that I can't feel anything.

Swim, damn it. Just swim.

I lift my hand in a doggie paddle, and now my brain is the enemy as it gibbers in terror. I can't feel my arm. It's not just cold. It's not just asleep. I literally cannot feel even the dead weight of it. But it moves. Somehow it moves. I swallow the panic and swim.

Only a hundred feet. Isn't that what I just thought? The shore is only a hundred feet away. But now it is a *hundred feet away,* a seemingly endless distance, and each lift of my arms takes incredible effort, and I am not going to make it.

I'm going to die.

No, I'm wearing a life vest.

What difference will that make? I'm going to freeze to death.

No, Kit is there. He sees I'm in trouble. He will not let me die.

He'll save you? With what? A boat he doesn't have? Swim out and die trying? Run for a rope to throw that you cannot feel enough to grab?

Earlier we'd joked about life vests only letting you find the bodies afterward. Not a joke. Not a joke at all. When the tears come, I gasp with the sudden heat of them scorching down my face, and they shock me from my gibbering panic.

I am swimming. I did not stop to flip out. I am still moving, and the waves are helping. They threw me from my board, but now they are helping. They're pushing me along, and all I need to do is stay alive. Keep up my pathetic dog paddle. Movement will help. Don't surrender to the cold. Just keep going.

I think I have it under control. Then something white surfaces in front of me, and my arms fly up, water filling my mouth as I flail, first in terror—*holy shit, Sadie's body!*—and then intention—*must get Sadie's body.*

The waves hit harder now, the splash and foam of them obscuring my vision. I can only see something pale. Then I realize my arm is over it. I have it under my arm, even if I can't feel it.

I have Sadie. Oh, thank God, I have Sadie.

Thank God?

I have Sadie's *body.* The friend I still loved, no matter how much her betrayal had cut me. I loved her, and I grieved for the loss of her friendship, and I had imagined a day when we would reconcile. Now she is gone, and I am holding her body, and I am damn well going to get it to shore, no matter what.

I keep pushing on, blind and numb, heading in the direction I know is the shore. I can dimly see the blur of it ahead, trees rising in a wall of darkness. I have Sadie by her arm or leg or *something*. I see a scrap of pale shape every time I lift my arm to claw at the water, the other arm needing to do most of the work because I cannot let go of Sadie. I absolutely cannot—

A wave grabs me. It catches me off guard, seeming to come from the front. Have I gotten twisted around? Am I imagining the shore and heading out to sea?

Sea? No, a lake. It's a lake.

Isn't it?

My brain seems to stall, thoughts evaporating. Where am I? Why is it so cold? I must be dreaming. I'm so tired, and I just want to keep sleeping, but this silly dream won't stop. I'm floating on the waves, and then I'm flying. I'm in the air and flying, and there's a voice. Is that Kit? I'm definitely dreaming. Kit is at home, wherever home is these days for him.

A hoarse cry, and then I'm falling. I hit the ground and it's like startling awake, reality slamming back.

"Laney!" Kit's voice. "Oh God, Laney. I couldn't feel my legs. I fell."

Lake. Paddleboard.

Sadie.

I convulse, and I can sense something below me, even if I can't feel it. Then Kit is there, rubbing my arms.

"Laney? I need to get you to the house. Just give me a second. My legs. My *fucking* legs."

Kit never uses that word. I do, more than any English teacher should. I totally blame Jayla's influence.

And that is not what I should be thinking, but my brain keeps threatening to slide back into shock. No, hypothermia. *Shit!* This is hypothermia.

I close my eyes and struggle to focus.

"Laney!" Kit shakes my shoulders, or I presume he does from the motion. "Don't go to sleep."

"Not," I mumble.

Focus. Concentrate. I'm on the beach. Kit came in after me. That's the "wave" that carried me to shore. He can't walk because his legs are numb. That means I'm not the only one in trouble here.

"Okay, okay," he says. "I can do this."

His arm goes around me.

"I can do this," he says through gritted teeth. "Need to get you someplace warm."

He manages to get onto his knees. Then I feel the faintest tug at my arm and realize it's clenched tight.

"You need to let this go," he says.

I convulse again, the memory hitting. "No! It's . . ."

I look down at my arm. It is not holding Sadie. It's holding some piece of . . . I don't even know what. Is it the damn trash bag?

In my half-blind state, I'd bumped into something white and grabbed it, thinking I had Sadie's body, and now I could almost laugh. My arm has a death grip on a chunk of debris, maybe a foot long.

I drop it. As it falls to the ground, I blink. It's a piece of beige leather. The top part of a boat seat. And there's something on it. Black permanent marker scrubbed and sanded in an attempt to erase it from the leather. Only part is left, the rest ripped away, but I know what it said.

Dean Peters, 2022!

I know what it said because I'm the person who scrubbed and sanded, cursing the entire time. I'd contacted the renters and told them what I'd found and they'd laughed it off.

Kids, huh?

Kid, my ass. That *kid* had been their seventeen-year-old son, who'd thought it was just fine to write his name on a leather seat—his full name, because what the hell was I going to do about it? Call the cops?

This is from my boat.

It's a piece of the captain's seat. The entire leather top of the captain's seat, *ripped* off.

"Kit?" I whisper.

His arms go around me, the pressure telling me he's holding tight, even if I can't feel his touch.

"I've got you," he says. "I'll get you inside. I swear it, Laney. I've got you. This time, I've got you, and I'm so sorry—" His voice breaks.

"Kit?"

I try to point at the piece of leather, but my arm only lolls onto it. When I try to form a full sentence, my tongue won't cooperate and I can only jerk my chin at the leather. He finally gets it, and even then only frowns at the seat cover, as if he can't figure out what it is or how it got there.

"Ours," I say.

I mean to say "Mine," but the boat *was* ours, and that's what comes out.

"Our boat."

He reaches for it, and it falls through his numb fingers. "That's . . . that's from . . ."

"Graffiti. Renter. Scrubbed."

He rocks back on his heels. "That's from our boat? The seats? How—?"

He looks out at the water, horror dawning. Then he jerks his attention back to me.

"We need to get you inside," he says. "We'll figure out . . . We'll figure it all out later."

He gets his hands under my armpits again, and I start to shake, and when I start, I can't stop, my whole body quaking so bad he can barely keep his grip on me.

"S-sorry. C-can't."

"Shh, shh. I've got you."

He lurches, as if on stilts, and twice he almost falls before getting his balance. Then it seems to get easier, and he's walking, with me huddled against his chest, in near convulsions of shivering.

"The shivering is keeping you warm," he says. "Don't try to stop it."

Another three steps. Then he warns, "I'm going to shout," before he does it. His voice rings out over the crash of waves.

"Jayla? Jayla!"

A few more steps before he bellows for his sister again. It's after the third time, when he's starting to shake himself, with the exertion of carrying me when he can barely walk, that a shout returns.

"Kit!" Bare feet slap rock. Jayla's voice. "Laney? Oh my God. What happened? Did you capsize? The storm, the damn storm. You shouldn't have—"

"Laney," he says. "In the water. Hypothermia."

"Fuck!" she shouts. "Garrett!"

Then Madison's voice. "Laney? Kit? What happened to Laney?" Her voice rises with every word, and I want to tell her I'm fine, but my teeth chatter too much to form words.

Other hands grab me, and as Kit relinquishes me, he says, "I'm sorry," and I know it's not because of what happened—he had nothing to do with that. It's that he's handed me to Garrett. He had to.

"Get her inside," Jayla says. "Fuck! Kit? Can you walk?"

"Help him," I manage.

Garrett says, "Looks like Laney wasn't the only one who went for a swim. Yeah, help him to the house before he collapses."

Garrett carries me inside, and when that first wave of heat hits, it actually hurts. Needles prick everywhere, and I squeeze my eyes shut against the sudden rush of sensation.

Garrett lays me on the sofa while Madison shouts orders. Blankets. Wet clothes off. Don't rub our skin. No hot water. Leave the wood-stove off for now. Let us warm up naturally.

I'd made her take first aid last year, when she started talking about spending a weekend on the island with friends. She'd grumbled about how boring the course was, and how she'd never remember anything. Obviously, not quite true.

Kit is able to talk first, and he adds to the instructions. Before long, I can feel all my body parts again, and I'm curled up with a hot cocoa and a plate of s'mores roasted on the woodstove fire, both of us being warmed enough for Madison to get the heat going.

"Bring more cocoa," Madison calls to Garrett in the kitchen. "They need sugar."

I'm not sure we need *that* much sugar, but Kit winks at me and calls, "*All* the sugar."

He's at the other end of the couch. We're both cocooned in blankets, having needed—as Madison correctly said—to get out of our wet clothing.

"Ready to tell us what the hell happened out there?" Jayla says. "I'm guessing the canoe flipped in the waves?"

I shake my head. "There is no canoe."

I don't mean to be that blunt, but I'm still mentally frozen.

"No canoe?" Garrett says, coming in with two more mugs of co-coa. "Did someone steal it?"

Jayla cuts in. "Please tell me you did not try heading to shore with the kayaks. Those damn things tip *without* waves."

"The kayaks are gone, too," Kit says.

"Then what . . ." Jayla stares at me. "You did *not* go out on that fucking paddleboard. A kayak is bad enough, but I don't know how anyone rides a paddleboard and thinks it's safe, much less *fun*."

"Laney paddled out a bit to check on something," Kit says. "She had her life vest."

"What the hell could be important enough to paddle out in a storm?"

"It's not a storm yet," Kit says, trying for patience. "She wouldn't do that. It seemed fine and . . ." He glances my way. "It was important. She thought she saw . . ."

"Parts of the boat," I say. "I noticed debris on the water earlier, and then I saw it again and remembered spotting it before falling into the crevice. This time it wasn't far from shore. Yes, I shouldn't have gone out. Yes, Kit trusted my judgment, and I took advantage of that. But I had to know."

"It wasn't . . . ?" Madison begins.

"It wasn't," Jayla says firmly. "It couldn't have been. But everyone's on edge, and I get why your aunt had to be sure, even if I really wish she'd waited for it to wash to shore."

"Laney?" Madison looks at me. "It wasn't part of the boat, was it?"

"What I saw at first was garbage from the boat," I say carefully. "Jayla's coffee cup. Then the trash bag with the litter scattered."

"Which you then tried to clean up and fell in," Jayla grumbles. "First you fall into that crevice, then you nearly freeze to death cleaning up trash. You might love nature, Laney, but it clearly doesn't love you back."

"At least you're both fine," Garrett says. "Even if I do agree with Jayla. Mother Nature is a bitch. Does anyone else want cocoa? I'm going to make myself some."

"You said *first*," Madison says, moving from her chair to sit on the edge of the couch. "You said that's what you saw at *first*."

I glance at Kit.

He opens his mouth.

"We found part of the boat," I blurt, saving him from being the one to say it. "I grabbed it after a wave knocked me off the board."

"Part of the boat?" Garrett frowns. "Something fell off it?"

Again, Kit and I exchange a look.

"No," he says, beating me to it this time. "We found part of the captain's chair. The top piece of material." When Garrett's mouth opens, Kit says, "It was undoubtedly from Laney's boat. There was graffiti from a renter that she tried to scrub off."

"I saw that," Jayla says. "Some asshole— Wait. Part of the captain's chair? The leather? How . . . ?"

She trails off as realization hits.

"The boat . . . sank?" Madison says, her voice a whisper.

"That doesn't make sense," Garrett cuts in. "Floating garbage might, if the boat hit the shore and sunk, but part of the seat? Like it came off?"

"It . . ." I begin.

"It's on the beach," Kit says. "You can examine it. The leather is torn, which doesn't seem possible, but the canoe and kayaks . . . They aren't missing. They're destroyed."

"How?" Garrett says.

"They're in pieces," I say. "Little pieces."

"Like someone hacked them up with a machete?"

"No, like . . ."

"It looks like a bomb," Kit says. "Everything that was on ground level is in small, twisted pieces."

"So someone blew up your boats?" Garrett says. "The kayak, the canoe, and the motorboat." He goes still. "Which means Sadie did *not* take the boat. Like I said." He strides to the windows, jabbing a finger out. "My sister is out there. On this damn island. She couldn't have left because the nutjob who killed your cleaner blew up all your boats, including that one. So we abandoned her out there, on the island, with a killer."

"All her things are gone," Jayla says.

"But she didn't leave on the boat because . . ." All the color drains from his face. "No. That's not— No." Before anyone can speak, he bears down on me. "Someone put a bomb on your boat, and if my sister took it . . ." He can't finish.

"We don't know that," Kit cuts in. "Yes, her things are gone, but she might have been planning to leave and then the boat wasn't there, so she's somewhere on the island, cooling off. Maybe she's even in the boathouse. No one searched it."

I remember what I saw in the water. Sadie's face. Sadie's body.

No, that's what I *thought* I saw. A blink, and it was gone.

Kit continues, "I shouldn't have said it was a bomb. I meant that's what it looked like with the canoe and kayaks, but it couldn't have been because the structure is intact."

Garrett's face screws up. "The structure is intact? Speak English."

"The shed wasn't touched," I say. "The boats, the life vests, the oars, they're all in pieces, but the paddleboard was left in the rafters—as if it wasn't noticed—and there's no damage to the shed, inside or out."

"That doesn't make sense."

"It doesn't. Which—"

"None of you are making sense," Garrett snaps as he stalks to the door. "I'm done listening. *You* don't even know what you're saying. I don't know why I expected better, all things considered."

That barb strikes hard, and I fight the urge to snarl something back. Not in front of Madison.

"I'll go with you," Kit says. "Give me a second to find dry clothing."

Garrett stalks out without pausing.

Kit looks at me. "Do you have any clothing renters left behind?"

"There's a box of your stuff in my storage room."

"Oh. Right. I never . . . uh, told you what to do with it."

"I thought you might want to come out here sometime," I say, as lightly as I can. "And if you didn't, I'd have added it to the box for renters who arrive in September with nothing but shorts and tank tops." I start to rise, blanket wrapped around me. "I'll show you where it is."

"I'll get it," Madison says. "Then I'm going out to see the shed."

Another exchanged look between me and Kit, but there's no rea-son to keep her from doing that. Better that we all see it and try to come up with a rational explanation.

There isn't one. You know that.

I need one. I know *that,* too.

FIFTEEN

Once they're gone, I get dressed. Then I come down to find Jayla in the great room.

"You're still here," I say.

"I thought no one should be alone. Is that a problem?"

I shake my head. "No, I was hoping you'd stayed." I fold the blankets. "I saw something out there. Or I thought I did. That's why I fell overboard—frantically going after it."

"You saw part of the boat?"

"Worse. Now I need my most rational, no-bullshit friend to tell me I was imagining things."

"You were imagining things."

I give her a look as I sit on the couch.

"What?" she says. "I don't even need to hear what it was. That's how well I know you. If you're questioning it, then you already realize it was that big ol' imagination of yours at play."

When I pull over a pillow, she says, "Well, tell me anyway. What was it? Alien? Shark? The Creature from the Black Lagoon?"

"Sadie," I blurt.

She blinks. "What?"

"I thought I saw Sadie. Dead. Floating in the water."

"Oh, Laney." She moves to sit beside me. "That was flippant of me. So you saw parts of the boat floating around and it made you think you saw Sadie. That must have been awful."

"I saw her before the boat parts. But I *had* seen the garbage, and I *had* seen what happened to the canoe and kayak, and I *had* heard Madison talking about the dead bodies at the bottom of the lake. In that moment, it really did seem to be Sadie's body. Her face. Her hair. But then it disappeared. Which means I was imagining it. Right?"

She leans a shoulder against mine. "You might not have seen parts of the boat yet, but that's what you expected to find. Even if you were making excuses for how the trash got out there, you knew it could mean that the boat sunk. I wouldn't say you hallucinated her. Just that you saw something from the boat, and you mistook it for her."

I nod. "That's why I wasn't going to mention it. Even to Kit."

"Because it seems to confirm the possibility no one wants to hear."

"That Sadie's dead. That she was on that boat when it went down." I gaze out the windows across the room. "We're pretending that's not what happened, but it is. Someone set off small bombs in the kayaks and the canoe. They missed the paddleboard in the rafters. Then they set a larger one on the motorboat. I don't think they meant for us to be killed. They were just cutting off our exits to scare the shit out of us. The motorboat was supposed to explode in the middle of the night. Except Sadie was on it."

"Maybe."

At the doubt in her voice, my shoulders sag with relief. "You think it's possible she *wasn't* on it. That they pushed the boat out into the lake, where the bomb went off, and she's holed up safe on the island."

"Maybe." Jayla folds her hands on her knee, gazes away from me. "Or maybe I was right the first time."

I pause to figure out what she means. "That Sadie's behind it?"

She looks over. "Doesn't that make more sense than her hiding in the boathouse because she's angry?"

Yes, but that dominoes back to everything else that's happened.

Would Sadie blow up all of our boats to trap us here? I want to laugh at the idea—she's not Kit's movie-style ex, cursing the world because I don't have a bunny to boil. She's also not a demolitions expert.

But she could find someone who was and charm him into getting what she needed. And if she didn't intend for anyone to get hurt? Just wreak havoc?

"Jimmy Morton?" Jayla murmurs. "Bianca Ramos?"

In middle school, Sadie read a bicycle-repair manual to sabotage Jimmy's prize BMX bike when he cheated on her. And she used an industrial magnet on Bianca's laptop, because she's the one he cheated with. We thought it was hilarious at the time. Harmless pranks, like when Kit and I put tape on the wheels of all the computer mice in the lab. Or when we stuck USE OTHER DOOR signs on *all* the school entrances.

Now I realize, in the case of Jimmy's bike, it was pure luck that he didn't get hurt.

"The boats, maybe," I say. "Even the stagings, if she managed to get the security codes from Kit and snuck out here. But Nate?" I shake my head. "That goes too far." I shake it harder. "No, it *all* goes too far."

"I think she set up that profile for me," Jayla says.

I frown, and then remember what she'd been saying last night. "The dating profile?"

She nods. "She's the one who warned me about it. She called, all hesitant and apologetic and 'I hate to bring this up, but you should know.' She said someone from our high school friend group found it."

"And she said *I* did it?"

"Oh, you know Sadie. She's never that obvious. I looked at the profile and . . . I wanted to be sick. Here I was, trying to come out of the closet, and someone posted a straight dating profile for me on a hookup site with photos that . . ." Her jaw flexes. "Me in a bikini. Me eating . . . a hot dog. I know it sounds silly. I wasn't naked or anything."

"They were private photos, ones that suggested you were looking for a hetero hookup."

She nods. "I was humiliated and freaking out, and you know what happens when I get upset like that. I lash out. I called Sadie back, ranting about who the hell would do that, blaming this person and that person. Not that I ever have a shortage of enemies. She asked how you and I were getting along. That was just after we . . ." She shrugs. "You know."

"Went on an actual date, and it was horrible and awkward and weird?"

"Yeah. After that horrible, awkward weirdness, we weren't exactly hanging out, but you had teachers-college admissions and I had law school admissions, so we were able to pretend we were just terribly busy."

When I don't answer, she says, "Fine. *I* was able to pretend I was terribly busy. The truth is . . ." She throws up her hands. "I was flailing, Laney. Still figuring it all out. Did I like girls? Did I like both? Did I like anyone? It was always so easy for you. Everyone thought you'd be the one I could talk to about it, and I couldn't. Instead, we decided to try dating, and that was an unmitigated disaster."

"Back up," I say. "You felt like you couldn't talk to me about your sexuality? Did I do something wrong?"

"Yes. Yes, you did. You were Laney. You knew you were bi in fucking *middle* school. Your parents never batted an eye when you told them. How could I tell you that I was struggling? That my parents are amazing, but this isn't what they wanted for me? That I wasn't sure it's what *I* wanted for me?"

"I'm sorry if—"

"Oh, I know it wasn't all peaches and cream for you. I was there. I heard what kids said. I saw you struggle—the guy who dumped you because he didn't think he'd be 'enough,' the girl you liked who thought you were a curious straight girl and reamed you out for it. But even when things weren't easy, you didn't have a moment of self-doubt. I was *all* doubt and questions, and I didn't think you'd understand."

"I'm sorry you felt that way. I'm sorry if I seemed like I wouldn't have listened or would have pushed you into making a decision."

"You wouldn't have. It was just . . . Indecision doesn't suit me. I was embarrassed and I hated that. So when Sadie called, I blurted it all out. Not my tale of lesbian woe, but how you and I tried going out and how it was awkward and I'd been avoiding you. She was . . . Well, she was Sadie."

Easy to talk to. A genuinely good listener. The kind of friend who, long after you've written them off and declared them untrustworthy, you still find yourself taking their calls and even sending them the occasional touching-base text.

"And she suggested I might have set up that dating profile for you," I say. "Not to be cruel. Just good old Laney goofing around. Maybe needling you a little. I'm a practical joker, and I don't always know when to quit." I glance over. "Close?"

"Yeah. She asked who could have had those photos. They were from when my parents took you and me to Costa Rica after grad."

"So it looked like I put them up. Except we'd shared our vacation photos with Sadie, whose parents wouldn't let her go."

She nods. "Without ever actually accusing you, she convinced me it was you, and that hurt. It hurt so damn much, and now I look back and wonder whether it was *supposed* to hurt. A double whammy. Maybe Sadie didn't just put up that profile to be a bitch but to drive a wedge between us. More revenge for . . ." She shrugs. "You know. Siding with you. When . . . it happened."

When *it* happened. The thing we don't talk about.

I tense before rolling it off.

She continues, "Hell, *everyone* sided with you. They knew who was telling the truth. What Sadie did? Picking him over you? Making you feel—" She takes deep breaths. "See? Even now I am furious on your behalf. It brought *us* closer together and drove *her* away."

"You think the profile was revenge? Intended to break up our friendship. If so, it worked."

Now she's the one flinching. "I'm sorry, Laney."

"Whether it was Sadie or not, it absolutely wasn't me. I knew you were struggling, and posting that profile would be a spectacularly shitty thing to do. There's no practical joke there. It's cruel, and I would have hoped you'd know better."

She bites her lip and turns away.

"But you were in a vulnerable place," I say. "I knew that, and I gave you space when I should have pushed."

"You let me walk away without demanding an explanation?" she says, her gaze locked on mine now. "You presumed you'd done something wrong? Or the other person just changed their mind about you? Suddenly didn't want to be with you when that made zero sense?"

We aren't talking about us anymore. Oh, we are, but we're also talking about my marriage, and when I duck her gaze she sighs.

"You need to stop giving other people so much credit, Laney," she says. "Stop presuming they left for a valid reason, and not because humans are fucked-up individuals who make stupid mistakes, and sometimes, you're not the only one who's hanging back, presuming if the other party doesn't try to mend the rift, it's because they don't want it mended."

I look at her. "I do want to mend our friendship. And if you're referring to anything else . . ."

"It's none of my damn business," she says. "I agree."

"As for Sadie, the point is not what she might have done ten years ago, but what she might have done now. Yes, she can be petty, even cruel, but what's the point here? Staging those scenes to drive me away from Hemlock Island? That's clever revenge, if I do say so myself. She thinks I 'stole' Kit, and so she steals what I have left from him? Brilliant. But blowing up my boats? Trapping me on the island *with* Kit. That's like a freaking romance plot."

She snorts. "That's one fucked-*up* plot . . . if it includes being trapped with your estranged BFF, your teenage niece, and the bastard who—" She clears her throat. "Not a romance plot."

"True. But you get my point. If Sadie's still angry with me, still wants Kit, why trap me with him and then hide?"

"That supposes she does still want Kit. Or that she thinks she has a hope in hell of getting him." She glances at the window and then back to me. "They had a fight last night. Did you hear it?"

"I heard them in his room and got the hell away as fast as I could."

She stares at me. "Did you think—? Wait, is *that* why you didn't want to go in and ask him about the gun? You thought they were in bed together? In your house?" She waves a hand. "Staying out of it. Point is that they argued. Has he mentioned it to you?"

I shake my head. "You?"

"Nope," she says. "He hasn't mentioned it to anyone. Because I get the feeling that if Sadie took her revenge last night, it wasn't just about you."

Bomb," Garrett says as he strides into the house. He doesn't hold the door for Kit and Madison. He doesn't even pause to make sure they lock it once everyone's inside. He has his answer, and because it's a logical one, nothing else matters. It's as if we're at a crime scene back home and not trapped on an island, possibly with a killer.

"Someone blew up the boats," he continues as he walks to the liquor cabinet. "Asshole move, but what do you expect? They're trying to scare you off. That poor Nate kid died, and they used his body in their sick scheme. Then they blew up the boats, and now Sadie is sulking somewhere, waiting for us to come coax her out. She pulled shit like this as a kid. I thought she'd outgrown it but . . ." He shrugs and pours a finger of whiskey.

There. Everything neatly tied up. Logical explanation. Nothing scary happening. Nothing at all. He just feels like downing a shot of hard liquor at nine in the morning, that's all.

I look at Kit. He's got his thousand-yard stare on. Ignoring Garrett and thinking it through, though I can't mistake that look on his face, the one that tells me he's not buying this story Garrett is so desperate to sell.

"That wasn't a bomb," Madison says.

Garrett wheels on her. To her credit—God, I love this kid—she stands firm and lifts her chin. "Tell me what kind of bomb does that?"

"How the hell should I know?" he says. "I'm not on the bomb squad. That's obviously what it was. Only thing that makes sense."

"Not to me."

"Because you're a kid." He downs the whiskey. "Okay, we need to find Sadie. It's a pain in the ass, but whoever set those bombs could still be on the island, and I might want to let Sadie sulk it off, but we can't take the chance she'll get hurt. We need search parties. Comb the island. Find her. Bring her in."

Jayla and I look at each other.

"That's presuming—" Jayla begins.

"What about the storm?" Madison says at the same time, having not noticed Jayla speaking. "And the fact we don't have a boat? Or a phone? Or any way of getting help?"

"We'll figure all that out later," Garrett says. "After we find Sadie."

Jayla looks at me.

"We need to be careful," I say. "Really careful. Not only could someone be on the island, but it's possible Sadie hasn't come back because she's hurt. Maybe she was near the bombs. She could have hit her head. She might be confused, frightened, not thinking straight. Even if we see her, we must be careful."

Jayla nods. That satisfies her concern that Sadie is behind this. Personally, I don't think we're going to find Sadie. I'm not saying that I definitely saw her in the water, but I think it's very possible she was in that boat. But no one wants to hear that, and unless we're sure, we need to look, in case Garrett is right. We can't focus on escaping the island until we're sure Sadie isn't out there, in need of rescue.

"Garrett?" Jayla says. "Are you okay searching on your own?"

"'Course," he says gruffly.

"Then I'll take Mads. Laney and Kit can search the boathouse. They know all the nooks and crannies."

I can ask Kit about his fight with Sadie. That's what Jayla means, and I agree. This is a piece of the puzzle we need.

SIXTEEN

Kit and I head to the main boathouse.

"How are you feeling?" he asks. "Is anything numb?"

"No numbness. No dead spots. No dizziness. No disorientation." I smile over at him. "I know the hypothermia and frostbite symptom list, and I'm fine. I suspect I'll have a few drowning nightmares in my future, but physically I'm okay. You?"

"Definitely nightmares in my future. Like those ones where you're trying to punch in a phone number and can't get it right? Except it'll be standing on the shore watching you drown while I wave my arms and shout, like that'll help." He makes a face. "And that is *not* the lighthearted answer I meant to give."

I reach to squeeze his arm. "You didn't just stand on the shore. You came in after me and nearly died of hypothermia yourself. That is so much worse."

He chokes on a sudden laugh.

"But you also saved my life," I say. "I don't think I was going to make it to shore."

"You would have."

"And this is definitely not the lighthearted conversation either of us needs." I swing open the boathouse door, and we step into the gloom within. "Or maybe 'lighthearted' isn't the word we're looking for, considering why we're out here. Let's just avoid topics that will make us feel even worse."

"Works for me. No discussing the stock market."

Now I'm sputtering a laugh. "Exactly."

I flip on the light before we let the door close. Then I lock it. "Hear that?" I call out. "It was the door locking, Sadie. If you're in here, you're not sneaking off."

"You really think she's in here?"

My expression answers for me, and Kit nods as we start our search. We stick together, as if by silent agreement that—however much Garrett seems to think there's no threat on the island—we disagree enough that we won't even split up to search a four-hundred-square-foot boathouse.

Without the boat in here, there are only a few obvious places to check. First, we open the storage locker, where all the life vests and paddles are kept. Inside are . . . life vests and paddles.

Next we shine a flashlight into the gap under the floor, where the water laps against the wood. Without the boat in place, the water level is lower, but having both experienced how cold that water is today, we don't spend long checking to see whether Sadie has ducked under, submerged to her neck. A quick sweep before we proceed to the most likely hiding spot: the rafters.

When Kit and I designed the boathouse, there was plenty of room in the rafters. After all, we expected this to be our summer home. When school ended, we'd retreat here, and I'd write and Kit would practice his music, having convinced himself he could just pop back to shore every few days for a meeting. Yes, that was ridiculously naive for both of us, but it was the dream. As such, we'd want to host friends and family, and we'd need a place to store extra kayaks, paddleboards, and deck chairs. Kit was a corporate CEO—providing high-end kayaks and luxury lounge chairs to our guests would be like normal people providing extra towels and new toothbrushes.

Hemlock House was finished late in the summer of 2019. We had a month here, and we were far too greedy to invite others up. That would come next year . . . and then the pandemic scuttled plans for guests and those extra "amenities."

When I took over the island post-split, the boathouse had a beautiful loft area, completely empty. No problem, right? That's where I'd "hide" my watercraft from renters. Yeah, that didn't last long. When I realized they'd been using my kayak and paddleboard, I moved them to the private shed only to discover that the now-empty loft proved too great a temptation, and not just for children.

After cleaning up far too many condoms, I decided the loft needed major changes . . . and not only because the evidence of carousing couples reminded me of how Kit and I used that empty loft space.

"Where are the floorboards?" he says when we climb up.

"I had to remove them. Safety hazard."

"Hiding the ladder wasn't enough?"

"Nope, that only made it a bigger hazard. I got a middle-of-the-night call from a renter threatening to sue after their son fell. He'd shimmied up, got a splinter, fell into the water, and hit his head."

"Oof. Yeah, when we were kids, we'd have totally tried that."

"He was thirty-six."

We climb up and balance on a rafter.

"The boards can be replaced," I say. "I did leave a few." I point to the shadows. "They're over there, where I hide some of the outdoor stuff." I raise my voice. "Hear that, Sadie? If you found my cubby-hole, we're coming to pull you out."

When I start to crawl over, Kit lays a hand on my ankle.

"May I?" he says, with a look that adds a "please."

I hesitate. Like Jayla said, my default response is "I've got it."

I'm fine. I can handle this. Nope, I got it. Thanks, though.

If Sadie has blown up my boats, then I'm not dealing with the teen-age girl who'd badmouthed me behind my back and cost me every friend except Jayla . . . and, apparently, eventually Jayla, too. No, as shitty as that was, it pales compared to this, and I can't be the fool who throws herself into the line of fire when she's the primary target.

I nod and move onto a side beam to let Kit pass. When I fall in behind him, he stops so suddenly that I death-grip the beam before I fall.

"You smell that?" he says.

I don't, not until he continues on and I move into the spot he vacated. Then the smell hits and a memory flashes. A memory from last night, picking up this same smell and dismissing it as a dead animal, only to discover—

I detour around Kit, taking another beam, even as he says, "Hey!"

I reach the storage spot. Not only have I made it hard to access, but I've blocked it in with plastic bins bearing labels like CANNED BEANS and OLD TOWELS to further throw renters off the scent of hidden treasure. I yank out the "towel" box, which is empty. The stink of decomposition fills my mouth and nose, and I double over, gagging.

Coming from another angle, Kit gently picks up a box, only to realize it's empty and shove it aside. Our flashlight beams converge on a spot where someone has pushed away the expensive deck chairs that I store up here. In the middle of that space, there's a heap of what looks like hair.

No, it's fur. Lumps of fur and decomposing flesh and bloodied bone with whip-like tails.

"Are those rats?" Kit says.

Holding my breath, I move closer as Kit does the same. It takes me a moment to figure out what I'm seeing. There's so much fur and bone and gore that my brain decides this is clearly *not* a rat. And it isn't. It's *six* rats, their decomposing bodies arranged in a circular pattern. In the middle of that circle? Their tails, knotted together.

"What the hell?" he whispers.

"Rat king," I say before backing up fast and twisting to get fresher air.

I take a moment to breathe with my hands over my nose and mouth, inhaling the smell of s'mores and hot cocoa instead.

When I turn back to Kit, I say, "The story goes that rat tails can get knotted together. The result—all these conjoined rats—form a 'rat king.'"

"It's not true then. Just a story?"

"Depends on who's telling it. There are lots of supposed cases from medieval times, especially in Germany, but they might be hoaxes. It's never been observed in the wild. At least, not in a way that proves the knotting came naturally."

"Well, this one didn't," he says. "Unless this 'rat king' happened to die in a ritualistic circle."

I look over to see a circle scorched into the wood.

"Have you even seen rats on the island?" he asks.

I shake my head.

"Then we've found another piece of staging."

I look at the grotesque spectacle. With a shudder, I start to turn away when—

"Kit?" I say carefully.

He's already moving off and looks back. "Hmm?"

I don't speak. I just stare. As I do, one of the bodies twitches.

"You didn't see that?" I say.

"See what?" He moves back over and follows my gaze. The same body twitches again, and he jerks back with a curse.

Relief washes through me . . . followed by the realization that actually seeing the dead move is not a cause for relief.

"It twitched, right?" I say.

"Um, yes." He takes a deep breath and then gags as the smell fills his lungs.

"Don't inhale," I say.

"No kidding." His voice is shaky. "Tell me there's a logical explanation."

"Hey, I'm the horror buff, remember? My answer to moving corpses will always be zombies."

I say it lightly—still riding that high from realizing I'm not hallucinating—but when another rat twitches, I nearly fall off the ceiling beam. Then I spot something.

I look around and find a piece of wood, left over from the deconstruction. Using the end of it, I flip over the rat that moved first.

"I could have done that," Kit says. "Note that I said that *after* you did it."

"Oh, I noted it."

The rat twitches again, but this time, the cause is clear. Pale maggots crawl through the decomposing flesh.

"Logical explanation supplied," I say, shuddering as I inch away. "Which means I'm not hallucinating, and we don't have zombie rats."

"Just Sadie, the missing frenemy."

"Your childhood called. It wants its vocabulary back."

He sticks out his tongue, only to catch a taste of the stench, judging by his horrified expression. I laugh and motion for us to retreat.

"No Sadie," he says. "She'd never hide up here with this smell."

We make our way back down to the ground level.

"You don't think she's on the island, do you?" he says as our flashlight beams skim the interior.

"No."

"You think she was on board the boat. That she's . . . dead."

I consider telling him what I saw, but I don't see how that helps, especially when I no longer think I could have seen what I thought I did. I also have a better explanation for what happened to Sadie, one that is going to let us set this aside and move on, at least for now.

"No," I say. "I just don't think she was on the boat when it blew up. If she's the one who set the bomb, does it make any sense to trap herself on the island with us?"

"Get to shore and then set the bomb . . . after sending the boat on a general course back to the island so we find the pieces."

"That's overly complicated, isn't it?"

He says nothing, and we head outside.

"Yes, then," I say. "It's overly complicated. You just don't want to say that."

"Actually, no. This morning I'd have said Sadie couldn't have done any of this. Now . . ." He scratches his beard and looks around. "I've been seeing the side of Sadie she wants me to see. I think she's done things to drive people away from you."

"Jayla told you."

"Told me what?"

I head for the forest beyond the boathouse, which is the other part of our search area. "It's okay. Jayla talked to me about the dating profile."

"Profile?"

I glance over. "That isn't what you were talking about?"

"Uh, no. Jayla hasn't said anything to me. I'm guessing she thinks Sadie was responsible for whatever made you guys go your separate ways after college, something to do with a dating profile?"

"I don't think any one person—or event—could be blamed for that. There was a lot going on. Law-school and teachers-college application stress. Jayla coming out. Us ending up on opposite sides of the country for years."

"But Sadie did something to drive the wedge in further. To hurt you both."

"Sadie thinks . . . What happened with Garrett . . . She thinks I destroyed her family and Jayla helped."

Kit's voice hardens. "*You* didn't destroy anything. That was all Garrett."

"But if you're Sadie, and you're convinced that I lied and that Jayla supported my lie, then I destroyed Sadie's family with Jayla's help."

"Sadie can feel like that at sixteen. Not at thirty-two."

I stand on the edge of the forest and look in. With the dark clouds looming overhead, even this sparse bit of woods looks like a sylvan portal to some dark world, one stray patch of light turning a dead tree branch into a gnarled finger, beckoning us in.

I push off the feeling. I love this bit of woods, those dead trees, the stories those twisted branches tell of times long past.

I find the path and stride in.

SEVENTEEN

I need to talk to you about something really awkward, Kit," I say once we're in the forest.

"About Sadie, I'm guessing."

"Yes. I'm not asking about your relationship. That's none of my business, which is what makes this really awkward."

He stops. When I keep walking, he strides in front of me and turns around. "You think I'm sleeping with Sadie?"

"That'd be none of my business."

"Did she say we were?"

I hesitate.

"Not in those exact words, right?" He swears under his breath. "Because that's not Sadie. She just insinuated it, and since you know we had a one-nighter before you and I got together, it makes sense, especially if she's showing up here after I canceled drinks . . ." He shakes his head. "Let's clear this up right now. Outside of business, I haven't had any contact with Sadie since we got married."

"If you did—"

"You'd understand. I heard that, and I know you mean it, which is why I wouldn't lie. We *were* supposed to have drinks last night. Discussing business. She's been pitching marketing projects to me, some of which I've bought. Yes, talking over drinks was her idea, and yes, it's not the first time, and yes, I've gotten the sense she's hoping it'll lead to more, but it hasn't and won't. I can spot that particular trap a mile away. I have money, and Sadie likes money."

I shake my head. "She likes *you*. She has for a long time, and she thinks I . . . Well, hopefully she doesn't seriously believe I married you to spite her, but she does have a crush on you. Has for years."

His brow furrows. "Sadie?"

I manage a small smile. "That is who we're talking about, right?"

He shakes his head. "It's not like that. Wait—she thinks you stole me from her? How? It was one night. I was in a rough place and . . ."

When he trails off, I brush a hanging vine out of the way and say, "I don't need the details, Kit."

"No, actually you do. I didn't tell you before, because it felt like blaming Sadie when I might have been wrong, and it's not as if I need to justify sleeping with someone before you and I got together. When I say she's interested in my money, that's not a lack of self-confidence, Laney. She's the one who got in touch with me, right after it was announced that I was taking over the company. She wanted to talk business, and then Mom had a cancer scare, and there were a few weeks there where I was convinved I was going to lose her . . . while Dad was still recovering from his heart attacks. That's when it happened. A night of comfort and companionship turned to sex, and I won't lie—I needed that. But she started telling people we were a couple and showing up at my condo."

"Well, you *are* really good in bed." I lift my hands. "Just saying."

He laughs, the sound carried on a whoosh of breath as he relaxes. "Thanks, but even I'm not that good. I just happened to have a job opening she thought she could fill, and it wasn't in the marketing department."

"CEO's wife."

He falls in beside me, and we resume walking. "Yeah. She apologized later for coming on so strong, but it still . . ." Hands in his pockets again. "I screwed up when Anna died. I know I did. It was the worst time of your life, and I was nowhere to be found. I hurt you."

I open my mouth to say no, it was fine, I understood. After all, we'd been separated and on the road to a quickie divorce. Instead, what comes out is a single word.

"Yes."

"I know," he says. "And while there's no excuse, if there's an explanation, it's Sadie. I couldn't stop thinking about what she did, taking advantage of me when I thought I could lose both my parents. I wouldn't do that to you. When Anna got sick again, I wanted to see you. I wanted to be there for you. I wanted to help with the expenses. But I worried it would only make things worse, so I settled for little things. Things you wouldn't know were me."

I think back to the anonymous gifts that'd come when Anna was in hospice care and after her death. Endless little things, for her, for Madison, for me, for my parents, from meals to gifts to housecleaning services. We'd presumed different sources—various friends and family being thoughtful. A few of the extravagant things I even suspected came from Kit's parents. But his parents had helped under their own name and they'd come to visit, as had everyone else on my list. Everyone except Kit, who'd slipped in twice to see Anna when I wasn't there, who'd taken Madison out a dozen times to cheer her up and give me a break. I figured that was his sole contribution. I should have known better.

"I'm sorry, Laney. I screwed up, and I hurt you more."

I answer carefully. "I won't say it didn't hurt, but I understand why you kept your distance when she was dying. And I really did appreciate all those things you did."

The path reaches a fork, and we head left, toward the water.

"You argued with Sadie last night," I say. "That's actually what I needed to talk to you about. The rest is good to know, but this is the important part."

"What did we fight about, and could that be a reason for her to blow up your boats."

"Somehow, I don't think anything could be a reason to strand us, let alone destroy the boats, but was your fight something that might have upset her more? She was already mad at me."

I explain why—what Sadie had said in the laundry room—and he squeezes his eyes shut.

"So that's the real reason she was here," he says.

"I think there were multiple reasons, but that was one of them."

"Agreed. Which is exactly what we were arguing about. She said she came here for me, because when she got my message, she knew I was falling into your trap." His hands fly up. "Her words, not mine. That was the start of the fight."

"Okay."

"She thought all this staging was a setup. Everyone knows you love horror movies. So you pretended to find all this stuff, maybe for book publicity."

"Uh-huh."

"And then you decided you could use it for something else. Getting me back."

"Uh-huh."

"You had Madison call and tell me everything, saying you were heading out here, just the two of you, after finding ritualistic symbols. Naturally, I would fly to your side."

"Which you kinda did."

"Yep, I'm predictable. That's why Madison *did* call. She knew I'd come, and she wanted me to come, and I was fine with that."

"But Sadie thinks I put Mads up to it."

"Yep, and I said that proved she didn't know either of you . . . which led to a whole different argument."

"I can imagine."

"Then she brought up the same subject she did with you, and I said hell no. The timing was so wrong. That means, yes, she was angry with me. I should have said that, but since everyone already figured she took off in a snit—and the evidence supported it—I didn't want to stir up more trouble by saying she'd accused you of luring me out here."

"Between her fight with me and her fight with you, I don't think there's any doubt she tried to leave and take the boat."

"The question is whether she also set the bombs."

We stand on the promontory, looking out at the lake. Waves no longer lap at the rocks. They crash with enough force to splash our shoes, and Kit eases me back from the edge.

"One hell of a storm coming," I say, and the wind whips my words away.

Kit puts his arm around my waist. The half embrace is tentative, unsure of its welcome. When I lean against his shoulder, his arm tightens, and I take a moment to breathe in the smell of the lake, close my eyes, and imagine this is just a storm.

Two years roll away, and I'm standing here watching a storm with Kit's arm around me. We'll settle on the rocks, high above the crashing waves, and we'll break out wine and crackers and cheese, because that's what normal people do, right? Picnic in a storm? We'll laugh at that—it's so us, isn't it?—and then the sky will open, rain drenching us before we can even pack up the basket, and we'll only laugh some more. Then I'll reach for his shirt and pull it up, joking that I'm helping him out of his wet clothes, and soon we'll be lying in the grass, reveling in each other and in the glory of a summer storm.

Roll back time. Please. I don't want to be in this moment, in this hellish perversion of a wonderful dream where I get Jayla back and I find peace with Kit and maybe even Sadie.

Sadie . . .

Fuck.

I squeeze my eyes shut and steel myself to continue this shitty, shitty conversation. Did my former friend blow up my boats and trap us on this island? Or is my former friend lying dead at the bottom of Lake Superior?

I open my eyes, ready to talk again, and something below catches my eye. I start to crouch, and Kit must think I'm falling—despite being two feet from the edge. He grabs me so fast we nearly *do* fall.

"There's something down there," I say just as thunder booms over the lake.

Kit cups his hand behind his ear. I shake my head and point to the surf below.

He motions for me to stay where I am. Then he inches forward. Careful, so damn careful. That's Kit. Either cautious to a fault or diving in headfirst.

"Look, a wedding chapel. You wanna?"

"Wanna what?"

That grin, that glorious grin that made my brain spin in twenty directions. "Get married, of course."

I laugh.

"You think I'm kidding?" he says. "I dare you to marry me, Laney Kilpatrick."

"You dare me? What are we? Five?"

"Dare you, dare you, double dare you."

I shake my head, sobering. "If you were ever serious about that, Kit, we'd need a prenup. The biggest, most ironclad prenup ever."

"Which is why I am serious. Screw all that. Marry me, Laney. Tonight. Now. Before you overanalyze it."

"Before I overanalyze it?"

"Before we both do." He grabs my hands. "Come on. Let's do it."

I squeeze my hands into fists, nails digging in, and when Kit glances at me, my expression is neutral.

"See it?" I ask, pointing down.

He peers over the edge. "I see something. Wait? Is that . . . ?"

He lies facedown on the rock. I stay where I am. I don't trust my eyes right now. Not my eyes or my judgment.

"Whatever it was, it went under the overhang," he says. "I can't see it."

"Did it look like . . . ?"

He meets my eyes and nods grimly.

I wrap my arms around my chest. "Are we sure?"

He shakes his head.

"What do we do about it?" I ask.

He peers down again. "There's some stuff snagged on the rocks. I can get to it safely, I think."

"You think? Or you're sure?"

"I'm sure." He manages a smile for me. "No more polar dips today. If I can retrieve it, I will. If not, I'll come back up."

He means that. He might have swum out in freezing water to rescue me, but he's not going to take that risk to answer a question. Unlike his ex-wife, who paddled out in a storm to answer hers.

I still worry as he climbs over the edge. I lie down and plaster myself to the rock, my head and shoulders over the edge to watch his descent.

If he slipped and fell in, would I dive after him?

Absolutely.

That's love, and I still love him. I always will love him. It shouldn't be that way. Something as brief as our marriage should die like a roman candle. One blaze of glory, imprinted on the retina for a few moments and then fading. This wasn't that. This was a flash fire, and I am scarred for life, and I wouldn't want it any other way.

That's the bitch of it, isn't it? I got hurt. Hurt so damn bad, and I don't care. Give me the chance, and I'd do it again. So yes, if he slips, there is no question what I'll do, just as there'd been no question what he'd do. Does that mean he still loves me? I think so, and that should matter. But it's not always enough, as *fucking* unfair as that is.

Kit pauses to shoot me a thumbs-up and a grin, and I lift my face to let the wind freeze-dry my tears before I return the smile. Our eyes meet.

Love you, Kit. I always will. And that's okay. I'll deal with it. I'll live with it. I have to.

I let my gaze hold his long enough that he won't think I'm pulling away, upset. Then I focus on scanning the rocks below. I know what I'd seen. We both did. There was no mistaking it. A bright pink carry-on suitcase, smacking into the shore below before disappearing under the rocks. There's a tiny cave under the rocky overhang. That's where it'll be, but there's no getting it now without going into the water. Instead, Kit heads for what looks like a piece of clothing thrown onto higher rocks.

He finally reaches his target and disentangles the piece of black and red fabric. He pulls back to a safer spot, and shakes out the piece. Then his hands run over it, as if trying to make sense of what he's seeing. It's torn and soaking wet, but I know what it is long before he does.

Panties.

A pair of fancy lingerie ones, the sort you don't wear for everyday. The sort you wear for a lover.

Yesterday, I'd watched Sadie wheel that bright pink suitcase up to the house. Now it is down below. I know it is, even if we both wanted to be sure.

Her suitcase.

Her panties.

Panties she brought in hopes that she might need them. That Kit would turn to her for comfort, as he had once before.

I should see that lingerie and be furious. She came to *my* island hoping to hook up with *my* ex? Or I should laugh. Seriously, Sadie? You thought Kit would do that?

When Kit realizes what they are, he almost drops them, fumbling before wadding them up and stuffing them in a pocket. That *should* make me laugh. His expression should.

You really thought you had a chance with him, Sadie? He barely wants to touch your clean undies.

I don't laugh, because I am not sixteen. I am not going to take one moment's vindictive pleasure in seeing how deluded Sadie had been. Oh, I would, if I were convinced she was only after him for his money, but whatever else she has done, here she was her genuine self.

After hearing her pain on that call, when she accused me of stealing him, I believe Sadie genuinely cares for Kit, and once again, we actually have something in common. I feel her pain. I won't say I'd ever want Kit to end up with her, but I can still feel a sympathetic pang.

On the heels of that comes a slap of real pain. Sadie's luggage is down there. Indubitably her luggage. She did not set a bomb and push the boat out. She did not get to the Fox Bay marina, set a bomb, and push it out.

What happened is this: Sadie argued with me, and she argued with Kit, and in her anger and humiliation, she fled, and some bastard had the boat rigged up to explode in the middle of the night, only she was on it.

Oh God, Sadie.

I'm sorry. I know if you were here right now, after what you did to Kit and Jayla, I would want to throttle you myself. But once upon a time, I loved you. I missed you, and I regretted what happened between us.

If you're dead . . .

If.

Tears well.

There is no if, is there? Stop with the fucking ifs, and the fucking alternate explanations, and face the goddamned fact that Sadie—

Something whispers beside me. Not the whistle of the wind, which is loud enough to drown out everything but the surf, and it should certainly drown out a whisper. Yet even as I know I could not have heard anything, I also know I did.

Not just heard it.

Felt it. I felt movement under my fingertips. Under my entire body. A vibration.

Under the rock?

That makes *no* sense.

"Laney?"

Kit's lips move, the wind whipping away my name. I barely notice. I am turning my head, following that sound that I could not have heard, the whisper I could not have sensed, the vibration I could not have felt.

And then I see what I cannot be seeing.

I see Sadie.

EIGHTEEN

There's a bush to my right, maybe ten feet away, and Sadie's hands are pulling it down, her face peering through, as if she's crouched there, spying on us.

I blink hard. That face will disappear. It must, because I am hallucinating. I am lying on a rock watching Kit climb as a storm whips up, with my friend's body somewhere out there in the lake. I cannot be hearing her whisper. I cannot be feeling whatever I felt. I sure as hell cannot be seeing her. I will blink, and she will be gone.

She is not gone.

Sadie is right there. Staring at me. And her face . . .

Something is wrong with her face.

"Kit?" I say, the sound coming strangled.

Sadie pulls back. She does not disappear. The leaves spring back as she releases them, and she withdraws. Then there's a blur of motion through the thin branches as she takes off.

I leap to my feet and run after her.

"Laney!" Kit yells.

I don't turn back to him. I can see the undergrowth moving ahead, and it tells me where she is, and I don't dare look away. I wave over my head for him to follow me. Then I steer inland, farther from the treacherous rocks.

I reach the bush just as Kit catches up.

"Sadie!" I shout, the word snatched up by the wind.

I've lost sight of her. She's past the patch of undergrowth and somewhere farther down. I take a second to turn to Kit.

"I saw her!" I yell. "I saw Sadie."

His lips form a curse, and he bears down to run alongside me. We keep going until we're past that undergrowth. Then I stop and peer around. There's nothing here. It's rock with some shrubby trees.

I didn't see her. I couldn't have. There's no place for her to—

"There!" Kit shouts.

I follow his finger. He's pointing past the edge of the rock. It drops off to a bit of stone-covered shore, and I catch a blur of movement down there in the shadows.

We run to the edge. The rocks jut only five feet above the rocky strip, and we scramble down easily.

We're on the west side of the island now. The wind is driving from the east, and this cove is quiet, the water only lapping at the stones. I can barely see, though, and I look up to see black clouds rolling in fast, shoving aside the gray ones.

Kit turns on his flashlight, and I do the same with the one I'd grabbed from our stash. There's no sign of movement, but there are dozens of places to hide along here, where the water has worn into the rock, leaving tiny pockets and caves, each of them black as night.

"I saw her," I say. "I'm *sure* it was her. I could see her face."

He nods. "I only caught a glimpse of someone moving, but if it wasn't Sadie, it was her doppelgänger."

I exhale. We are agreed then. Nothing to prove. No need to hedge in case I was mistaken.

We walk along the shore with our flashlight beams crisscrossing as we check each cave-like divot big enough to hide a person. When

Kit spots something, it's a piece of fiberglass with looping script on it. A single word: "Wicked."

The Wicked Witch of the North. That was the name of our boat, a joke between us.

We continue. We'll reach the end soon, just after the shoreline curves to our right. We take one step around that curve and a figure appears.

It's Sadie. Undoubtedly Sadie.

She's poised on a rock. Perched like a gremlin, knees bent and splayed, arms hanging down. One arm hangs wrong, the palm unnaturally facing out, as if her shoulder is dislocated.

We can't see her face under the shadows of an overhang, but it's her, from the pale heart-shaped face to the heavy pendant necklace to the sopping-wet blond hair. There's something on her cheek. Something red and ugly. With a gasp, I realize her cheek is torn open to the bone.

"Sadie!"

I leap forward. She turns and takes off, and I stop, blinking. The way she's running, bent over in a lurching lope . . . It's like the uncanny valley of movement, where I see what looks like a person moving but my brain screams it's not right. The muscles, the bones, nothing is moving the way it should.

She's hurt. I can see that arm swinging, and I'm sure the shoulder is dislocated. One of her legs keeps buckling too. And her cheek—dear God, it was *ripped* open. She is badly injured and has suffered some kind of head injury that numbs her to what should be agonizing pain.

Despite her horrendous injuries, she clambers up the rock and disappears as we race after her.

"She's hurt," Kit says, as if we've been thinking in tandem. "She's badly hurt, and she's confused."

I nod. "We have to get to her. She needs help."

She needs a doctor. She needs a *hospital*. And how the hell am I going to give her that?

Someone blew up the boat, and she was on it. She heard or saw something and had time to jump, but not enough time to escape the concussive wave of force.

I start climbing the rocks.

Kit catches my arm. "Be careful, Laney. Please. We will get to her. We will help her. But she's not thinking straight."

"I know."

I scrabble on the rocks, and nearly fall, and Kit has to boost me. Then I need to help him. The rocks are loose and lichen-slick. How the hell did Sadie get up in her condition?

Because she's not thinking. She's not pausing and worrying and taking the easiest path.

We reach the top. It's forest up here, and I stop to search the trees with my flashlight beam. Thunder rumbles, and I fall back, only to have Kit brace me. He reaches past my elbow to silently point, and when he does, I see a patch of white.

Sadie's long-sleeved white jersey. She'd changed into it before the campfire. As I watch the spot, it moves as she shifts. She's hunkered down, and although I can't see her face, I know she's watching us.

I take a step, but again, Kit stops me. He leans down to my ear.

"She can see us," I whisper before he speaks.

"I know."

She spotted me at the cliff edge. I know she did, and she must have heard our shouts, down in the cove, away from the howling wind.

"She's hiding," he says.

"Hiding and running." I swallow. "From us."

"She's confused. *Really* confused. The last thing she did was argue with both of us. She might not remember that but . . ."

"She senses she's upset with us, and she's hiding. She's scared. Of us."

"I think so."

"Would it help to get Garrett? One of us keep an eye on her while the other gets him?"

A firm shake of his head. "We are not splitting up. If that means we need to go back together and bring him, that's what we do."

"Or if it means we catch her? Bring her in? Whether she wants it or not?"

He hesitates.

"You're right," I say. "She's traumatized, and we can't traumatize her more."

He gives a shaky laugh. "I was thinking she might attack us if we try. She's given you more reason than anyone to write her off, but you can't."

I pull at my sweatshirt sleeves. "I'm naive."

He kisses the top of my head. "I was thinking good. Kind. A hundred other things, none of them naive. You're also right. Not about traumatizing her. I don't think we can worry about that. But if we have her in our sights and we walk away, you won't forgive yourself if anything happens." He pauses. "We both won't."

"So we have to catch her."

I look at that spot, where the white patch keeps moving. She's too far to hear us—we can barely hear each other with our mouths at the other's ear—but she can see us, and she is not moving until we do.

"Who do you think she's less angry with?"

He gives another strained laugh. "I don't dare guess."

"One of us is going to have to slip up behind her, and whoever stays here should be the one she's less worried about. The one who'll make her less nervous."

"If it's a matter of who'll make her less nervous, I'm going to guess it's never the Black guy."

I make a face.

"Not true?" he says.

"Sadly agree in general, but not with Sadie."

"Not with the Sadie in her right mind. Forget that part, though. In general, a guy is always going to be more frightening than a woman, right?"

"Granted, but she also likes you better. Whatever anger she has toward you, it's temporary. I'm the source of her deep-seated . . ."

"Jealousy?"

"More like anger. Resentment. Whatever it is, I have a feeling she'll stay if you do."

The corner of his mouth lifts. "You could just say you want to do the sneaking up."

"I didn't until I thought it through." I squeeze his arm. "I will be careful, and I will stay where you can see me. I'll pretend I'm going back for help. Whether she's in any mental condition to understand or not, she will see me leaving."

"And then?"

"I sneak up behind her, and when I am close enough to cut off her escape—but not close enough to be in danger—I'll signal for you and we'll trap her."

"Together?"

"Absolutely together. But remember, please, that she's badly hurt. Even if she attacked me, there's a limit to what she can do."

"Yeah, but there's also a limit to what you'd do to *her* when she's already hurt."

"I'll be careful."

NINETEEN

I promised to stay in Kit's line of vision, but I also need to stay out of Sadie's. That's tougher than I expected, but if I'm going to prioritize, I need to go with the first part. I made a promise to Kit.

"I'm going back to the house to get Garrett," I shout, as if to be heard above the wind. I jab my finger in the direction of the house.

"Good idea!" he shouts back.

I take off at a lope. I don't look toward Sadie. I must pretend that I am completely absorbed in my task. I run through the forest and aim for a tree that's toppled, roots jutting into the air. I circle around those roots, and for those moments Kit won't be able to see me, but neither will Sadie. It'll look as if I'm continuing toward the house.

I stop and hover behind the roots. Catch my breath. Then hunker down and make my way along the trunk. When I peek, Kit is looking in the other direction. Then he checks his watch, as if impatient and glances my way. He spots me, nods and quickly looks back at Sadie. His lips move, as if he's speaking, but I can't hear anything.

Hell, I can barely *see* anything. If Kit weren't in a light-gray hoodie, I'd lose him. The sky is night-dark now. Distant thunder rumbles. Then a flash of lightning has me diving to the ground before I'm spotted.

I check my own clothing. My sweatshirt is pale pink. That comes off, leaving a black T-shirt below. I shiver, but bundle up the sweatshirt and leave it behind. Black tee. Black sweatpants. I'd rather have a hoodie, but my hair is dark. Good enough.

I continue past the branches of the tree. By that point, I'm behind Sadie's line of vision. I rise up to see over the leafy top. The hood of Kit's sweatshirt seems to turn in my direction, and I wave one pale hand. He reaches out, as if entreating Sadie, and I hope that's him saying he sees me. I'll make sure of it once I'm closer.

I turn my attention to the bushes where she's hiding. I can see a sliver of her white jersey. I'm definitely behind her. Good.

In a glance, I set my path. It's mixed forest up here. Foliage has dropped from the birches and ash, and I have to avoid dry piles of leaves, but most of them aren't at that stage. The evergreen trees will be my friends in this. They lean toward Charlie Brown Christmas tree territory—with the lack of soil and competition for light—but they're thick enough for me to use, and I creep from one to another.

I'm darting between two when Kit puts out his hand again. Okay, that's definitely an "I see you" sign. He knows how dark it is, and that I might not notice him looking my way.

Three more trees, and then I'll be right behind Sadie, and I can ambush her. Yes, I suggested I'd just spook her into running, but if I can grab her unawares, that's better. She shouldn't keep moving in her condition.

I don't even know how she *is* moving in her condition.

Sheer will. Like me in the water. I couldn't feel my arms and legs, but I'd kept going. She can't feel the pain, and she keeps going.

I run to the next tree. When my foot hits unexpectedly dry leaves, I startle, but even I can't hear the sound over the wind. Take a moment. Catch my breath again.

On to the next tree.

I'm halfway there when the sky opens. Rain slams down with such sudden force that I gasp. It's like falling into the lake this morning.

I'm soaked in the blink of an eye, the bitter rain making me shiver, as I'm mentally plunged back into the icy lake.

I'm *not* in the lake. Not drowning. Not fighting the waves. I'm on land, and I'm wet, but I'm fine.

I look past the tree.

There's no sign of Kit. There's no sign of anything. It's like being caught in a downpour in the car, the windshield suddenly as useless as leaded glass. I can make out blurred shapes, but they're all dark.

I stand there, at the side of the tree, rain pummeling me. It runs off my brows and into my mouth and even my nose when I breathe. I wipe a hand over my face. Useless. I blink. Still nothing but trees.

Kit's there. He must be.

A blur to my right. A pale shape running at me. I turn to meet him, and Sadie barrels into my side so hard we go down in a tumble of limbs and drenched fabric. I scramble up, ready to fight, only to see her looming over me, her eyes wide.

There's something wrong with her eyes.

I catch only a glimpse of them before they're hidden by the pelting rain, and all I can tell is that they're wide. So wide. Fear pulses off her, making my own heart race.

"Sadie," I say, as loud as I dare. "You're hurt—"

Her face lowers to mine, and I brace myself. Her cheek hangs open. Oh God, the skin just flaps there, bloodless, and I see her jaw-bone and teeth.

"Help me." Her lips form the words. "Please."

She's on top of me. Pinning me to the ground, but I don't think she realizes it. She's barreled into me and knocked me over, and now she's over me, her eyes wild and empty at the same time. Her pupils are blown. That's what I'd noticed earlier. They are impossibly huge, the blue irises barely a ring.

Head injury. Traumatic head injury.

No shit, Sherlock.

"Laney," she says.

She recognizes me. Thank God. Recognizes me and somehow, deep in that damaged brain, perceives that I'm not a threat. That however angry she's been with me for half our lives, I still care about her. She can still count on me.

"I'm here," I say. "I'm going to help you."

I reach up, tentatively. My fingers wrap around her good arm, and she seems to slump in relief.

"I'm sorry," I say. "Whatever happened to you, I'm sorry. We need to get you inside. Kit will help."

"Kit?" She pulls back, wrenching from my grip. "No."

"Kit will—"

"No, no, no." Her voice rises until I can hear it over the wind and rain. "He did this. Kit did this."

"What?"

"Help me. Stop him."

I open my mouth to argue and then shut it. She's confused. The last thing she must remember is being angry with Kit, and her brain has twisted that into thinking it's because he's the one who did this to her.

"Okay," I say. "Forget Kit. I'll get you back—"

Another blur appears in the rain, and this time, it materializes into Kit. When he sees Sadie over me, his eyes widen in alarm and he rushes forward. I start to say I'm fine, but she rolls off me. Her one arm shoots out, hand palm-up to ward off Kit, the other twisted and drooping.

At first, I see only her expression. The undeniable terror in her eyes. There is a moment when my gut twists, when the most bruised part of my heart screams that Kit has done something to her, that I have misjudged him, because deep inside me, that battered corner *wants* to have misjudged him, to be able to tell myself I didn't lose a good man.

Then I see Kit's expression—his utter bewilderment—and that doubt evaporates. His bafflement only grows as she scuttles backward.

"I'm not going to touch you, Sadie," he says. "I thought you might be hurting Laney. I can see you weren't."

He leans her way, only a lean to speak over the wind, and she hunches into herself like a dog ducking a blow. He straightens fast. When he looks at me, I tap my head, and he nods. Yes, of course. She's confused.

Kit hunkers down to her level, and it's the most nonthreatening pose ever, but she shrinks in, her good shoulder rising as if trying to shield herself.

"D-don't," she says. "P-please. I'm sorry. Whatever I did, I'm sorry."

Kit looks at me, his own confusion growing.

"She thinks you hurt her," I say.

"What?" His eyes saucer. "I didn't touch you, Sadie. Whatever happened—"

"Saw you." Her chest expands, as if drawing in breath. "Saw you, saw you, *saw* you!"

"What did you see?" he asks.

"You!" she spits the word. "Outside my window. Told me to come out. Go with you. Leave with you."

"I . . . I would never."

"Liar!" She rocks forward. "Saw you."

"You're saying you saw me outside your window, and I called up and asked you—"

"Waved to the boat. Beckoned to me."

Kit looks my way. "I . . . I don't understand."

She hallucinated it. Saw what she wanted.

Her deepest desire come true.

The core of so many fairy tales. Something in the woods. Something beckoning. Your true love, calling to you.

I shiver. That's my imagination again. I'm cold and drenched and exhausted.

Sadie must have dreamed Kit was outside her window saying he wanted her to leave with him. Then she got on a boat, and it exploded.

I'll explain that to Kit later. For now, I shake my head, telling him not to unravel her delusion. There's no time.

"Kit?" I say loudly. "I need you to go away. I have to help Sadie, and you can't be here."

He hesitates. Oh, he knows what I'm doing. He's just not sure he can play his role. Finally, he squares his shoulders and gives an angry wave, as if to say "Screw both of you," and stomps off.

I turn to Sadie, and I watch her expression for any sign of satisfaction, proof that she's playing a role herself. She only shudders with relief.

"Okay, let's go," I say. "I'll get you to the house."

I put out an arm to help her up, and she takes it. As I get her on her feet, her one leg buckles. I've seen it do that before, and I don't pay any attention now. It's just a reminder that I need to take this slow and support her.

We move at a snail's pace. We're a few hundred feet from the house. I have a spot out here, where I write sometimes, and it's close enough to the house that I can run back and grab a cold drink or use the bathroom. Now it seems impossibly far, like being in the water again, looking to shore.

Sadie wants to move faster. She keeps pulling at me, and I keep tugging her back.

"Need to get home," she mumbles when we get into a dip where the wind dies and her voice can rise above the battering rain. "Let Milo in. Raining."

"Milo?" I say, trying for a casual note. "Is that your cat?"

She nods, chin bobbing to her chest, that flap of flesh bobbing with it.

"I didn't know you have a cat," I say. *Keep her calm. Don't let her go into shock.*

She just keeps nodding.

"We'll get you home," I say.

"Key. You need the key." She stops suddenly and starts patting her pockets.

I squeeze her good arm. "I have it. Let's just keep walking. We're almost there."

She takes another step. Her leg buckles again, and this time I look. When I do, I gasp. There's bone sticking through the bottom of her yoga pants. *Bone.*

"Sadie?" I say.

She resumes walking. The bone in her lower leg peeks out and pulls in, and my gorge rises.

How is she walking? How *the hell* is she walking?

I take her elbow. She pulls away without seeming to notice I grabbed it. She's just moving. Blind to everything.

I grasp her arm tighter, and she spins. Her leg gives way, and I catch her, but she rips from my grip and grabs my forearms. Both hands dig into my arms so hard I let out a yelp of pain and shock. I try to yank free, but she has me in a vise grip.

That's not possible. Her shoulder is dislocated.

Sadie yanks me to her until my face is mere inches from hers.

"You made me a promise," she says, and it's a guttural rasp, but somehow I hear it over the wind and rain. "You made an oath."

"Oath? I-I don't know—"

"You promised to look after me. I gave you everything, and you made an oath and you *broke* our pact."

My brain reels to comprehend what she's saying. Broke a promise? Made an oath? Maybe I once said something that she took as a promise. *We'll always be friends. I'll always have your back. I'd never hurt you.* Words between children too young to anticipate the possibility of a situation that would rip them apart.

But broke a *pact?*

I remember the hex circle on the basement hatch, the symbol on the rocks, the one painted around the rat king.

I don't understand.

Because they're not connected. Because this is Sadie, horribly injured and out of her mind with confusion and pain. The woman is walking on a com-

pound fracture. Trying to run with it. Do not expect anything she says to make sense.

"I'm sorry," I say. "Whatever you think I did, we'll talk about it, but I need to get you back to the house."

She wrenches my arms, her fingers digging in. "You owe me, girl. You owe—"

"Laney!"

Kit shouts right behind me. I'd forgotten he was following us, only pretending to have stormed off.

Sadie's hands slam into me, and it's an impossibly superhuman shove that sends me flying off my feet. I smack into a tree, pain rocketing through me. My feet slip on the now-wet leaves, and I start to slide, but something stops me. Pain rips through my shoulder.

"Don't move!"

It's Kit. He's there, holding me still. Rain sluices over his face. He's pushed his soaked hood off, and he's leaning over me, looking at my back. He says something I don't catch. Then he takes my shoulders, very gently.

"There's a broken branch puncturing your shoulder. It's not big. It's just—" He aims a lethal scowl over his shoulder. "Damn her. I know she's not in her right mind, but . . ."

"It's okay." I sound a lot calmer than I feel. "You said it isn't big? No danger of bleeding out if I pull away from it?"

He shakes his head. "It's just part of a branch. The rest must have already broken off."

"So a sliver."

"A big sliver, but yes."

I nod. "I need to pull straight forward. Can you watch to be sure it's not longer than we think?"

"That was my plan." He manages a half smile. "Those first-aid courses are really paying off, huh?"

I return the semi-smile, but then my mind goes straight to Sadie. How the hell is a first-aid course going to help us with her? What if it doesn't? What if she dies because we don't know enough to help her? What if she dies because we can't find her? She's long gone. Run off into the forest again.

When I glance around Kit, his thumbs rub my shoulders. "We'll find her, and we'll help her."

How? Sadie isn't on the mainland. She's not sending a boat. We don't have a boat. We're trapped, and whoever hurt her could still be—

"Laney?" Kit's face comes down to mine.

"Pull off carefully. Got it."

He doesn't say that was *my* instruction. He just kisses the top of my drenched hair.

"Count of three," he says. Then he positions himself where he can see the piece of wood. "Keep it slow. Three, two, one . . ."

I start to ease forward. Pain makes my knees buckle, and I throw myself forward instead. My knees do give way then, but Kit catches me and holds me against him.

"That was *not* slow," he says.

"It hurt too much."

He gently embraces me. "I know. Now keep still while I take a look."

I do that. His fingers carefully prod where the branch stabbed me. Then he tugs the fabric from my skin. I feel heat, as if blood trickles down along with the rainwater. A dull throb of pain, but nothing more.

"Will I survive, Doc?" I say.

"In my nonexpert opinion, yes." He moves back to look at me. "It's a puncture wound, like a nail, and it's hard to see how much it's bleeding in the rain, but it doesn't seem too bad. We need to get you inside, though. Get it bandaged. Make sure nothing's left in there."

I shake my head. "Sadie—"

"Attacked you. Grabbed you. Shoved you into that tree." He lifts his hands. "I know she didn't mean to, but she did it, and that makes her dangerous."

"She's hurt. Really hurt. Not just her face and shoulder. There's bone sticking out of her leg, Kit."

Kit rubs his beard. "Okay, that's . . . I'm not even sure what to say. She was *running* on that leg."

"I definitely saw bone."

"I'm not doubting it."

There's something wrong with her. That's what I want to say, and it's ridiculous, isn't it?

Of course there's something wrong. She's badly hurt.

No, something's really wrong.

She running on a compound fracture. She's out of her mind.

No, I mean . . .

I don't know what I mean. Something in her eyes. The way she grabbed me. Hurled me with a dislocated shoulder. What she said. That guttural voice.

You promised to look after me. I gave you everything, and you made an oath, and you broke our pact.

Am I losing it? Hypothermia can have lasting mental effects. Confusion and disorientation, just like I'm seeing with Sadie. Am *I* thinking straight?

"We need to get you to the house," Kit says firmly. He hugs me, being careful with my shoulder. His mouth moves to my ear, letting him lower his voice. "If we see Sadie, I'll try to bring her in. If we don't, I'll leave you in Jayla's hands and take Garrett. Sadie will come out for Garrett. We'll find her, and we'll help her."

I nod against his chest.

Another light squeeze, and then he releases me.

"Let's go."

TWENTY

I take the long way back to the house. Kit *knows* I'm taking the long way and says nothing. This is the direction Sadie ran. I keep telling myself we're bound to see her. How much farther can she go on that leg? Yet I don't catch so much as a glimpse of that pale shirt or her blond hair, even when the downpour subsides.

"Storm's letting up," Kit says beside me. We can talk in normal voices now, and the sun filters through gray clouds overhead. "We'll get Sadie, and we'll figure it out."

Figure it out how? Hope that someone decides to head out for an autumn boat ride while storm clouds still threaten?

I don't think I've ever comprehended what would happen if I were stranded on the island. All those times Kit tried to buy me a sat phone, even he hadn't pushed too hard. After all, we had a motorboat and canoe, and even a kayak could do in a pinch, Plus, I never came up without letting multiple people know where I'd be and for how long. Then there was Nate, who always "popped by" if I visited for more than a few days.

"Did you ask Nate to check on me?" I say.

The question startles Kit, but after he recovers, he shrugs. "I wish

I could take credit, but it was his idea. I knew you'd want to be able to write undisturbed, but when he suggested it, I agreed."

"And paid him."

It's not a question. Kit knew how to strike that perfect balance, like he had with those anonymous gifts while Anna was sick. Nate would have volunteered, and to assume he wanted pay would be insulting. Yet Kit would find a way to compensate him.

"I . . ." He shoves his hands in his pockets. "I opened a college fund for him. His aunt helped. When he was ready to go back to school, she'd have told him it was some kind of post-pandemic scholarship fund for students experiencing hardship."

His hands dig deeper into his pockets, shoulders rising as he must think the same thing I do. Nate won't need that fund now. The money will go to his funeral instead.

"His aunt has a couple of kids still in high school," Kit says. "I'll make sure they're covered if they want to go to college."

I loop my arm through his and say nothing. Kit isn't looking for virtue points. That'd be easy to do in his position. Sprinkle money here and there and point neon arrows at it. He follows his parents' example and just does it, and if he's concerned it'll draw attention to him as the benefactor, he slides it under the radar and hopes the connection won't be made. *Genuinely* hopes it won't be made.

"Earlier, I asked when Sadie last contacted you," he says. "That wasn't a random question."

"Okay."

"You said it was after we got married."

"Right."

"Did you—?" He stops short to look off to the left, but when I glance over, there's nothing there, and he keeps walking.

"Did I what?" I ask when he doesn't continue.

He shakes his head. "I know you didn't, and I *should* have known, but I was never quite certain about the state of things between you two."

"Between me and Sadie?"

"I know what happened and that you weren't good friends after that, but you weren't sworn enemies either. So it made sense, at the time, that you might have said it. In passing. A confession to an old friend who knew . . . all the complications."

"You do realize you're not making any sense, right?"

"I'm fumbling."

"I see that," I say.

"Fumbling because I'm looking back, wondering how I could have been so stupid, and realizing that you're going to wonder the same thing, which does not help my case at all."

"Okay. I'm going out on a limb and guessing Sadie said something to you. She claimed I said something. Confessed it."

He doesn't answer, which is an answer.

I soften my voice. "Was it about me being bi?"

"What?" He looks over sharply. "Uh, no, Laney. I've known that since I was, like, twelve."

"I don't mean that I confessed to be bi. That's hardly a secret. But did she say . . ." I take a deep breath. "I know we talked about it, in the early days. About what it meant for me being married to a man. Would I be missing something? Would I want—need—an open marriage? I said no, and I meant it. If I married a woman, I'd have felt the same. It's about the person for me. Did Sadie say I confessed that I missed women? That it wasn't enough, being with you?"

He shakes his head. "I'd have known that was bullshit. If you felt that way, you'd have talked to me, and you wouldn't be confessing it to her."

"Okay, so what *did* I supposedly confess?"

"It was about . . . Well, not *about* Garrett but—"

He keeps talking. I don't hear it over the blood pounding in my ears.

A confession. About Garrett. Something Kit shouldn't have believed, but he did. A lie Sadie told.

A lie about the fact that I'd confessed. But a lie she believed to be true.

And so had Kit. At least for a while.

No. Oh God, please no.

When Kit left me, he made excuses. So many excuses, most of them mumbled and half intelligible, and maybe it seems like I should have demanded answers, but I'd been too hurt to chase them. He didn't want me. That was all that mattered. He'd changed his mind and no longer wanted to be with me.

When the pain faded to a dull ache, when my pride slunk back, I thought about asking for that answer. We were divorced, so it couldn't sound as if I was begging him to come back.

I had considered the possibility there was more to it than falling out of love. The way he'd left, the way he'd thrown Hemlock Island in my lap and tried to heap more gifts on it, I'd seen guilt.

What if he'd had a pandemic fling? Restrictions had eased, and we'd been cooped up together so long, and yes, I hadn't minded the closeness, but maybe he did, and he had an affair. Hell, maybe a one-night stand.

This had been the real reason I'd wished I'd insisted on an answer. If he had a fling, we could have worked it out. Extenuating circumstances—quickie marriage, pandemic anxiety—would have made me a whole lot more forgiving than I might otherwise be.

But what if that wasn't the answer? What if *this* was it? If Sadie said I confessed that I'd lied about Garrett . . . and Kit—my *husband*—believed her?

"Laney?"

I see his mouth moving. He's in front of me, holding my arms, his face swirling with panic and worry. But it's not his voice I'm hearing.

"Laney!"

Madison? Why is Madison—?

Shit! Madison has been out here the whole time. In the chaos, I'd been thinking she was in the house, safe. I'd forgotten she's with Jayla looking for Sadie . . . who is out of her mind and dangerous.

"Madison!" I whirl, searching for her.

"Right here." Madison appears from behind rocks. "I thought I heard your voices. Did you find her?"

Jayla rounds the rocks. "The only thing *we* found was rain." She plucks at her drenched shirt. "I feel like I went for a swim, and not a nice one." She shivers. "I was trying to persuade the kid to get inside and change into something dry before we catch pneumonia."

"That's not how you catch pneumonia," Madison says. "Or a cold. We just spent two years in pandemic hell, and you *still* don't know how viruses spread?"

"Yeah, yeah. I know it. I was just hoping you didn't. It's a good excuse for getting inside."

"We saw Sadie," I say.

They both turn to stare at me.

"Fuck," Jayla says. "So I was right. She's behind this bullshit and hiding on the island."

I shake my head and glance at Kit, but he seems to be only half listening as he looks out over the landscape.

"She's . . ." I measure my words, aware of Madison soaking them in. "Hurt. Badly hurt. I think she might have been on the boat."

"When it exploded?" Madison says.

"Maybe she jumped off before it did. Heard a noise or spotted the bomb. We noticed her suitcase was in the water, and when we saw her, she was drenched even before the rain started."

"You couldn't get to her," Madison says.

"I . . ." *Careful. So careful.* "We couldn't call to her with the wind, and so we chased her."

"Chased her?" Jayla frowns. "She ran away?"

Kit snaps back from wherever his mind had been. "She's badly hurt. A blow to the head or concussive shock from the bomb. At first we thought she didn't recognize us, but then she attacked Laney, and she accused me of being the one who hurt her."

"What?" Madison says.

"She's really confused. But she's also—"

"What the hell is going on?" Garrett's voice booms as we turn to see him striding from the direction of the house. "Are you searching for my sister or hanging out chatting?"

"No, asshole," Madison says. "We're talking to Kit and Laney, who saw your sister, and we're getting the story so we can help her."

Garrett stops short and swivels on me. "You saw my sister?"

I nod. "She's out here, and she's hurt and confused."

"And again, my fucking question, louder now. You are standing around chitchatting after you *found* my sister?"

"What the hell is your problem?" Madison snaps.

I step between them and lower my voice to address Madison. "His sister is missing, and he's panicked. Same as I would be if you were missing."

Cut him some slack. That's what my tone says, and Jayla's lips tighten at that, but she doesn't interfere. Yes, in this instance, we need to cut Garrett slack. Just not as much as he demands.

I turn to Garrett and keep my voice calm. "We are discussing it because she's not in her right mind."

"She attacked Laney and Kit," Madison cuts in.

"The point," Kit says, "is that Sadie's dangerous. That's not her fault, but it doesn't change the fact she is. We were making sure Madison and Jayla knew that before they went running after her, as they understandably would want to."

"Would they?" Garrett says. "Does anyone here give a shit besides me?"

"Yes," I say firmly. "I think we've proved that. Now, if we can divide into groups, we'll go after her."

"Uh, Laney?" Madison says. "Is that blood dripping down your back?"

"It is," Kit says. "And that saves me from being the one who brings it up. You need that looked at."

I start to protest.

"I also don't think Madison should be out here," Kit says. "Not Laney or Madison."

"Why not me?" Madison asks.

"He's right," Garrett cuts in. "You need to go inside, kiddo. Sadie would never hurt you in her right mind, but we can't take a chance she'll mistake you for your, uh, aunt." He jabs his index finger at Kit. "You come with me."

"I was going to check Laney's shoulder. Then I can—"

"Jayla will do it. Or the kid can do it, if Jayla wants to come with us. But if Sadie's hurt and she's not coming back willingly, I'm going to need help."

Jayla takes my arm. "I'll look after Laney. Mads will help. You guys hunt for Sadie. You have one hour. Then we need a check-in."

TWENTY-ONE

The injury to my shoulder really is as simple as a bad sliver. After they check it, Madison insists I have a hot bath, in case the cold rain . . . I don't know, triggered my hypothermia? Whatever her reasoning, I don't argue. I need to clean the wound, and I need to rest the leg I injured earlier, and I need to warm up. Afterward, Madison bandages my shoulder while Jayla takes a hot shower.

"What happened with you and Sadie?" Madison says as we throw our wet clothing in the dryer.

I shrug. "She's not thinking straight, and she grabbed me and then pushed me into a tree."

And accused me of breaking a promise. A pact. Not just that, but when she said it, her voice . . . it wasn't her voice.

Madison is watching me expectantly, and I realize she must have said something else.

I shake off my thoughts. "Sorry. I'm a little out of it myself."

"I said I didn't mean what happened just now. What happened to you guys as friends? I always figured it was just the normal thing, where you outgrow a friendship, like me and Catelyn. But with the way everyone's been acting, I started to figure there was more to it, and there seems to be something with her and Kit." She makes a face.

"Or there was? In the past? That would explain the . . ." She searches for a word. "The tension. Awkward, right, if she had a thing with Kit and then you guys got married. But then Jayla's thinking Sadie might have blown up your boats and now she attacked you, and people don't do that over a guy."

Oh, they do, but I get what Madison is saying. She knows I wouldn't "steal" Sadie's boyfriend, and I wouldn't be jealous of Kit's past. If Sadie had been over the top with her own jealousy, I'd have steered clear and locked my doors.

"It's—" I begin.

"Don't you dare say 'complicated.'"

I smile and lean against the washing machine. "Okay, I won't. But what I would have meant by that is that it's old history, and it's not really my place to discuss it."

Her cheeks pink. "Discuss it with me, you mean. Right. That makes sense."

I hug her. "It's grown-up drama that started as teen drama, and you know what that's like. I can say two things. One, Sadie has issues with me, and they have nothing—" I stop and veer around that land mine. "They aren't issues with you. If she did hurt you in her current state, it'd honestly be because she mistook you for me, which would take some seriously bad lighting."

She rolls her eyes, and then says, "And the other thing?"

I meet her gaze. "Don't hold it against her. Whatever she's done, it's between me and her. It's past history that Sadie can't quite let go of, but I wouldn't want that to turn you against her. When we find her, forget all that and focus on her as a person in need of help."

"Don't judge. Except with that Garrett guy. I can totally judge him."

When I hesitate, she frowns. "He's an asshole, Laney. Please don't tell me I need to give him the benefit of the doubt too, because that is *not* happening."

"There you two are," Jayla says, walking in as she gently towels off her braids. "I thought you'd be in the office showing your aunt what we found."

"Found?" I say. "In the office?"

"On your laptop."

"Your laptop is fine," Madison says quickly. "Don't freak her out like that. No one did anything to your laptop, Laney. But Jayla and I were talking while we searched. I wanted to check into this theory that whoever stages that stuff was trying to buy the island. I was thinking that if I wanted to buy an island, I'd want to see it first. Easiest way to do that?"

"Rent it," I say.

"Yep. So Jayla and I came up with a list of red flags to look for. We were going to give them to you, but since you were in the tub, and you don't lock your laptop, and I know you trust me not to look at your private stuff . . ."

She trails off with a sidelong look of uncertainty, waiting for me to say yes, it was fine. When I do, she relaxes.

"Good," she says. "So we went on a cyber-spy mission through your rental email folder. We started by looking at people who were here right before it all started. The first thing found was the hex circle under the crawlspace carpet, right?"

I nod. "The people who rented Hemlock Island before that were seniors with young grandkids. Unlikely suspects. However, no one would have moved the crawlspace carpet until I came for a visit, so it could have been two, three, even four renters before them."

"That's what I thought. So, like I said, we had a list of red flags we checked against. The suspect we found, though? They did something different."

Madison waves me from the laundry room into my tiny office, where my laptop is open on the desk. She sits and brings up a tab. On it is a message from a renter, and when I read it, I let out a string of profanity.

"Aunt Laney!" Madison says with a grin.

I pull over the stool and take the laptop. I can't believe I missed this one. Well, yes, I can, because when I'd been considering suspects for the staging, I'd had certain renters in mind. The trust-fund twentysomething couple who'd treated the island like a hotel room they could trash and have Mommy and Daddy pay the bill. The older couple who'd said they were renting it for themselves and instead let their college-aged son and his friends have it for a party weekend. Or the several groups of renters with teenagers.

The ones Madison and Jayla pinpointed were a couple in their early forties on a getaway. As unlikely to be staging occult nonsense as the elderly pair and their preteen grandchildren.

So what's in the message that has me swearing? Something that had seemed so innocuous at the time. They were the sort of renters who have a laundry list of questions before they commit, common questions that I have canned answers for.

One of their questions was about the security system. That's not unusual. I might stress how remote Hemlock Island is, but people still think of the lower Great Lakes in summer, with endless passing boaters who might decide my island looks like a good place to pull over and camp. They want to be certain they'll be safe from intruders.

I'd given the canned answer, and this guy came back wanting to know what type of system we had. He'd apologized for being a "pain in the ass," but he owned a security company, and there were plenty of rental properties that claimed to have good security, only for him to discover they'd bought some cheap system online. I'd sent back a link to our system and steeled myself for him to tell me it was trash in hopes of selling me his company's product. Instead, he'd said that was a great choice, and I never heard a word about it again.

This guy is a security professional. He knew what kind of system I had before he came out. If I'm wondering how someone could get access to my secured house? Here's my answer.

"That could be a coincidence," Jayla says. "If you brought this to me wanting to legally pursue damages, I'd laugh you out of my office. But then . . ."

She leans over and pulls up an email. It's from one of the companies that has tried buying Hemlock Island. This one bypassed Kit and came straight to me.

"Note the area code and first name."

I do—it's a Detroit area code, from a land-development company, the letter sent directly from the CEO, whose name is Rachel Rossi. Then Jayla flips to the rental agreement for the guy who asked about security. She points to the phone number. The area code is the same . . . and his wife's first name is Rachel.

I swear under my breath.

"Do you know how much I'd love to have internet access right now?" Jayla says. "It'd be an easy check to link that letter to that renter. Then we have our third piece of evidence."

She opens another tab, with a message from a person who rented the property shortly before the grotesque wind chimes were found.

> Hello! I'm hoping to rent your lovely island for a fall getaway!
> You hosted friends of ours—John and Rachel—this summer,
> and they can't stop raving about the place!

John and Rachel. Security-company guy and his presumed land-developer wife. I don't remember much about this "friend" couple, and I zip through my messages to find the reason: they did nothing memorable. They had no questions and paid in full. They'd come for a weekend and left without so much as breaking a plate, giving me no reason to contact them later. They'd five-star-reviewed Hemlock Island, and so I'd mentally entered them onto my ideal guest list and returned the five-star rating for them . . . on their brand-new renters account.

They'd also paid by e-transfer, which came from a corporate account identified by a string of numbers.

John and Rachel's "friends" didn't rent Hemlock Island that

weekend. John and Rachel did. They'd come on site, done whatever additional research they needed. They might have set up the wind chimes, or they might have just found a spot to moor a boat so they could access the island whenever they wanted.

I push back from the desk. Then I march into the great room and change my admin codes on the security system.

"You think they also took the gun?" Madison asks.

"Yes," I say. "If they can crack the security system, they could open the locker. I don't think they're prowling the island with my gun, though."

Jayla nods. "They took it so you don't shoot them *while* they're prowling the island."

"After we found that hand, we'd go straight for the gun. They couldn't take that chance, so they've removed it. Logical?"

"Yep. They rented the house the first time to check out the island, make sure it lived up to expectations. Which it would—it's exactly what you claim it is: the perfect luxury getaway. They drew the hex circle and figured out the security system while hoping they wouldn't need either."

"Because two weeks later, they sent a lowball offer through the wife's company. Being spooked, I'd naturally agree. Instead I refused to even negotiate. So they got serious. Came for another weekend and upped their game with the wind chimes and the boathouse staging. Oh, Kit and I found something else in the boathouse earlier, too. That'd be part three, along with scratches in the closet."

"Only when they staged part three, Nate was here," Jayla says. "They misjudged their timing, and he caught them. There's a fight. He dies . . . and they go full out. Use his body. Destroy the small watercraft. You show up with a team of friends to investigate, and they try to trap us here—making you realize how isolated and dangerous this place is. They set a bomb on the boat, except Sadie decided to abandon us, and was on the boat and is now badly injured." Jayla crosses her arms. "These bastards are going away for a very long time."

Is that the real story? Does it explain everything that's going on here? A couple of investors got in over their heads, intent on their prize, and the more things went wrong, the further they were willing to go? In for a penny, in for a pound.

There's more to this. You know there is.

Should I point out the parts that don't make sense? Like what I saw in Sadie's eyes? What she said to me? How the hell she's running with bone sticking out of her leg and do *not* tell me that's from brain trauma.

Jayla and Madison don't know any of that. I should tell them. Just casually say it and get their impressions.

Are you fucking kidding me, Laney? You're going to "casually" tell Madison about Sadie's leg? If you think that is at all appropriate, turn in your guardianship papers right now.

Jayla then. Take her aside and get her read on it.

I consider that. Then I see Madison's face as she looks at me. No, as she *watches* me. Watches for a sign that I doubt the story Jayla is telling.

Madison needs me to believe it. She trusts me, and she relies on me to keep her safe, and it doesn't matter what's actually happening out there. What matters is that she feels I have this under control.

I do have it under control. I've changed the security codes. We are safely in the house, and the guys will be back at any moment. With any luck, they'll have Sadie, and everyone can judge the situation for themselves.

"We need to get ready for Sadie," I say as I slap shut the security panel. "She's badly injured, and we have no immediate way off this island, so we need to care for her."

"What are her injuries?" Jayla says.

I hesitate. Then I plow on. "A dislocated shoulder. A cheek in need of stitches. A compound fracture on her leg."

"Compound?" Madison frowns.

"Badly broken," I say. "All the bathrooms have first-aid kits. Let's start gathering those. We also need clean clothing, towels, and hot water."

We divvy up the tasks and set to work.

I'm in the laundry room looking for my sewing kit. I know I have one here somewhere, and it might not be the best idea for stitching up Sadie, but we're going to need something. Sanitize the needles. Clean the thread. Pray it's better than leaving an open wound.

Now if only I could find the damned kit. The problem is that, well, I'm not a seamstress. I can barely thread a needle. But I am a bit of a squirrel when it comes to freebies. That's how I was raised. We were comfortably middle-class, but my parents had ascended there from childhoods where every penny counted. On vacation, if we opened a bottle of hotel shampoo, we took it home. And if it was a fancy hotel, we'd reason that the amenities were included in the price and take home the unopened ones, too. All this is to say that my "sewing kit" is actually a box of mini sewing kits from hotels. Because someday, I'm going to need to fix a button or whatever.

Now I need to stitch up my former friend's gaping wounds . . . and I have no idea where I stashed that box. I only know that it exists and it's in the laundry room. Somewhere.

I'm searching a cupboard when I catch a glimpse of movement out the window. I slap the door shut so I can look past it.

I'm hoping to see Kit, to know he's okay. Yes, after what he said in the forest, I . . . I'm not sure how I'll deal with that. But it doesn't change the fact that I'm worried about him out there with a woman who thinks he's responsible for her horrific injuries.

Let it be Kit, and let him have Sadie.

It's gotten dark again, and for a second, I think the day has passed into night. It certainly seems as if it's been that long. It's barely past noon, though. The darkness is the clouds reminding us that the storm hasn't dissipated yet.

I squint and lift my hand to shield the reflection from the laundry-room lights. Someone lurches from the forest. Even before I see a figure, that movement tells me who it is.

Sadie.

She's stumbling now, barely able to stay upright. She's at the west side of the house, where the forest comes up to the patio.

Where we found Nate's hand.

She takes three steps and collapses in a heap. I jolt, as if from a stupor.

Sadie is there. Right there. Collapsed from pain and exhaustion and God knows what else, and I'm just standing here watching.

I run from the laundry room. In the hall, I stop short, my bare feet squeaking on the polished hardwood.

Voices sound overhead. Jayla and Madison upstairs, down by Madison's bedroom. I pause for two seconds. Then I veer into my office on the way to the back door. I grab a pen and stickie pad from the desktop. As I run to the door, I write "Sadie is outside. Getting her. Stay in here!"

I slap the stickie note on the patio door. Then I set the alarm to rearm once I'm out. I yank on my drenched sneakers, open the door, dash through, and lock it behind me.

As I race across the patio, a voice whispers that it would only have taken a shout to bring Jayla and Madison. Less time than it took to write a note.

I can tell myself I didn't have time to explain, but the truth is that I don't want Madison out here with Sadie until I know it's safe. I am not being reckless. I am tipping the balance of risk from Madison to me.

I run over to where I saw Sadie.

She isn't there.

I'm in the wrong place. All I saw was that she came out of the forest over here somewhere. The angle is different. She must be on the other side of that bistro set—

She's not there, and once I'm standing in that spot, I see blood to my left, in the direction of the laundry-room window. More blood is smeared on the paving stones.

I turn, and it really seems like twilight here, in the gloom of the trees under a gunmetal-gray sky. I can't see—

There! I catch a glimpse of Sadie's white shirt, moving erratically into the forest.

I glance over my shoulder at the house.

I shouldn't go far.

I should have brought Jayla. Insisted Madison stay inside and brought Jayla.

Oh, hell no. I'm not leaving Madison alone *anywhere* on this island.

I look between the house and Sadie's retreating form.

I can do this. Sadie's lurching, barely mobile. No more running and climbing for her. I can catch up with her easily.

Should I? What if she attacks me again?

She's barely moving, remember?

I remember her face, twisted with rage.

You promised to look after me. I gave you everything, and you made an oath, and you broke it. You broke the pact.

I remember the feeling of her fingers digging in. I have bruises on my forearms from her grip. I have bruises on my back from hitting that tree. That wasn't normal strength.

Make up your damned mind. Are you going after her or getting the others?

My feet are answering for me, have been since I saw Sadie's retreating figure. I'm already at the edge of the forest. I can still see her lurching away. I take a deep breath . . . and then I run in after her.

TWENTY-TWO

I've lost Sadie.

I don't know how the hell that's possible. I had her in my sights, and then I stumbled over a fallen branch. It really was no more than a stumble, with a quick recovery, but when I looked up, she was gone.

I know she didn't race off with a sudden burst of speed. She must have fallen. The damned forest is nearly night-black again, and I'm stumbling around without a flashlight, hoping to catch a glimpse of her white shirt.

I should turn back.

I *will* turn back.

I just need one last look, enough to let me face Garrett and say, in all honesty, "I did my best."

No, screw Garrett. It's Madison I'm thinking of. I need to be able to stand in front of her and honestly say that I did my best to save an old friend.

I'm heading for a tree. The island is half covered with trees, more than one would expect on this northern hunk of rock. But they seem to flourish here, and this is the most impressive and implausible of all—a massive oak, gnarled and gorgeous.

Is it silly to have favorite trees? I do, at least on Hemlock Island, and this is my most favorite of all. When I saw that someone carved their initials in her, I'd been ten times more outraged than when someone defaced my boat. I'd spent hours gently sanding out the initials.

As much as I respect the age of this grandmother tree, I love her even more for her thick and climbable branches. In that sense, she does indeed remind me of my own grandmothers, who even in their twilight years would put out their arms to let Madison climb up to her safe spot in their laps.

I rub my hands on the tree and murmur a warning. *I'm going to climb your branches again. Hope that's okay.* Then I heave myself onto the lowest branch and continue up two more until I reach a wide one worn from me lying on my stomach, plotting and dreaming.

Today, that branch serves a new purpose. It lets me see deep into the dark forest, where I might catch a glimpse of Sadie's shirt or hair. I lean out but it's all trees and dying foliage, browns and grays and greens.

"Sadie?" I call. "I know you're here! Let me help. Say something. Lift a hand. I don't want this for you."

My eyes prickle with tears. *I never wanted any of this for you. For us.*

When this is over, we need to sit down. I understand what you want and why you want it. After what you've done, to Kit, to Jayla, to me, I'm not sure there's any coming back, but if there is steady ground we can find, I want to.

"Sadie?" I say. "Please. Whatever you think I did, I swear—"

Movement. It's off to my left, and my heart stops as I squint into the darkness.

Don't be a rabbit. Don't be a squirrel or a mouse or a fox.

Be Sadie. Please, please, please—

I glimpse pale skin through a bush. A hand, I realize. The blur of a pale hand lying palm down on the ground. The fingers work, clawing at the ground, as if Sadie is trying to drag herself, no longer able to walk.

I scramble down the tree and race toward that bush. When my foot slides on wet undergrowth, I go down hard on one knee.

Breathe. Relax. She's there, and she's not going anywhere. I can still see her hand. Her fingers just keep clawing at the ground in a slow, robotic way, as if running on instinct alone, unaware that she isn't pulling herself anywhere.

Must keep moving. Must keep going.

Like me in the lake.

I resist the urge to reassure her that I'm coming, which might not be reassuring at all. She's barely functioning. Don't stress her out. Don't panic her.

I take two more steps, completely focused on that moving hand. Then I stop.

Something about the hand is wrong.

Everything about this is wrong, Laney, and you know it, and yet you keep insisting it's normal, just bad people doing bad things.

No, that isn't it. It's not the way her hand is moving or its position. It's . . .

It's not Sadie's hand. It's wide, with thick fingers and square nails and a smart watch. A men's smart watch on a man's hand.

Garrett.

Shit!

I leap forward, and I will fully admit that as I do, I'm not thinking "Oh my God, Garrett is hurt!" I'm thinking "Where's Kit?" Kit was with Garrett, and if Garrett was hurt, Kit would still be with him . . . unless he's also injured.

No, if Garrett was hurt, Kit would go back to the house and bring help. Garrett is a big guy. It's going to take at least two of us to move him.

"Garrett?" I say.

The hand keeps moving. There's a moment where I have a horrible flash of Nate's hand sticking from the ground, of his body seeming to twitch of its own accord. But this isn't that—I can see an upper arm and the bulk of a torso, almost obscured by the bush.

"Garrett?" I say again.

I take another step. Then I stop. It's a smart watch—I can tell by the blank screen—but it's gold, and not just gold colored.

That isn't Garrett's watch.

That isn't Garrett's hand.

That isn't Garrett.

My heart thuds, stealing my breath. I force myself to take another step, while braced to run, as my brain screams this is a trap.

The man lifts his head. I couldn't see it before through the bush and the gloom. He must have been lying facedown. Now he lifts his head, and I am looking into the face of a stranger. Yes, it's still partly obscured by the bush, but there is no doubt that this isn't Garrett. It's a dark-haired man with tan skin and a beard. And he's looking right at me.

I stumble back. The man's mouth moves, but if he says anything, I can't hear it over the blood pounding in my ears.

There is a stranger on my island.

You just figured that out? Weren't you all huddled in the house earlier, locking the doors against this exact situation?

Yes, after finding that hand, we barricaded ourselves inside and then tried to flee on the boat because someone killed Nate and buried his hand and lured us outside to find it. That had seemed clear. But in the hours that passed, we'd convinced ourselves it wasn't true. Sure, someone did kill Nate. Sure, they did stage his hand and lure us out, but they must have left before the storm hit, and if by some chance they missed that window, they were hiding, waiting for their chance to flee.

They killed Nate accidentally, and the last thing they wanted was for us to find them. We'd be careful, but we were safe.

How the hell did we decide *that?* How did I delude myself into thinking it was safe to charge out here after Sadie?

Because we needed to believe it. Sadie was out here, hurt, and we needed to believe we weren't in imminent danger from anyone on this island.

Now I'm staring at a stranger. He's lying on his stomach, his hand outstretched, fingers clawing the ground. As I stare, he makes a noise. A low moan. As if he's injured.

He's faking being injured. So badly injured that he can't get up.

Luring me in.

Get back to the house. Get back there now.

He's between me and the house.

Then go around him, for God's sake.

I don't run. I don't dare turn away from him. With my gaze fixed on that hand, I back up until there's twenty feet between us. Only then do I veer and run.

TWENTY-THREE

I'm running for the house, and I've gone at least a hundred feet be-fore I realize I can't reach Hemlock House this way. Not directly, at least, unless I want to wade across a storm-swollen creek raging with icy water. I either need to go back and around the way I came or continue on to the bridge that Kit and I built our first summer here. I glance over my shoulder. There's no sign of the man giving chase, but I can't see into the forest, and he might be ten feet behind me and running fast.

Keep going. I know this island. I know every inch of it. If he's behind me, I'll get away. I have the advantage.

Do I? If that's the guy who set all this up, then he's rented my island twice, maybe visited even more often. He could know it as well as I do.

He's *not* behind me—at least not right behind me—and that's all that matters.

I swerve north, away from the house. The bridge is up ahead over a patch of rock. Rock that's slick with dead leaves and pools of rain-water.

Another glance over my shoulder before I let myself slow down enough to get over that rock without falling. Then I'm at the bridge. As I cross, each footfall booms.

That bridge over the creek doesn't seem safe. Are you sure it's safe?

Little Billy jumped off that bridge into the creek and cut his foot on the rocks. Don't you realize what a temptation that is for children?

Why aren't there rails on that bridge? What if someone slips?

Voices of past renters ring in my ears, swirling with the rage of realizing a past renter did all this. Killed Nate. Mutilated his body. Hurt Sadie.

Fuck you. Fuck you all. You are never setting foot on my island again. This is mine, damn it. Mine.

"Not yours."

The whisper sets me stumbling as I hit the end of the bridge, and my ankle twists. My arms windmill as I get my balance and then whip around.

There's no one here. I'm surrounded by twenty feet of open rock on all sides.

A breeze snakes past, seeming to whisper as it does, making me give myself a shake. The wind is picking up, and I'm out here, panicked and alone and hearing voices.

I pause and look around again.

There's no sign of the man who'd been lying on the ground.

Could he have really been hurt?

Damn, I hope so.

Unless . . .

I wrap my arms around myself and stare back the way I came. Back in the direction of the man. I'd told myself it must be the person who staged all this. John Sinclair, Security Guy. Is that the only answer?

What about the Abbases? The couple who'd been frightened off the island?

No, it couldn't be them, because my boat was still at the Fox Bay dock.

What if they chartered another boat? Got someone to take them back to the island?

I remember the voice I heard on the phone. Dr. Abbas. A Middle Eastern accent, like his surname. The man I just fled from had dark hair and light brown skin.

Oh God.

What if that was Dr. Abbas?

I can't run back to him. I can't take that chance. I just need—

At a blur of motion, I wheel. It's off to my right, away from the house, heading up that bluff toward the gazebo. A figure striding in that direction. Dark skin. Short dark curls and a beard. Light gray hoodie.

"Kit!" I shout, but the wind whips my voice away.

I run toward him. Still going the other way, he breaks into a jog, and then a run, as if he's spotted something on that bluff. I shout louder, but he's too far to see me now.

I pick up speed. Soon I'm at the base of the bluff. The route Kit took is along the edge, and I'm ready to head up the trail and cut him off, but the dirt path is flooded and slick with mud. I pick my way over to his route. It's not as close to the edge as it seemed, and we use it all the time for the view. The rocks here are rough enough that they aren't rain-slick, and I climb easily. I'm nearly at the top when I spot something below.

A boat, tucked into a small bay.

I stop and stare down, as if at a mirage. Then I look up to where Kit disappeared. Is this what he saw? It must be, and he's taking the route down the other side. There's another path here, one I discovered on my own—a safe trail to that little bay, where I could sit on the rocks and write as the water crashed beneath my feet.

I start down. I'll meet Kit at the small bay, and we'll check the boat and pray it has keys. Hell, if it doesn't have keys, we'll grab oars and row it to shore.

From what I can see, it's a small fishing boat with a little motor that makes it undersized for Lake Superior, at least this far out. Does it belong to the people who staged this? They bought or rented this little boat to sneak onto the island? Probably. All that matters now is that it's ours. Our way back.

I'm almost to the bottom when I stop.

There's something dark in the bottom of the boat. I squint down at a spot on the stern. A big dark patch.

I take two more steps along the ledge and then bend to peer down at the boat.

That's not a black spot. It's water. The boat is listing to one side, and the port side of the stern is filled with water. I climb down to the next ledge, and from that spot, there's no mistaking what I'm seeing: a gaping hole in the metal. When I take yet another step, I can see it's more than a hole. There's a rip through the metal all along the port side, with a hole at the stern, as if someone tore along it with the giant can opener.

Rocks tumble down across from me, and I look up, expecting to see Kit having come down the opposite route. It's just a squirrel, peering at me before racing back along the path.

I stand and look for Kit, but there's no sign of him. Is he not down yet? Or did he already see what I did?

I turn around and trudge back up the bluff.

Another boat destroyed. Another way off the island gone.

I speculated that it belonged to the couple who staged this. But they wouldn't trap themselves on this island.

Unless they didn't mean to. What happened to my boats was catastrophic. This is a rip in the hull, the sort you get when you take a tiny metal boat too close to sharp rocks.

Any other time, I'd be chuckling at the irony of that. They trapped us . . . and got trapped with us. Right now, though, all I can think is that I've lost a chance to get to shore. What if it was damaged *after* they moored it? What if we'd found the boat sooner? What if I'd looked down when I'd been here in the wee hours of the morning?

I stop short at the top of the bluff. Something sways at the periphery of my vision, and it rockets me back to when I'd come up this hill and seen what looked like a wind chime on the gazebo. Tiny objects swirling on strings, clacking like bamboo wind chimes.

I catch the same motion, and I freeze, my heart hammering with the remembered horror of what I'd seen, that moment of revulsion and fear before my rational brain took over and said it was just feathers and animal bones.

Feathers and animal bones. That's what I remind myself as I turn. If there is something there, that's what it will be, and there might *not* be anything. A trick of the light. Distant movement of branches behind the gazebo. There could be nothing—

There's something there. In the exact same place where that macabre wind chime had hung. It's another wind chime. Or it seems to be. The last had been constructed of perfectly sized branches, equally spaced and tied with red yarn. Now, knowing what we suspect, I picture Rachel Rossi—or her assistant, more likely—sitting at a desk with a pile of supplies from the nearest craft store, constructing the perfect "outdoorsy" wind chime frame, and then adding the bones to make it appropriately spooky.

This one is different. This one looks like it was made by a kid at summer camp, forced to participate in the daily craft, slapping together something that vaguely approximates a wind chime frame. Randomly sized sticks, still shaggy with tree bark, lashed haphazardly together.

John and Rachel, stranded on my damn island, frantically trying to use the time to scare us even more, forced to build with whatever they have at hand. The "string" hanging from each arm of the chime looks like . . . kelp? It's thick and white.

As for what they used as chimes . . . Minnows? Or at least the ones I can see from this angle seem to be minnows. Long and thin and pale. On the far side, they've strung something heavier, making the whole thing tilt, weighed down.

I shake my head. Is that supposed to scare me? Fish tied to sea-weed? It makes me wonder whether Sadie isn't the only one who bumped her head.

I continue on, not bothering to get closer to the gazebo. I don't need a closer look at that wind chime. I need to get Kit up here and tell him about the man I saw and decide what to do. If it's John Sinclair and he's actually hurt, I don't give a shit. If it's Dr. Abbas, that's a whole different thing.

I jog to the main path down to my cove. There's no sign of Kit. I frown and peer over the side, where I can see the entire route. He isn't there.

I pause and look around. Where else would he have gone?

I haven't seen him since he disappeared heading up toward the gazebo, when I presumed he headed down the other bluff path. I haven't heard him either. The wind whips around me, but it's not so loud that I shouldn't have heard him make a sound—or that he wouldn't have heard me.

"Kit?" I say. Then, louder, "Kit!"

The wind seems to slide across the back of my neck, ice cold. I hear Sadie's voice earlier, saying she'd seen Kit outside her window last night, that he'd beckoned her down, motioned for her to leave with him. I remember Kit's bewilderment. That wasn't him. I know it wasn't him.

So what did *I* just see?

Kit leading me up here, onto this bluff, toward the gazebo.

Leading me away from the house.

I whirl and run. I get two steps before movement flickers to my right. It's the wind chimes. The damned—

I stop, feet nearly flying out from under me. I'm on the other side of the chimes now, closer to them, out of the glare of the overcast skies. I'm staring at the minnows tied to the end of the strings of kelp. From the other angle, they'd seemed gray, almost silvery. From this one, they are pink and white, with red tips.

I take a slow step, my gaze fixed on those chimes. With each step, my brain screams for me to run. Just run. Tell myself they are min-nows, and get the hell out of here.

I can't do that. I must know what I'm seeing. I must confirm what I think I'm seeing.

I stop as the smell hits me. The stink of rot. My hand flies to my mouth as my gorge rises.

They aren't minnows. They're long, thin, pale fingers with red nail polish. A woman's fingers, ragged, as if ripped off—

I double over, choking on bile. Then I grit my teeth. I need to get back to the house. I brush my hair back as I straighten, and I train my gaze past the fingers, not seeing them, not thinking about them. Move past the chimes and see only the frame—

My hand slams to my mouth as a scream bubbles up in me. I stare, unable to wrench my gaze away, as much as my brain shrieks for me to do exactly that. Don't see. Don't think. Don't process. Don't even try to understand what I am seeing.

I'm looking at the frame of the wind chimes. From a distance, I'd seen rough-hewn sticks covered in dark bark. They are not sticks. They are ribs. Rib bones, streaked with blood and dotted with gore. And the pale kelp hanging from the end of those ribs? It's intestines.

My brain keeps shrieking at me. Telling me I am not seeing what I am seeing. It's sticks and kelp and minnows.

Kelp? Minnows? What the hell kind of sense does that make?

What kind of sense does *this* make?

I am looking at the remains of a woman. I know that. There is not one second when I can honestly tell myself I'm imagining this. A woman has died, and I am seeing what is left of her.

Part of what is left.

Another image flashes. That bloodied hair on Sadie's pillow. Not her hair. We'd told ourselves it might be Nate's but now I know it is not.

Get back to the house.

Get back to the house *now.*

I can't move. I'm rooted to this spot, staring at this thing. This thing that used to be a woman.

I don't understand. I do not understand, and I don't want to understand. I don't know who this woman is. I don't want to think of what happened to her. I cannot comprehend what kind of person did this to her. I only know that I need to get back to the house, because whoever did this to her is out here.

Get back to the goddamned house, Laney!

I can't move. I can't—

Madison! Madison is in the house, and you have to get back to her. Get back and put her someplace safe, make absolutely certain she does not set foot outside. Get in the house and lock the doors and stay there. Just stay there until someone realizes you're all missing and comes for you.

Get to Madison.

Take care of Madison.

That's what finally does it. I think of Madison, and the spell breaks, and I'm turning—

One of the fingers moves.

No. It's the wind. Just the wind. Now move—

There is no wind. It's gone. Completely gone, leaving the bluff in still silence.

I turn toward the wind chimes. One finger twitches. I stare at it. Then I step toward it.

What the hell? What the absolute fucking hell are you doing, Laney?

I need to know. I need to understand, because if there is a chance— even the faintest chance—that I am actually seeing that finger move, without wind or insects or any plausible explanation, then it is not a person who did this.

Not a person? What, an animal attacked her and crafted this thing?

No. Not an animal. Not a person. A thing. Something—

Are you hearing yourself? Something?

I silence the screaming voice. I know what I have seen today. I saw Nate move. I saw Kit where Kit could not have been. I saw Sadie running with bone sticking through her flesh. I heard that voice coming from her. I felt those fingers digging into my arms.

Now I am seeing a severed finger move, and I am damned well not leaving until I am sure.

But Madison—

I cannot protect Madison if I don't know what I'm facing.

The finger has gone still. I count to three, and nothing happens. There. I really was just seeing it move in a stray breeze. I can get back to—

The finger curls up at the joint and then falls again. Up and down, as if it is trying to claw the air, slowly and rhythmically.

Like the man lying on the ground.

I'm stepping back when another finger moves, in that same slow clawing. Then another, and another, and I'm tripping over my feet to get away, backpedaling as fast as I can. When I stumble over a rock, I look down to see the circle I'd noticed in the early hours of the morning, when I'd been out with Jayla, before I fell into the crevice. The roughly drawn circle with hatches. The circle drawn in blood. What seemed to be stick figures of two people. A man and woman, holding hands.

I'm backing away from it when I spot something in the long grass behind the circle. My brain says that something is missing. I take a moment, and then I remember there used to be a spindly tree here. We'd always joked about its tenacity, growing in such an inhospitable place. A lone strip of earth that spawned both a tree and a patch of tall grass. Now the tree is gone, but I can make out the stump of it behind the grass. The stump, and something else.

I pull back the grass, and my knees give way. I drop to the rocky ground, the pain barely registering as I stare at the head of a woman. A head jammed onto the remains of that thin tree stump.

She's facing me, her eyes thankfully shut. She has dark hair. Dark hair like the bloody clump left on the pillow, and I can see where that clump and more was ripped from her scalp.

She's white, maybe in her forties. Her head has been ripped from her body, ragged bits of flesh hanging down. I look at her, and I know I should be heaving everything from my stomach, but all I can feel is horror and pity.

Who are you? What the hell happened—

Her eyelids open.

TWENTY-FOUR

I fall back with a scream, landing hard on my ass, scrabbling back as I stare at empty pits where the woman's eyes had been. The lids flutter. Then her mouth opens and closes, and I—I don't even know what I do.

The next thing I know I'm on my feet and running as fast as I can, slipping and sliding on the rock and running, tearing down the bluff.

Someone calls my name. Shouts it. I don't slow. I don't even process whether the voice is male or female. I just keep running.

Hands grab me, and I twist, flailing and punching as I try to get free.

"Laney! It's me. Kit!"

I see his face, a flash of beard and dark eyes, and I remember that figure running up the bluff, and I fight harder. It's not Kit. Another trick. Another trap.

"Laney!" His hands tighten on my shoulders.

"Not you," I say, barely processing that the words come out loud. "Not you, not you, not *you*."

"It *is* me. Laney! Please! Stop!"

I fight harder, clawing and kicking now. I need to get away. Need to get back to Madison and Jayla and the real Kit.

His hands tighten, but he makes no move to stop me from clawing and kicking him. He just keeps saying my name, growing frantic, begging me to stop.

"Provost Steakhouse," he blurts. "That's where we went to dinner the first time. After we touched base again. When you came home for Anna. You got a . . . some huge drink. It was blue, and I got one, and it nearly put me under the table, and then I found out yours was a mocktail. You thought I knew and—"

"Kit."

He exhales. "Thank God. Yes. It's me. Garrett is . . ." He waves absently. "I heard you scream and—"

"Gazebo," I blurt. "A wind chime. It was . . . It was . . ."

The words stop in my throat, and I can't speak past them, can't *breathe* past them.

"There's another wind chime?" he says slowly. "Okay. Should we go see—?"

"No!" I start to shake, and I try to explain, but again, the words won't come. When I saw that horrible thing—that thing that had been a living person—I'd known what it was. I'd had no doubts about my mental state. Now, with Kit holding me and the cold wind whipping past, it's like a hug and a slap at once, reassuring me that I couldn't have seen such a thing while smacking me for being so foolish as to think I had.

"All right," Kit says. "I'll take you back to the house, find Garrett and we'll investigate."

"No!" I shake my head wildly. "P-please, don't. Please. Just . . . in the house. Please. Get in the house. All of us."

Another quick hug. "Got it. We'll go inside." He pulls back and shouts, "Garrett! We're going in." Then to me, "The asshole took off. Went chasing what was obviously a damn squirrel."

"You—you didn't find . . ."

He takes my arm to steady me as we set out. "There's no sign of Sadie. I don't think Garrett's going to give up, but that's his choice.

It'll be dark in a few hours, and we're not spending the night searching for her. We can't."

"N-no more searching," I say. "No more being outside."

"Agree," he says grimly.

We continue on until I see the bridge. That snaps my thoughts back into focus.

"Man," I blurt as I wheel to Kit. "There—there was a man. On the ground. Hurt. I thought it was a trap, so I ran. Then I thought I saw you and went up onto the bluff." I shake that memory off. "But first there was a man. We should check. I don't know if it's Dr. Abbas or the security guy."

He frowns. "Security guy?"

"We think we found who was behind the staging." My heart rate slows as I find something to latch onto. "A couple who rented the place. The guy—John—was in security and asked questions. It seems his wife—Rachel—was one of the people who tried to lowball me on the property."

I quickly add, "She's not one you passed over," but he doesn't seem to hear me. Any guilt he felt has been wiped away by everything else. Taking blame right now smacks of selfishness.

Remember that *when you start feeling awful about letting Madison come along.*

No, that's an entirely other level of guilt, and one I'll deal with on my own.

I'm centered now, as if talking about the people behind the staging shifts this all into the realm of the ordinary. Horrible and unthinkable acts, but still acts committed by regular people.

"I'll show you where I saw him," I say as I straighten. "If he's still there, we'll decide what to do."

"And if he's not, then we know he's out there, and we need to stay inside."

That's not the only explanation if the man is gone, but I nod. Keep it in the realm of the believable. Forget what I thought I saw on the bluff. Nothing moved. I hallucinated that. The rest was just staging, and if the man is gone, that proves it was a trap, and he's alive and fine.

Does that make sense?

I don't care. It's the story I'm going with if the man is gone.

Kit takes my hand. Our fingers entwine, holding on as tight and firm as we can. We will not get separated. I will not take off if I spot Sadie.

I tell him where I saw the man, and in thirty paces, I see my tree. I point to it and explain that's where I spotted him from.

"Good idea," he says. "Climbing for a better vantage point."

"It didn't help me find Sadie."

"Which we can't worry about. If you need someone to keep saying that, Laney, I'll do it. If you need someone to lock the door and change the code so you don't go after her, I'll do that. I'll be the bad guy here."

"You're definitely not the bad guy here," I say softly. "But you won't need to do any of that. I'm . . ." The wind chime flashes and my gorge rises. "I'm not going out again. Like you said, if Garrett wants to keep searching, that's his choice. We can't stop him." I point. "Over there. That bush. I saw the guy's hand—"

"I see it," Kit says.

The man's hand is exactly where it had been, arm outstretched, fingers rhythmically clawing the ground.

"What's he doing?" Kit says.

"I don't know. He was doing that before. Like he's trying to drag himself along, only he hasn't moved."

Kit curses under his breath. "He's definitely hurt then. Mentally, too. Like Sadie."

Like Sadie.

"Hit on the head," he says.

No, I don't think so. I swallow, but I say nothing.

After this, I will tell him what I saw at the gazebo. I will tell him and Jayla, and they can do with that what they will, whether that's deciding I'm suffering mental confusion from the hypothermia or declaring there's a deranged human killer out there or reaching the same unfathomable other conclusion.

That I was not hallucinating.

I can tell myself I was, but I know better.

I saw those severed fingers move. I saw those eyelids open. I saw that woman's decapitated head try to *speak*.

That is not the work of a deranged human killer.

"All right," Kit says. "Let's get a closer look."

He doesn't add "carefully." His fingers just tighten on mine, and that says it for him. We are not letting go of each other even to move toward this injured man.

I squeeze Kit's hand. Then we take a step. A second step veers us around that bush. A third follows, and then we can see the man's entire upper body, and Kit relaxes a little, as if he'd feared what I first did: that I was only seeing a hand, severed from the rest.

The man's torso lies on the ground. What looks like a torn tarp lays over him, as if someone covered him up and he managed to crawl just this far from under it before his strength gave out.

There is no question now that he's injured. Blood smears his shirt and his neck and his exposed forearms. It's spattered all around us.

Blunt force trauma. That's what springs to mind. When Kit glances over, I realize I've said it aloud.

"A hard blow to the head," I whisper. "Or a sharp one. That'd explain the blood spatter."

"And his mental state."

The man doesn't even seem to have registered us. He's still clawing at the ground with that one hand, the other twisted at his side. His eyes are open, his gaze straight forward.

"Sir?" I say, and even as the word leaves my mouth, I mentally smack myself. *Sir?* Where the hell did that come from?

Yet Kit repeats it, as if acknowledging that this man is older than us. A middle-aged man with gray threads in his dark hair and a gold watch, and yes, that last shouldn't inspire respect, but it's ingrained in me. Like with Jayla and Kit's parents, when I'd been so aware of their social standing that I'd called them Mr. and Mrs. Hayes for a decade after they insisted I use their first names.

"Sir?" Kit says.

The man stops his clawing. His face turns our way, eyes still blank, but face lifting as if searching for the source of that voice. Blinded by the blow to his head?

I start to crouch, and Kit lowers himself with me, both of us carefully dropping to our knees, hands still clutched together.

Up close, I don't think this is Dr. Abbas. The light brown skin is obviously a tan, the sort that screams artificial for northerners in October. I could be wrong, of course. I'd never want to make the mistake of presuming a man with a Middle Eastern accent and an Arab surname couldn't look white. But my gut says this isn't Dr. Abbas.

"You're hurt," I say. "Can you tell me your name?" I add, "You've been hit on the head," as if I need an excuse for asking his name.

The man's gaze lifts in our direction. His pupils are huge, and his eyes are dull.

"Do you remember your name?" I say.

His mouth works, but it had started working before I finished the sentence. Is he answering the question? Or just trying to speak? No sound comes.

"Can you keep talking to him?" I say to Kit. "I'll get a look at his injuries. See if it's just his head."

Kit hesitates, but then releases his grip on my hand. We're still close, and I'm the one moving farther away. I can't imagine this man leaping up and attacking, but if he does, Kit will be ready.

The man doesn't seem to notice when I move away. I walk around the bush to where I can get a better look at his head. Before I can bend, I spot something lying a few feet away. It takes a moment to realize what it is, so incongruous in this setting.

"There's a credit card over here," I say.

Kit gives a strangled half laugh. "A what?"

"A platinum Visa. Oh, there are other cards, too." I point. "Looks like his wallet is right there."

"Fell out of his pocket when he got hit?"

"I guess. The credit card is closer. May I pick it up?"

He knows I'm really asking if it's okay for me to take those two extra steps away to retrieve this possible form of identification.

Kit nods. I scoop up the card. It is indeed a platinum Visa, the sort even Kit doesn't carry. Oh, he certainly has the credit rating. He just doesn't like the flash of a high-end card. This guy does. Gold watch. Multiple platinum cards, from what I see scattered beyond. And when I see the name, I am not surprised.

"John Sinclair," I say. "The security guy."

Kit makes a noise in his throat. "Exactly how wrong would it be to just get up and walk away?"

"If I knew for certain he murdered Nate, I'd do it in a heartbeat."

The man—Sinclair—doesn't react. His head is wobbling, like that of an infant struggling to focus. I'm about to toss aside the card when I stop. I motion to Kit that I'm getting the rest of the wallet contents, and he nods. I do it quickly, scooping up the wallet and cards and shoving them into my pocket. We need all the data we can get on this asshole. Even if he didn't kill Nate, he's done so much more, and he is going to pay—

I see the wind chimes again. See the woman's head staked on a stump.

Rachel Rossi.

His wife.

Whatever happened here, he was hit on the head, so severely that he was left for dead under a tarp. Then his wife was killed, her body torn into pieces and—

Don't think about that. At least it wasn't the Abbases. I have enough on my conscience already.

I move toward Sinclair. He's still looking in Kit's direction, but Kit is hunkered down, his face set in a look of barely contained fury that lessens only when he glances my way to be sure I'm all right. Then I'm on the other side of the man, crouching. Kit tenses, but Sinclair gives no sign of noticing me. He's beyond that, his head injuries too severe.

I frown and lean closer. Kit tenses more, and I say, "There's no blood on his scalp."

Kit lifts one shoulder in a shrug. "Might be a closed wound."

"Then where's the blood coming from?"

His wife.

Rachel.

Was Sinclair knocked out before she was killed? Before she was torn apart? Or did he witness that?

"I think it could be shock," I say, my voice low. "On the bluff, the gazebo, what I found." I swallow. "It was a woman. The remains of a woman. His wife, probably."

Kit flinches. "Shit. You think he saw it happen."

"Maybe. He could still have been struck on the head. Knocked out. Covered up. Left for dead. I'm just saying the blood might not be his."

"All right."

I reach for the tarp. "We'll make sure of that. If he's not suffering from any life-threatening injuries, then we need to leave him and get to the house. Figure out what to do with him later."

And if that means we leave him in the sights of a killer who might realize he's not actually dead?

So be it.

I have my priorities, and whatever John Sinclair might have witnessed, however horrible that would be, he isn't one of them.

I need to get to Madison. Warn Jayla and keep Madison safe.

I tug at the tarp. It sticks, and I pull hard enough that I topple backward. When Kit lets out a gurgling gasp, I scramble up, ready to launch myself at Sinclair, certain he's attacking Kit.

Kit has fallen back, arms behind him, bracing himself up, as if Sinclair had indeed lunged at him. But the man hasn't moved. He's lying there, just as he was, his head tilted toward Kit.

"Kit?" I say. "What—?"

Then I see it. Or I don't see it. That's what my brain screams. It shrieks that I am not seeing something I absolutely should be seeing.

My gaze is fixed below Sinclair's torso, where I've yanked the tarp aside, and I should now see the rest of him.

I do not see the rest of him.

I see his torso and then there is nothing below it.

It must be the angle. The leaves. The dead vegetation. Or even the earth itself. It's covering the lower half of his body. He'd been buried, the tarp haphazardly thrown over the spot. He managed to crawl out, but he's still half buried.

That is the answer.

It must be the answer.

"Laney?" Kit's voice is so choked I can barely make out my name.

I shove up to my feet. Change my vantage point. Take one decisive step in that direction, knowing I will collapse with relief when I see that I'm right and Sinclair is only half buried.

I take that step and—

"No!"

Kit shouts, lunging to stop me, but it's too late. I see what he's already seen, and I drop to my knees, retching. My brain fires wildly, random electrical flashes of bright light, as if it can erase what it just saw.

I told myself Sinclair's lower half was buried. Under dirt. Under vegetation. It's not. There *is* no lower half. It's gone. As I think that, that inner voice lets out a hysterical laugh.

Gone? Don't be silly. What do you mean, it's gone?

I mean there is nothing below Sinclair's torso except a trail of blood and gore and intestines. My brain tried to erase that image, but it cannot, and even with my eyes squeezed shut, I can see it.

Kit's arms are around me. He's trying to tug me away from the sight, but I twist out of his grip and open my eyes.

Sinclair's torso lies on the ground. His one hand claws the ground again, and his face has turned our way, those blank eyes fixed not quite in our direction. His mouth moves, as if he's trying to talk. But his bottom half is gone. Not just his legs. His entire bottom half, from the waist down. It's been ripped away, the flesh as torn as his wife's fingers, as her neck.

"He's . . . dead, right?" I rasp.

"I . . ." Kit manages. "He . . . he has to be but . . ."

"He's dead," I say, firmer now. "There's no way he's alive. Not like that. It isn't possible."

"It isn't."

"But he's moving," I say. "You do see that. I'm not hallucinating."

"You're not."

"What exactly do you see?"

Kit swallows, glances over, and then turns away. "His hand is moving. His mouth is moving. His head is turned our way."

Exactly what I'm seeing. I should be relieved. I'm not losing my mind. I am not relieved. I am the farthest possible point from re-lieved.

Let me be wrong. Let me be hallucinating. Even let me have lost my mind, fallen over the edge of reality and plunged into madness. That is better than this.

"On the bluff," I say. "His wife's . . . Her head. Her eyes opened. Her mouth moved. Someone—some*thing*—ripped her apart and stuck her head on a—"

I scramble to my feet, pulling him up with me. "Inside. We need to get inside. Now!"

Kit doesn't answer. He just grabs my arm, and we run.

TWENTY-FIVE

We're at the patio when a voice from the forest shouts, "What the hell are you doing?"

It's Garrett. Kit ignores him, but I shout back, "Get in the house."

We near the door to see Madison running for it from the inside, having heard us. She jabs the security panel as I reach for the sliding-door handle. A hand grabs my shoulder, and I barely have time to spin around before Kit's fist flies out. It hits Garrett in the jaw, and the bigger man stumbles and then bounces back with a snarl of rage. Garrett swings, but Kit grabs his wrist and twists it away.

"You do *not* touch her," Kit says. "You do not *ever* touch her."

He shoves Garrett away. Madison has the door open, and Kit nudges me through while watching for Garrett to come at him. Garrett does, but it takes a moment. He didn't expect that from Kit. Oh, Kit might be a tech CEO and a band kid, but he was also captain of the football team in high school. Never the guy spoiling for a fight, he's always been the one getting between two guys who are. That's why he made captain. He was the player who commanded the most respect . . . while not being afraid to get in the quarterback's face if he had to. When Garrett does bounce back, it's only to wrench the door from Kit's hand.

"What the hell are you doing?" Garrett says. "My sister is out *there*." He jabs a finger at the forest.

"Get inside," I say.

"I am not—"

"Get the fuck inside, Garrett," I say. "Or I am locking that door and leaving you out there with Sadie and whatever the hell did that to her."

"A bomb did that—"

"Inside. *Now*."

He moves past the door, just enough for Kit to get it shut and me to arm the security system.

"A bomb did *not* do that to Sadie," I say. "And I think we all know it. You saw the shed. A bomb didn't destroy my . . ." I trail off as I see Madison watching.

I freeze. I need Garrett to know what's out there. If he chooses to still search for Sadie, that is up to him, but he must know what we saw. Yet there is no way in hell I'm painting that picture for Madison.

"Mads?" Kit says. "I could ask you to come and make dinner with me, but you're not a child. You'd know exactly what I'm doing, and you deserve to be treated like the young adult you are."

My gut clenches, and I'm ready to leap in before he tells her anything.

He continues, "So I'm going to be bluntly honest. Laney and I really do not want you to hear this. I can give you the basics while we make that dinner, but we don't want you hearing the details, and if that pisses you off?" He shrugs. "Then it pisses you off. I'm sorry, but you are not listening to this conversation."

There's only a moment's hesitation before Madison nods. It's the "we" that does it. *Laney and I*. The united parental pairing, something she hasn't had since she was too young to more than vaguely remember it.

"Thank you for making this easier on them," Jayla murmurs to Madison.

Madison ducks, cheeks flushing. She mumbles something and then lets Kit lead her out of the hall.

When they're gone, I motion Jayla and Garrett into my office. Garrett's mouth sets, but he just stomps in. He makes a move to slam the door shut behind us. I catch it and leave it cracked open.

"In case Sadie comes to the patio door," I say, but I'm not thinking of Sadie; I'm thinking of Madison and Kit. I need to be within earshot.

"Out with it," Garrett says. "What did you find?"

"The people who wanted to buy the island," I say. "Who staged everything."

His gaze shoots to the door. "They're out there? Where? There's four of us. We can—"

"They're dead."

"Dead? You're sure?"

"That's . . . that's the problem," I say. "Kit and I are absolutely certain they're dead. I found the woman's head staked on a tree."

"What the . . . ?" Jayla says, and seems to lose the last word.

"It's up on the bluff, by the gazebo," I say. "There's also a wind chime. Made from her fingers and rib bones."

Jayla looks like she's going to be sick.

"Did you hit your head?" Garrett snaps. "You did, didn't you?"

"I did not hit my head."

"Then you're making up some bullshit story. Shouldn't be surprised. That's what you do. You tell stories, and I don't just mean professionally."

Jayla shoves him. It's as fast and unexpected as Kit's punch.

"Shut the fuck up and listen to her." She meets his gaze. "For once, listen to her."

I cut in. "Kit found me running back to the house. He wanted to go up the bluff, but I couldn't face it again. However, that wasn't the only thing I'd seen. There was a guy in the forest. Either injured or faking it to trap me. That's what set me running the first time, looking for Garrett and Kit." That's a lie, but I'm skipping the Kit-mirage for now.

I continue, "We went back to check on the man. It was the guy from the emails, Jayla. John Sinclair. The guy we suspected was behind this. Kit and I thought he was just injured, but there was a tarp. When we pulled it off . . . his lower half was gone."

"Oh God." Jayla's hand flies to her mouth.

"Bull*shit*," Garrett says. "You really think I'm stupid, don't you? I'm not a teacher or a lawyer or a fucking CEO. I'm just a dumb cop who'll buy any bullshit you three feed me."

"Why?" Jayla says before I can respond.

"Why what?" Garrett says.

"Why would we feed you anything? You honestly think, what, we've conspired to tell you about people being hacked *apart*? For shits and giggles? Hidden camera catches Garrett Emerson being punked . . . while his sister is running around the island, badly injured."

He crosses his arms. "Kit and Laney are the only ones who saw Sadie. They're also the only ones who saw this guy who was supposedly ripped in half." He turns on me. "This is revenge, right? You three cooked up this revenge scheme, and you're holding my sister hostage."

"After luring you to the island?" Jayla says. "Oh, wait. No. You and Sadie showed up uninvited."

Garrett goes to answer, but I cut him short.

"I wouldn't do this, and I sure as hell wouldn't do it with Madison around," I say. "But forget all that. Don't take my word for it. Go see Sinclair. Go up to the gazebo and see what's left of his wife. That's not all you'll see either. You'll see their bodies moving."

Jayla goes still. "What?"

"They are still moving. Her eyes opened. Her mouth moved. Her fingers moved on the wind chime. *His* hand moves. His lips move. His head moves. And before you ask, they are absolutely real bodies, not some kind of animatronic horror show. But don't take my word for it, Garrett. Go and check it out. She's up on the bluff. He's twenty paces west of the bridge, in a bush."

I wait for him to snarl and spit and accuse us of playing a Halloween prank. Instead, he says, slowly, "Kit saw this?"

"Yes."

"If it's a joke . . . If it's a prank . . ."

"Are we acting like it's a joke? A prank?"

"I . . . don't understand. What you're saying . . . it's not possible." He rubs his hand over his mouth. Then he stops. "Those things you found. The circles. The feathers and bones. You said they were meant to look like Satanic-cult crap. But they weren't *meant* to look like that, were they? They *are* that."

"What?" I say.

"Satanic cults. This is clearly the work of a Satanic cult."

I blink at him. "You're serious. A Satanic . . . ?"

"There's no such thing," Jayla snaps. "You're a cop. You should know that."

"I know there are people who fuck around with that shit. Circles and hexes. Even animal sacrifices."

"Because they're deluded or mentally ill."

He looks at me. "You said it was this couple, this Sinclair guy and his wife."

"We think they—"

"You figured they wanted the island. They didn't. They were playing with . . ." He waves his hands. "Dark forces."

Dark forces? I want to laugh. I don't laugh. Neither does Jayla.

After a moment, Jayla turns, almost reluctantly, to me. "You and Kit definitely saw them moving."

I nod. "We compared observations to be sure we were both seeing the same things. We were. Earlier, in the boathouse, when we saw the rat king, we thought it twitched, but it was only maggots. We wouldn't risk making that mistake twice. This wasn't a twitch. It wasn't final misfiring electrical signals from the brain. Sinclair's hand was clawing at the ground when I ran, and it was clawing when we came back. It was like he was trying to crawl, but on autopilot. Instinct. When we talked, his face turned our way, but his eyes wouldn't focus on us. Again, like instinct."

"I'm going to say a word," Jayla says. "And the first person who laughs gets smacked."

"No one's going to laugh," I say.

"Yeah, not at *you*," Garrett mutters. "Because you're a goddamn lawyer."

I look at him. "No one is going to laugh at any suggestions from now on. It'll only keep us from sharing information. We accept that this isn't natural, right? That a head can't open its eyes and try to talk long after it's been severed? That a man can't survive after his body has been ripped in half?"

Jayla looks sick, but I don't regret my choice of words. There's no room for euphemisms here. We must be one hundred percent clear what we are discussing.

"Agreed," she says. "There's no natural explanation for that."

"Also agree," Garrett says. "What word were you going to say?"

She looks at me. "Zombies."

"Voodoo," Garrett says.

I make a face at the word. I'd correct him, but I just said we weren't mocking ideas, and that veers too close, so I just say, "Haitian lore of sorcerers reanimating bodies."

"Oh, that bit I actually know," Jayla says. "It originated with slaves. It's a nightmare come true—even after death they're enslaved."

"Exactly," I say.

"Could that be what we're seeing?" Jayla says. "Not Haitian or anything like that, but the basic idea that someone has raised the dead to serve them."

"Necromancy," I say. "That's another very old idea. But the way they were killed . . ." I shiver.

"Ripped apart, you said," Garrett says. "Not cut up."

Jayla looks sick again.

"I don't think a person did it," I say.

"So this couple, they were messing around with dark magic," Jayla says. "They actually raised something or summoned something, and it ripped them apart and won't let them die."

Now I'm the one who feels ill. Are John Sinclair and Rachel Rossi still in those bodies? Still conscious?

"You know this shit," Garrett says, his voice low, gaze on me. "You knew that someone planted that Satanic stuff. You knew what could happen."

"Knew what could happen?" Jayla says. "That a hex circle might actually hex someone? Laney didn't believe that, and if she'd suggested otherwise, you'd have laughed at her. It's not like being a chemist and knowing the water is tainted. This is made-up bullshit. Or it's supposed to be."

"She still knew something could happen. And she brought us here."

"Brought?" Jayla sputters. "Kit snuck over to help her, and I joined him. Both of us knew what was found here. Sadie also knew and also snuck over, and presumably you knew too. We all came uninvited—"

"Not Madison."

That one hits hard enough that I suck in breath.

Garrett's gaze meets mine. "You knew, and you brought her."

"That is not fair," Jayla says, bearing down on him. "No one thought it was anything more than a prank."

"But it's not, is it?" He throws open the door and stalks into the hall. "My sister is out there, and I'm going to find her."

I hurry after him. "Please, don't. At least wait until—"

"Until what? She's dead? Dead and reanimated like some fucking zombie? There is something out there, Laney. Something that murdered your cleaning guy and your renters, and now it's after my sister.

I am helping her, and you are going to sit on your ass and look after Madison."

"I—"

"You brought her here!" he shouts, voice rising with each word. "You came because someone was doing God knows what on this island, and you brought our *daughter.*"

Jayla lunges at him. "Lower your goddamn voice, Garrett."

"Why? What difference does it make now? Anna's dead. The kid's dad doesn't want anything to do with her. Who exactly are we keeping up this lie for, Laney? Oh, I know. For you. To punish me and to punish Sadie. All my sister wanted was to get to know her niece. You stole that from her. Stole my daughter from me. Stole Sadie's niece from her. You got to stay in our daughter's life. *Aunt Laney.* And now you have her all to yourself. You get our daughter, and I *don't.*"

"Laney?"

The voice behind me is so soft I think I've misheard. Then I turn and see Madison there, her face pale, brown eyes fixed on me.

"Laney?" she says again.

"Stay with your mother, kiddo," Garrett says, his hand on the sliding door. "No matter what happens, you stay in here with your mother."

"You *bastard,*" Jayla hisses.

Garrett leaves. Jayla moves to lock the door. The alarm light flashes. I run over and hit the sequence to disarm and then rearm it. Then I slowly turn to Madison. Kit is behind her, breathing hard, as if he ran from the kitchen. He puts a tentative arm around Madison's shoulders, and when she allows it, he gives her a quick squeeze. Then he nods at me.

Do something, Laney. Take control of this. You only get one shot.

I step forward, and my eyes fill. "I'm sorry, Mads. You weren't supposed to . . ."

"Hear it like this?" One corner of her mouth lifts in a humorless quirk as her own eyes glisten with tears.

I take another step and reach out, even more tentatively than Kit. She falls into my arms, and I hug her tight.

"I was young," I whisper. "Younger than you. Your mom and dad had just found out they couldn't have kids, and your mom wanted one so badly."

She nods against my shoulder and snuffles.

"She was—" My voice catches. "She was an amazing mother."

Madison sags against me, a sob ripping from her, and I hold her tight. When she pulls away, it's only a little, just enough to see my face.

"She didn't want me to know," she says. "Even after she was gone."

I shake my head. "No, she *did* want you to know. There's a video I'm supposed to show you. She'll—she'll talk to you about it. I just . . . It wasn't time yet. She hadn't been gone long enough, and it felt like . . . It felt like . . ."

Jayla fills in the words for me. "Like giving you a new mother when you lost your own, Madison. A substitute. Laney wouldn't have done that until you were ready."

"And Anna is still your mom," I say. "She will always be your mom. I never regretted that."

"And my father? My biological one?" She tenses in my arms. "Tell me what that asshole said . . . That he didn't mean it like that. That he's not . . ." She glances over her shoulder at Kit. "Was it you? You guys grew up together."

He shakes his head, and her face falls in disappointment. Then she gives a wry smile. "No, if I do the math, Laney was fifteen. That'd make you thirteen."

"Yeah."

"I wish it was you," she says, her voice the faintest whisper.

Kit comes in and hugs us both. "I wish it was, too. But if you thought that's why I care about you? That you must be my daughter? No. I care about you because I care about *you*."

Tears fall on her cheeks, and I slip out of their grasp to let her hug Kit.

After a moment, Madison steps away from Kit and looks at the door. "It was him, wasn't it. That's what he meant. About me being his daughter and Sadie's niece."

"I was young," I say. "Really young."

"He's older than you." She looks at me. "How much older?"

"A few years." I make a face. "Let's not talk about that."

"He raped you, didn't he?"

My whole body convulses. Jayla inhales sharply. Kit looks at me, stricken.

"I . . . don't know who told you that," I say carefully.

"No one did." She backs up, arms crossing. "I could tell he'd done something like that by the way you act around him. The way Kit and Jayla act about him being around you. I figured he did something when you were young, but then it seemed weird that you wouldn't try to keep *me* away from him. Now it makes sense. He isn't that kind of a threat to his own daughter."

"He didn't . . ." I flounder. *Take control, damn it. This is her* father. *These are the circumstances of her conception, and you were never going to let her know those circumstances.* "I had a lot to drink. There was some confusion."

"Some confusion . . ." she says slowly. "In other words, you were drunk, and he took advantage. Of a fifteen-year-old girl. That's rape."

Jayla cuts in. "Does it matter, Mads? He's an asshole, as you already noted. That's all you need to know."

"Is it?" Madison turns to me and shrugs. "Fine, he's an asshole. Not a crime, sadly. So I should probably get to know him. Take my friends to meet him. Would that be okay?"

I flinch.

"Or go on father-daughter bonding trips. Just the two of us. You'd be okay with that, right? You have no reason to believe he wouldn't—"

"Enough," Jayla says. "We get your point."

"And I get yours," Madison says. "No one wants a rapist for a dad.

Only he's not my dad. He's just the biological contributor of half my DNA, and I might have hoped for someone more like Kit—smarter, nicer, cooler—but the guy I thought was my father is no prize either. I'll deal with it. But I want to know. That guy is going to expect something from me now, some acknowledgment that he's my father, and I need to know what kind of person he is."

Madison lifts her hands. "And before anyone says we'll talk about it later, this isn't the time, yadda-yadda, are we running after him? Going out there? Doing anything except waiting here and looking out for each other? No? Then you can tell me what happened. I want to know. In case he comes back, in case he tries to pull me off on my own and tell me his story, I *need* to know."

Kit looks at me, and that look tells me she's right.

"Let me put dinner in the oven to stay warm," he says.

TWENTY-SIX

We go into the great room. Outside, dark clouds hover a looming threat over the lake, and I almost laugh at that.

You think we're afraid of a storm? Right now, that's the least of our concerns.

Talking about my past is even less of a concern, but I'm doing this for Madison. While she might say she needs the information, that's only to guilt me into talking. We're trapped here, and she's just heard something that rips her world apart and jams it back together in a shape she can barely comprehend. She wants details because that is something she can focus on and, for a few minutes, pretend there is something more critical than being on an island with the undead.

I settle onto the sofa, and Madison takes the other end, turning to face me, her feet up and pressed against my crossed legs. Kit is in the kitchen, where I can see him puttering, giving us a chance to settle in. Jayla is in the recliner with her bare feet on the coffee table.

"I was fifteen," I say. "Sadie and Jayla and I had just started high school. We were best friends." I glance at Jayla, who's waggling her hand. "Fine. Sadie and Jayla were *my* best friends. I'd met Sadie in second grade. Then I met Jayla when we went to middle school. It was a slightly awkward three-way friendship, but mostly it worked. Anyway, it was a Saturday night. Jayla and I had been at Sadie's place that afternoon. Jayla had to leave right before dinner. I stayed, watching movies with Sadie. I lost track of time, and it was dark as I was leaving, and Garrett was just heading out. He offered me a lift."

"Was that normal?"

I scrunch my nose. "Not *ab*normal. He'd given me a lift before, when I was younger, right after he got his license. I didn't know Garrett well. It wasn't like with Kit, eighteen months younger than Jayla. Kit hung out with us, and it never felt weird. With Garrett, it would have been weird. He was four years older. Sadie adored him, and he was a good brother, so to me . . ." I shrug. "I just thought of him as Sadie's older brother. He didn't ignore me, but didn't pay much attention to me either."

"And you?" Madison asks Jayla.

"Same. He pretty much ignored me, but I got the sense that was more about . . ." She waves a hand around her face. "I didn't like going over to Sadie's. Her parents were . . ."

"Racists?" Madison says.

"The garden-variety sort. When your parents are rich and Black, people can be weird. Like, how did you *really* get that money? Black folks running a tech company? Who believes that?" Jayla rolls her eyes. "The Emersons didn't know what to make of me, so I limited my visits. Let's just say that I didn't *actually* have to leave before dinner that night."

"What?" I twist to look at her. "You never told me you were uncomfortable there. In fact, I remember getting the sense you were, but you insisted their air fresheners gave you a headache."

Jayla shrugs. "If I told you the truth, you'd have done something about it."

"Which would have made things harder for you."

"Nah, but you'd have made sure I never had to go to Sadie's house again, and at some point she'd have figured it out and demanded answers and . . ." Another shrug. "Drama." She turns to Madison. "The point is that Laney didn't know Garrett well, and neither did I, but she had no reason to think there'd be anything suspicious about him offering her a ride."

"I didn't think that," Madison says. "If there was, she wouldn't have gotten in."

"Oh, don't give me too much credit," I say. "I wasn't quite as mature as you at that age. I did *way* more stupid things. Like agreeing to go to a college party when Garrett invited me." I pull a pillow onto my lap. "Gran and Gramps were out at a party of their own, and your mom was married and gone by then, so if I was a little late getting home, no one would know. Here was a college guy who thought I was mature enough to go to a college party. He wasn't creepy about it or anything, and that made me feel like maybe I was pulling off this grown-up thing more than I thought."

"No one's blaming you for going to the party," Jayla says. "I'd have gone."

I meet her gaze, and she knows I'm quietly asking her not to defend me. Let Madison draw her own conclusions. Jayla and I have been through this countless times. Was I wrong to accept a ride? Wrong to go to the party? Wrong to drink at the party?

Jayla would defend my choices to her dying breath, as would Anna and my parents. I would do the same for Jayla, if she were in my shoes. But being in those shoes myself, I can see every angle where my choices could be attacked.

Why did you get in the car?

Why did you go to the party?

Why did you drink?

What were you wearing?

Are you sure you weren't flattered by his attention? An older boy? Good looking and popular? What would a boy like that see in a fifteen-year-old—?

Stop. Just stop.

I continue, "It really did seem like he was just being nice. Taking me along to a party as his guest—his sister's friend. We got there, and it was . . . a lot. The one time Garrett stepped away from me, two guys swooped in. He yelled at them, said I was just a kid, and stuck by my side after that."

"Like you'd expect if he'd brought you along to be nice," Madison says. "Not creepy."

"He wasn't creepy. At all. He hung out with me, and talked to me. I had a beer and then something stronger. Punch that packed a real punch."

Which he gave me. Convinced me to try it. Didn't mention how potent it was or tell me to slow down when I slammed it back.

I don't say that. I am walking a fine line here. I always expected, when this came out, that I could just pretend I'd been young and stupid and slept with my friend's older brother. I didn't see the dangers in keeping that part of Garrett from Madison. Now I do, but I will still proceed with caution.

I pluck at the pillow. "And that's pretty much the story. I had too much punch, and I woke up in a bed with Garrett."

"You blacked out?"

"I wasn't used to hard liquor. Gran and Gramps let me have a sip when I started getting curious but . . ." I quirk a smile. ". . . they made sure I had the kind that made me decide I was in no rush to drink more."

"Mom did the same to me," Madison says. "Gave me a half shot of whiskey."

"It's a valid strategy. But it also means that whatever was in that punch didn't taste like booze to me, so I had too much."

"And he had sex with you after you passed out?"

"No, no." *I don't think so, at least.* "I must have passed out later. I was just too drunk to remember anything."

"And too drunk to consent. Which he must have known. He was nineteen, and he took a kid younger than me to a party, helped her to get drunk, and had sex with her."

I let it stand at that. There are nuances, including the suspicion that Garrett spiked my drink with more than booze, but this is enough for her to never get into any dangerous situations with him.

I won't tell her how I woke up, panicked, and found him sitting there, completely chill, as if we'd had consensual sex. How he'd said we could keep hooking up but warned it had to be a secret, because people wouldn't understand. How I'd run into the toilet and puked, and he'd acted like it was just the booze. Acted like nothing had happened . . . right up until I insisted on getting myself home, and he realized something was wrong and told me I'd enjoyed it. He didn't insist I consented or hadn't been "that" drunk. Nothing like that. Just that I enjoyed myself.

"You had fun. You liked it. Remember that."

He'd done nothing wrong—that's what he'd been saying, and if I didn't get the message clear enough?

"You tell anyone, and it'll be my word against yours. Everyone knows you're a slut. You can't even pick a side. You like it all."

A slut.

Bisexual, he meant, which clearly translated to slut, even if—at barely fifteen—I'd never gone beyond kissing.

Had I really thought I could get away with only telling Madison that I'd been young? Pretending Garrett was just some guy I hooked up with? Trusting him around her and her friends if he wanted to be part of her life?

"So that's it," I say.

Jayla clears her throat, and when I look over, she shakes her head.

"She needs to know the fallout," Jayla says. "Sadie and Garrett are sure as hell going to give their version."

"Sadie didn't believe you, right?" Madison says. "When you accused Garrett, he denied it, and Sadie sided with him."

"I didn't accuse him. Or I tried not to. Afterward, I told Jayla, who convinced me to talk to my sister—your mom. They said they'd support whatever I wanted, and I wanted to drop it. There was nothing to be gained by going through with an accusation. And there was no reason to . . . until there was."

"You were pregnant, and he was the father, and you didn't want anyone acting like you'd knowingly slept with him."

"I didn't want him to have any right to you," I say. "That's why I told my parents the truth. If Garrett decided to take responsibility and be your father . . ." I shake my head. "I needed my story out there first."

"Garrett said it was consensual, right?" Madison says. "Sadie believed it, and that ended your friendship."

"It ended a lot of things. Their father believed me. Their mother didn't. Sadie's parents split up before you were born."

"They had other problems," Jayla cut in. "Even I heard the fights in the little bit of time I spent at their house. But to Sadie, Laney accusing Garrett is what broke up her parents."

"She begged me to take it back," I say, my voice low, as I remember her pleas, her tears. "Begged me to save her family."

"How the hell would that have helped?" Jayla says. "The problem was that one parent believed their son and the other didn't. Even if you lied and said you'd wrongly accused him, it wouldn't have changed *that*."

Kit comes in from the kitchen finally and walks over to where Madison can see him.

"Sadie wants to have contact with you, as your aunt," Kit says. "Laney won't want to interfere with that."

I open my mouth, but Kit lifts a hand. "That isn't to say you shouldn't have any kind of relationship with her, Madison, but there's a lot that needs to be discussed and Laney"—he glances my way—"is not necessarily the best person to discuss that with."

I start to protest. Then I stop. He's right, as uncomfortable as that is. What happened with Garrett was guaranteed to leave me with a lifetime of doubts and regrets, hammered in by every person who questioned my story. And the one who'd led the pack of deniers? My best friend.

Instead of cutting Sadie loose, I've accepted the guilt she piled on me, and there might always be part of me that wants to make it up to her. If I need to do that, fine. But I can't pull Madison into it. Sadie cannot be trusted with Madison, unless Madison is aware that anything Sadie says about me—or Jayla, or maybe even Kit—could be a lie. Someone else needs to talk to Madison about that. I'd pull my punches.

"Does it matter?" Madison says, her voice dropping as her gaze turns toward the windows. She wraps her arms around herself. "Is Sadie going to . . . survive this?" She turns to me. "Is she even alive?"

"I hope so. She was the last time I saw her."

"Was she? Are you sure?"

I flinch, and Madison twists to face me, hugging her legs. "Kit told me you found the people we think staged that stuff. Found their bodies. He said they were dead but moving. Reanimated."

"I had to tell her," Kit says. "Warn her. In case she saw something. And also let her know whatever's out there, it's not necessarily a person."

"Can we stop this?" Madison says, lifting her hands to her ears, her sleeves tugged over them. "Just stop, okay? No more protecting-Madison bullshit." She looks at me. "I get it. You're responsible for me, and you want to do this right. You're my guardian. You're my aunt. And you're my mother. That all makes it really complicated, and you're scared of screwing up. I see it at home, too. Renting that shitty house so I don't have to move out of my school district. Selling your motorcycle. Staying home every night, even if I'm out with friends, so you'll be there when I get back. I don't want you doing all this for me, Laney. I just want . . ." She waves her arms. "I want to be with you. Like before. I used to think how cool it'd be to live with you, and I feel like I ruined everything."

"You *never*—"

She presses her hands to her ears again. "I know, okay? I know you love me. I know you wanted to be my guardian. And I know this isn't the time to talk about any of this. So forget all that. The point is that I'm not a child, and I'm pretty sure I'm handling this whole thing better than any of you. We have dead people who aren't dead. Call them zombies or whatever. I get it, and I'm dealing with it, and I'm not trying to tell myself maybe there's a mistake, maybe there's a natural explanation." She looks across the three of us. "Can any of *you* say that?"

We don't answer.

"I didn't think so," Madison continues. "I have no idea what's going on, but I accept that it is. You said Sadie was badly hurt. Really badly hurt. Are you sure she's alive?"

We look at each other, but again, we don't answer.

Madison exhales. "Okay, so Garrett might be out there looking for his zombie sister. My father might be out there looking for my zombie aunt." She shudders. "Nope, that's weirder than the zombie part. Garrett and Sadie. They're Garrett and Sadie." She looks at me. "I know you're going to say we need to warn Garrett, but I've heard enough to know it's not going to work. He'll say we're all crazy, and we all hate him and Sadie, and he won't abandon his sister. Yes?"

"Yes," Kit says. "If he comes back—or comes near—we will warn him that it's possible Sadie is already dead—and dangerous—but I can't see him believing us."

"Then as shitty as it is, we need to do what he said. Stay in here. Hole up until tomorrow, when the Hayeses will send help."

I glance at Kit, my brows arching.

"I told Madison, but I didn't mention it to you," Kit says. "Because, at that point, we were trying to get off the island immediately. No one wanted to hear that it could be sometime tomorrow. Our parents know we're here. I was supposed to have dinner at their place tonight, and on the way here, I called to cancel. They know Jayla and I are on Hemlock Island with you and Mads, but we'll be back late tonight. I have a board meeting tomorrow morning and Mom is still on the board, so we were having breakfast to discuss strategy."

"When you don't show up, she'll know something's wrong," I say.

"Well," Jayla says. "First she'll call me, desperately hoping it means you and Kit got back together again. But she's going to know that's not happening." She glances at us. "Oh, not that you guys *won't* get back together. Everyone knows that's coming. But Kit's not going to skip a board meeting without at least boating to shore and calling to explain."

So help will come. That's an absolute. The moment their mother realizes they aren't back yet, she'll launch a commando search team, possibly with actual commandos. There's no point in having mountains of money if you can't use it to track down your missing children.

"Helicopters gonna land," Jayla says, as if reading my mind. "And that's tomorrow at the latest. Bridget expects me home tonight. If I don't check in before midnight to say I'm on my way, she'll call me. Within an hour, she'll be calling our parents, apologizing profusely but wanting to know if they've heard from us. Now, Mom might say Kit and I must be running late, and Bridget will buy that, but by the time Kit misses breakfast, the troops will be ready to launch. They know where we are, and they're coming for us."

"That's the important part," Kit says. "Help is coming, and that doesn't mean our parents taking a leisurely drive to the coast. There *will* be a helicopter, and it'll have everything and everyone we need, maybe even a doctor if they're worried enough. All we have to do is hold tight until—"

A shape lurches toward the huge bank of windows.

TWENTY-SEVEN

We all scramble up. Kit has the baseball bat, and Jayla scoops up a knife that must have been on the floor. When Madison takes a knife from the cushions, I feel like I missed a memo.

Kit opens his mouth, arm waving as if he's about to tell me to take Madison into another room, away from that massive window. But then the lurching figure triggers a security light, illuminating the twilight, and it becomes two figures.

Garrett, with Sadie over his arms.

Garrett is at the door, punching at the keypad. We all stand there, frozen. When the lock beeps a negative, he pounds on the glass of the door.

"The code," I say as I run forward. "I changed it."

Madison races in front of me. "No, Laney."

I stop. Behind her, Garrett pounds on the window.

"You changed the fucking *code* on me?" he bellows.

"Don't open the door," Madison says. "Stop and think about this. Talk about this."

I glance over at Kit and Jayla. Jayla nods, and Kit walks to the window.

"We need to speak to you first, Garrett," Kit says, voice raised to be heard through the triple-pane glass.

"My sister is—"

"We will do what we can for you, but you can't bring her in here."

"What the fuck?"

"Are you sure she's still alive?" Kit asks.

"What the *fuck*?" Garrett roars.

Madison moves in front of Kit. "The other people are dead. Clearly dead. But they were moving. Like Sadie."

Garrett starts to snarl a reply. Then he seems to remember who he's talking to. A moment's pause, and when he speaks, his voice is almost soft. "I saw the guy, kiddo. There's no way he could be alive, and yeah, he's moving, which is messed up. This is different." He hefts Sadie. "She wasn't just moving her eyes or her mouth or her hand. She was running, right up until she collapsed and passed out. She's alive."

"And what if she doesn't stay that way? What if she dies and comes back and tries to hurt us?"

He stares at Madison. Then his gaze swings my way, and his fist slams the glass so hard Kit yanks Madison back. Garrett doesn't seem to notice. His gaze is fixed on mine, and it boils over with hate. Actual hate.

I've always known how Garrett feels about me. To him, I betrayed a trust. I was supposed to keep quiet, and it wasn't like he'd broken into my bedroom, held me down, and raped me, right?

I was the source of a terrible experience for him. The experience of being made to face his actions and question whether what he'd done was wrong.

I got that. I didn't want to—Jayla would kill me for admitting it—but I understood. Garrett had been raised in a world where you had to trick girls into sex, a world where, sure, sex with a fifteen-year-old was illegal but that doesn't count if you're both teenagers, right?

Bringing a girl to a party and getting her drunk enough to have sex with you was a win.

I got that, and I have spent too much of my life wishing Garrett got it, too. Wanting him to realize what he'd done. Acknowledge his mistake and be changed by it.

Now I see the hate blazing from his face, and I know just how wasted those hopes were. This isn't a guy who is secretly ashamed of what he did at nineteen and just doesn't know how to deal with that. When he warned me to keep quiet—before I accused him of anything—he was acknowledging that he knew what he'd done.

Does he still know? Or has he rewritten history to a version that makes him the guy his mother and sister believe him to be? A guy falsely accused by a scared and pregnant girl who didn't dare admit she'd had consensual sex.

"This is *your* doing!" he says, setting Sadie down and pounding on the glass. "You did this. You put this zombie bullshit in our daughter's head, and now she's scared shitless, thinking her goddamn aunt is going to come back from the fucking dead, and you're just standing there."

"No, Garrett," Kit says. "We're all just standing here, because Madison has a point. We have no idea what's going on. But we know the dead aren't dead, and we know Sadie is very badly injured. So she is not coming in this house. We will give you what you need, and we will help in any way we can—"

"You bitch!" Garrett roars, pounding the glass. "You vindictive little bitch."

"No," Kit says. "Laney is the one who tried to let you in. If Sadie lives, it's because Laney gives a damn. I don't. Jayla doesn't. Sadie wouldn't do the same for any of us."

Jayla steps forward. "And *you* sure as hell wouldn't."

Garrett stomps across the deck. He disappears for a second and returns with a rock as big as his head. He heaves it back, ready to throw it at the window.

"Your daughter!" I shout.

That makes him pause.

I talk as fast as I can. "You told me to look after our daughter." I stumble on "our" but push the word out. "That's what we're doing. Kit has a breakfast business meeting with his mom. Their parents know where we are. When Kit doesn't show up, they will send help."

"They'll call the cops, who'll wait twenty-four hours."

I shake my head. "You forget who you're talking about. People like you and me call the cops. People like the Hayeses hire a damn SWAT team."

That makes him hesitate.

"Kit is their only son," I say. "Their heir." The Hayeses would never think that way, but it'll make sense in Garrett's world.

Jayla steps forward. "Without Kit, they won't get grandbabies. They won't be able to pass on their legacy. They lose their fucking shit when he goes *hiking*."

Also not true. Okay, well, yes, our off-the-grid summer house made them nervous, but only in the way it would make any parent nervous. I can see our reasoning penetrating, though.

"They will be here tomorrow," I say. "Like Kit said, we'll do what we can to help with Sadie. If she's resting comfortably and you want to come inside—"

"No. I'm staying with her."

"Then we'll give you whatever you need to stay out there, and we'll take shifts watching for trouble. If something happens, if something *comes*, we'll decide what to do then. But for now, Sadie is no better off in here than out there. You might not think she'd ever hurt Madison, but she attacked me. She went from pleading for help to attacking in an eyeblink. She's not in her right mind. You can't—"

"Fine."

"Thank—"

"It's for the kid." He lifts a finger. "And don't ever say I don't care about her."

"I never did, Garrett."

"Get the stuff, then. First-aid kit. Hot water. Towels."

"We'll get everything we can find, and we'll talk you through it."

TWENTY-EIGHT

Sadie's wounds have been cleaned and bandaged, and we've given them half the blankets and pillows in the house, overcompensating in the guilt of leaving them outside as the temperature drops. There's a propane fireplace on the deck, and we made sure Garrett got that working and tucked himself and Sadie into a warm spot by the door, where we can see them.

As we gathered and shared whatever Garrett might need, we picked at dinner. Now that Garrett and Sadie are settled, we're moving around the room, checking the doors and tidying up—whatever else our numb brains tell us we need to do.

I walk over to Madison, standing near the windows.

"Are we *sure* she's alive?" Madison says, her voice low. "She's moved a few times but . . . She's really badly hurt, Laney, and her skin doesn't look . . ." Her voice drops more. "Normal."

When I don't answer, she looks over. "Has he checked for a pulse? Breathing?"

"Probably not," I say.

"Should we tell him to?"

"I would have if I thought it'd do any good," I say. "He might refuse to check. Or he'll check and, if it's not there, he'll tell himself he feels it."

"He's a good brother," Madison says.

I put an arm around her shoulders. "He is. He's always been good to Sadie, and I'm sure he's good to his kids."

She nods. Then she says, "Do *you* think she's still alive?"

"I don't know. But as long as she's moving, he's going to insist she is."

"Even when he also saw that dead guy moving."

"Yes."

I wait for her to ask me what I think is going on. When she doesn't, I know it's not lack of curiosity—Madison inherited enough of that from me—and I realize the simple and wise truth of her silence. Does it matter what's going on? Whether we're dealing with zombies or something else? No, because it's not like pinpointing a cause to solve a mechanical issue. There's no step-by-step answer. We can only deal with what we see.

"Hey," Jayla says as she comes over. "Could I get your help cleaning up in the kitchen, Mads? Maybe rustle up something for dessert."

Madison's expression says I'm not the only one whose stomach churns at the thought of more food, but she gamely nods and follows Jayla. I back into the great room. Kit comes out of the hall, where he'd been checking locks for the dozenth time. Seeing me alone, he waves to the sofa. I walk to it and sit, and he lowers himself beside me.

"So," he says. "Moving on to another topic that this really isn't the time for, but right now, it feels like it's the time for everything we need to say." He pauses. "That sounds ominous. I don't mean it like that." He pushes on. "But since we're stuck in a holding pattern and trying to forget what's going on . . ."

I nod. I know what he's going to talk about, and I want to find some excuse.

No, Kit, you're right—this isn't the time.

The words won't come. No words can come. Just that mute nod.

He takes that nod as his cue. "Earlier I said Sadie told me something. Lied about it, I realize."

Now my words come in a blurt. "She claimed I confessed that Garrett didn't . . . do what he did."

He frowns, as if he can't quite hear me, though it's completely silent in here. "What?"

"She said I confessed that Garrett didn't 'take advantage of me' or whatever euphemism we care to use. That I claimed I'd lied or been mistaken."

"*No*. Absolutely not." He stares at me a moment, and then presses back into the cushions, his eyes squeezing shut. "That's what you thought when I said it was about Garrett. Of course it's what you thought."

His eyes open. "If Sadie ever said that to me, Laney, I'd never have spoken to her again. Hell, I didn't even realize your friendship broke up because she didn't believe you. She said it was the awkwardness after what happened and . . ." He flails. "I was Jayla's little brother. No one was telling me anything I didn't need to know. I overheard my parents talking about what Garrett did, so I knew that much, but the rest . . ." He meets my gaze. "If I knew Sadie didn't believe you, I would never have worked with her. Sure as hell wouldn't have hooked up with her, even *before* you and I got together. I can only imagine how bad that must have seemed, me keeping ties after what she did to you."

"I kept ties with her, too," I say. "I never blamed you."

"Well, I'd have blamed me."

He turns toward me, our knees touching. "What she told me was only tangentially about Garrett. She said . . ." He inhales, breath hitching. "She says you and her talked about how we got together, how we got married. You joked about there being alcohol involved. Then your conversation got serious, and you admitted it made you uncomfortable."

"Made me . . . ?"

"That I took you on a Vegas getaway, as friends, and then there was drinking, and we got married while you weren't . . . weren't sober. That it reminded you of what happened with Garrett."

I jerk back. "She said *what?*"

He opens his mouth, but I wave off the words.

"No, I get it," I say. "That was shock, not disbelief. You're telling me that Sadie said I compared our *wedding* to when Garrett *raped* me?"

"Not like that. She . . . You know how she is. She circled it and hinted, said a few things outright and then took them back, saying you'd spoken in confidence and she shouldn't say anything."

"She said exactly what she needed to say to have you suspecting I regretted our marriage."

"Yes. That you felt tricked, that maybe I'd gotten you drunk on purpose."

"Holy fuck!" I say, bolting to my feet.

Garrett turns at the window, and I see Sadie lying there, and I want her to be alive. Alive and well so I can confront her. So I can finally confront her and drive her from my life.

And I want to cry.

Mostly, I want to cry.

Kit says something to Jayla and Madison, who must have come running at my exclamation. I don't hear them. I just keep staring out the window at Sadie. After a moment, their footsteps retreat.

"I'm sorry," Kit says softly.

I half turn to him. "Why? You didn't do anything."

"I believed her," he says. "I shouldn't have, but she poked exactly the right spot. The place where I was vulnerable."

I sink onto the sofa.

He continues, "I regret that we'd been drinking when we went into that chapel, Laney. I regret it so damn much, and I have from the moment I came down from that high."

"You were drunk?" I say. "I didn't think—"

"No, I was fine. I mean the high of getting married. Of asking you to go into that chapel, and you saying yes, and then going through with it. Yes, we'd had a couple of drinks earlier, but I was sober."

"So was I." I meet his gaze. "I had two drinks two hours earlier. I could legally drive, and I could legally get married. I knew what I was doing, Kit. If you thought otherwise, at any time, you should have told me."

"I know. I thought of that, many times, but . . ." Now his gaze locks with mine. "If you *did* feel as if you'd agreed under the influence, would you have said so? Or would you have committed yourself to making the marriage work, because you care about me and you liked me enough to give it a shot."

I open my mouth. Then I shut it.

His lips twist in a wry smile. "Yep. Which is why I didn't ask. I knew if you were unhappy, you'd leave, and you might not have loved me yet, but I'd get there, and if I couldn't, then I'd let you go. I saw it as a chance to prove myself to the girl I've loved for most of my life."

My breath catches, and my eyes fill.

"Never said that, have I?" he says. "Never admitted it. Partly because it sounds corny, but mostly because, if you weren't happy with me, I didn't want to give you any more reason to feel guilty. You're too good at that already."

I want to say something—to say *so much*—but once again, words fail.

He continues, "I never thought you were drunk when you married me. I wouldn't have done that. But a bit tipsy? Maybe not making fully rational decisions? Yes. Afterward, I wondered about that. If so, I just had to convince you that marrying me was the best poor decision you'd ever made. Then along came the pandemic, and you weren't only stuck married to me—you were literally stuck *with* me, twenty-four hours a day, just the two of us. Any time things got understandably rocky, I worried more that I really had trapped you. Then Sadie said that, at a moment when I was already at my lowest . . . and she knew it."

He takes a deep breath. "She didn't say it out of the blue. She was asking how we were doing, and I was joking-not-joking about driving you crazy, me working from home while you were struggling with virtual teaching. I started blathering about how it had to be hard for you, coming back from Vegas with a husband instead of a hangover, ha-ha. I asked if you two had been in touch . . ."

"You wanted reassurance," I say. "You wanted her to say she'd talked to me, and I was happy and regretted nothing."

He nods. "Now, knowing how bad things were between you two, I feel stupid for expecting that from her. I set my own trap. After that conversation, I panicked and walked out, and I thought it was temporary. You'd come after me, and tell me you were madly in love with me, and everything would be fine." Another twisted smile. "Speaking of corny . . ."

"I *was* madly in love with you, Kit," I say. "I wanted to go after you. But you know what? You weren't the only one who worried their spouse might have stumbled into a marriage they didn't really want. When you left, that seemed to prove it."

His shoulders sag. "We made a mess of things, didn't we?"

"We made a royally fucked-up mess of things," I say. "But that's what happens when people like us go to Vegas as friends, wind up in bed, and get married after a couple of drinks. We are going to second-guess and overanalyze. Yes, someone might say a simple conversation could have cleared this up, but I don't think it would have. We set the stage for our own destruction."

"Not destruction," he says. "That was never my plan. Even though you didn't come after me, I wasn't done. Hell, when I signed the divorce papers, I wasn't done. It was a step in the new plan. We made a mistake. Time to undo it and start over. I'd win you back after you were free and clear. But then Anna died and you got custody of

Madison . . . and if I tried wooing you then, I'd have worried I was striking while you were weak, like Sadie did with me. I needed to bide my time, and then launch a fresh seduction with something like coming to the island to help you solve the case of the staged curse hexes."

"That's working very well," I say with a straight face. "It's been terribly romantic so far."

He sputters a laugh.

I sober. "I'm sorry you were dragged into this."

"I'm not." He holds my gaze. "Whatever happens, there will never be one moment where I wish I hadn't come. Where I would have rather you faced this on your own."

"On her own?" Madison says behind us. "Hey, watch it, Kit. She has me."

Madison walks in, followed by Jayla.

"For the record," Jayla says, "I am definitely wondering why the hell I agreed to come along. Love you, girl, but the next time you want an excuse to mend a rift with me, let's fly to a beach some-where, okay?"

"There's a beach here," Kit says. "Also, *you're* the one who asked to come along to mend that rift."

"No, I wanted to make sure you didn't do anything stupid."

"Mmm, no, pretty sure you said you wanted to talk to—"

"Enough." Jayla waves her hand. "The kid and I are sorry to in-terrupt your moment, but the light in the fridge is flickering. Are we in danger of losing our electricity? I don't know how this solar shit works."

"That's just the fridge," I say. "It does that. The storm means the system didn't recharge much, but we have a huge bank of batteries. I checked a couple of hours ago. We're at seventy percent."

"Whew. Okay, then, so—" Jayla turns to the window. "And it looks like Sadie is regaining consciousness. Let's hope Garrett got those meds into her, and she's not strung out on a fever."

Garrett is leaning over Sadie, who has lifted her head. She's on her back and trying to prop herself up on her arms. He takes hold of her shoulders, obviously telling her to lie down and rest.

From here, she looks fine. There's a bandage wrapped around her head to keep her cheek in place, but that's facing the other way, so all we see is the clean bandage. Above it, her eye is fixed on Garrett and her chin bobs, listening to what he's saying.

She starts falling back onto the deck, and he gets his hand in behind her head to lower it down.

He's a good brother. That's what Madison said, and it's absolutely true. Garrett isn't a monster. I never mistook him for one. People are never that simple. He did a monstrous thing to me, and I do not for one second believe I am the only person who has ever suffered at his hands. But he loves his little sister as much as Jayla loves her little brother, as much as Anna loved me.

Garrett protects Sadie and takes care of her, and right now, I am seeing the best of him, and I'm glad Madison is seeing it, too. I do not want her to be fooled, but she's too smart for that. I just want her to realize that her father—the person who contributed half her DNA—is more than what she's seen so far. She needs that.

Sadie is on her back again. Garrett bends over her, talking and smoothing her hair. Then she convulses, her back arching so fast her body strikes his, sending him toppling.

We all scramble to the door. My instinct is to block Madison's view, but she stays on Jayla's other side, thwarting me and Kit—intentionally.

Do not try to shield her. Protect her, yes. But don't shield her.

"She's having a seizure," Madison says.

Sadie's body jerks and spasms, every muscle tightening and contracting. Her heads slams into the deck before Garrett can get his hand behind it to cushion her.

"Watch her tongue," Jayla says. "Tell him to hold down her—"

"No!" Madison cuts in. "They don't do that now. A friend of mine has epilepsy. You're supposed to just let it run its course while making sure she doesn't get hurt."

Garrett has his hand behind Sadie's head, and his gaze swings up. When he sees us, his face contorts in rage and he jabs a finger at the door.

"I need to get her inside," he shouts. "Open the fucking door!"

Nobody moves. I meet Kit's eyes.

"No," Jayla says, too low for Garrett to overhear. "I'm sorry, but no."

"Jayla's right," Madison says. "The seizure isn't dangerous. It looks awful, but Sadie's okay."

I move to the window. "Just keep her from hitting her head. She'll be fine. We'll—"

"Fine? Fine? Does she look fucking fine?" Garrett meets my eyes. "You think there are monsters out here, Laney? No. The monsters are in there."

My heart twists, but even as Jayla strides forward to take over, I say, "You told me to look after our daughter. I will give you whatever you need to help Sadie, but you are not bringing her in here."

Sadie convulses, her body rocking up, head and feet barely touching the ground. Garrett tries to pull her down.

"No!" Madison shouts as she rushes to the door. "Don't try to stop the seizure! You'll hurt her!"

Garrett either doesn't hear her or doesn't care. He's pinning Sadie by the shoulders as her entire body jerks and heaves, limbs flailing.

Then she stops.

Sadie lies there for a moment, her chest heaving as if she's panting.

"She's breathing," Madison says. She's over at the door, and I open my mouth to tell her to get back, but she only presses her fingertips against the glass. "She's definitely breathing."

Madison's relief is palpable, and it brings tears to my eyes.

"She is," I say. "She's still—"

Sadie levers up. She hovers there, sitting upright. Garrett reaches for her, and she collapses against his shoulder.

"She's okay," Madison whispers. "She's—"

Sadie's head whips up, and Garrett screams. He falls back, hand to his shoulder, blood pumping between his fingers. A chunk of flesh hangs from Sadie's mouth. She spits it out and lunges for him with a banshee shriek.

TWENTY-NINE

Garrett's hands fly out, but he doesn't have time to get away before Sadie's on him, clawing and biting and howling like a cornered beast.

A blur to my left.

Jayla lets out a cry and lunges toward the door. That's when the blur takes form. It's Madison. Outside.

Madison is outside and running for Sadie and Garrett with Kit's baseball bat raised. I wheel toward the door, but Jayla's in my way, and we collide, each of us scrambling to get free of the other.

Outside, Madison starts to swing the bat at Sadie's head. Sadie has Garrett pinned beneath her. He's fighting, but she doesn't seem to feel his blows. Then her head jerks up just as that bat swings, and she leaps.

It happens so fast. Impossibly fast. One second she's on Garrett, and then she's on Madison, and someone is screaming.

I'm screaming.

I'm at the door, clawing it open, and it is like the worst kind of nightmare, where you only need to cross a few feet and somehow, you can't. I am moving, but it is not fast enough. Madison screams, and the world goes red. All I see is Sadie—the thing that was Sadie.

That thing has Madison, and there is blood. Blood flying. My niece's blood. My *daughter's* blood. My brilliant, beautiful, amazing little girl's blood.

I grab Madison. I have no idea how I got there, and I don't care. I only care that I have her in my hands, and I am ripping her away from that thing. Then Kit and Jayla are both there, dragging Sadie off.

Blood. Oh God, there is so much blood.

Madison's shaking, her eyes huge. Her mouth works. Saying my name.

Blood flows from her neck. From her *neck*.

There's a scream, and I think it's me. Then I see Sadie, held back by Jayla and Kit. I see Sadie. Actually Sadie—the woman I know—in those eyes, and I see absolute horror.

"M–Madison?"

I don't know if Sadie actually says the word or her lips just form the name. I can hear nothing over the pounding in my ears. I'm lowering Madison to the ground as my hand clamps against her neck. Jayla rushes to our side. Dimly, I see Kit give Sadie a shove, but she's already backing off, one hand to her mouth, horror in her eyes.

I see Sadie completely then—the bandages half pulled from her ruined face, bone jabbing against the bandages on her leg, her one arm twisted grotesquely. She meets my gaze, and I see Sadie in there. Oh God, I still see Sadie.

Her hand lowers from her mouth and her lips form the words "I'm sorry."

Then she runs. Lopes, hobbles, staggers. I don't even know what word to use. She goes. That is all that matters. She goes.

Kit has his shirt off, and he rips the sleeve free as Jayla paws through the bandages and supplies Garrett left scattered about.

"L–Laney?" Madison whispers, her eyes still impossibly huge. "Laney?"

"You're okay," I say, even as blood gushes through my fingers. "I've got you. You're going to be okay."

"I-I'm sorry. I shouldn't have—"

"No!" I say, the word harsh as I meet her gaze. "You did nothing wrong, and you will be okay."

Kit's there, using his torn sleeve to apply pressure to Madison's neck. Blood soaks through it in a blink. Jayla shoves bandages at us, but we just keep applying pressure.

"Laney?"

Madison's hands flutter, as if searching for mine.

I hold them tight.

"It's not the jugular," she whispers.

I want to sob, and I want to laugh hysterically. We're freaking out, and her voice is so calm. It's shock, I know that. But it pulls me back to earth and grounds me.

"Need to stop the bleeding," she says.

"I know. We're working on it."

"Keep my head raised above my heart."

We're already doing that, but she's in too much shock to know, so I only nod and keep pressure on that spot, staring as if I can will it to stop bleeding. Seconds tick past, and the bandage stays white.

Has the bleeding stopped? How much blood has she lost? Yes, it's not the jugular or carotid, but it *was* something, and I have no idea what or how bad the injury was and I can't answer that without opening the bandages, which I'm sure as hell not going to do.

"Laney?" she whispers.

"We've got it," I say. "I think the bleeding stopped and—"

Madison's head lolls, eyes shutting. I let out a noise. I don't even know what kind of noise, I just feel it rip from my throat as her grip relaxes on my hand.

My fingers fly to Madison's face, cupping it.

"Madison?" I say. "Mads?"

A hand grips my arm. Kit's voice. "She just lost consciousness, Laney. She's still breathing. We need to get her inside."

Don't move her. That's what I want to say. *Do not touch her. No one can touch her but me, and we are leaving her right here and waking her up so I can be sure she's alive.*

So I can be sure my baby is alive.

I physically force myself to move away, hands lifted as if in surrender. Kit gently slides his hands under Madison's shoulders and knees. Then he very carefully lifts her, his gaze fixed on her mouth, as if watching for any hitch in her breathing.

Jayla runs ahead and opens the door. I follow anxiously, my whole body twitching. Then we're inside and Kit is moving toward the sofa. I recover enough to scramble past him and open up the sofa bed.

He lowers Madison onto it. I force myself to wait until she's situated. Then I'm checking her breathing, her heart rate, everything I can to assure myself she's alive.

She's breathing. It's shallow, though. Weak.

"She's lost too much blood," I say.

"Can we do something about that?" Jayla asks.

I run to the first-aid book we'd pulled from my library when we'd been trying to help Sadie. It's over by the window, where we'd been relaying instructions. I'm halfway there when I see Garrett.

Garrett.

We forgot about Garrett.

He'd been lying only a few feet from Madison, but no one had even registered it. We'd been so focused on Madison. Now I see him, and he sees me. He's on his side, doubled almost in half, one hand pawing at the glass, leaving bloodied smears.

His lips form two words. "Help me."

"Garrett," I say. "Oh God. Garrett."

Jayla runs over as Kit stays with Madison.

She sees Garrett and whispers, "Fuck."

He's hurt, and I have no idea how badly. There's blood everywhere. A chunk of flesh hangs over one eye. Blood soaks his shoulder. There's more blood soaking his midriff, where his shirt is torn, but he's hunched over, one hand to his stomach, and we can't see his injuries.

"Laney?" Jayla whispers. "Is that . . . ?"

I follow her finger. She's pointing at his hand. At first I don't see what she's indicating. Then I do. What looked like a pinkish red knuckle isn't a knuckle at all. It's a bulge of intestine.

"What did Sadie do to him?" Jayla whispers.

"It wasn't Sadie," I say. "It was whatever I saw in her before. Sadie's still in there." *She came back and saw what she'd done to Madison. That's why she ran.* "But there's something else, too, and it . . ." I shudder.

"It can do that," Jayla says. "Whatever *that* is."

It can do worse. So much worse.

"What do we do?" Jayla says.

I look at Garrett. He's alive. Undoubtedly alive, his face a mask of shock. He starts to shake, but his gaze stays on mine, pleading.

"We can't bring him inside," she says.

"I know," I say. "Then I have to go out there and try to help him."

"The hell you are."

I rip from Garrett's gaze and lock with Jayla's. "The hell I *am*. Madison nearly died going out there to save him. When she wakes up—because she *will* wake up—I am not telling her that I sat here and watched her father die."

"I'll do it," Kit says from the sofa bed.

"No, I—"

"Let me rephrase that. I *am* doing it." He rises so I can see him in the growing darkness. "Not to pull guy-rank here, but if something goes wrong, I can subdue him more easily than either of you two. Yes, I know that whatever's out there gives Sadie some kind of superhuman strength, but Garrett's not at that stage yet. If I see any hint that it's not him, I'm getting back in here and leaving him to die. Could you do that, Laney? Or would you wait to be sure?"

"Go," Jayla says. "I'll cover you."

Kit motions for me to switch spots with him. I pause only a moment before doing it. He's right. I'll hesitate before running back inside. I'd need to be sure. Kit won't.

"I'm going to take a look at his wounds," Kit says to me. "Then I'll come back in and get what I can. If anything happens, don't come out after me."

"That better not apply to me," Jayla says. "Because if anything happens, I sure as hell am going out after you."

He manages a weak smile. "Oh, I'm counting on it. But Laney stays with Madison."

"Agreed," Jayla says.

I don't answer. He's right, and I will stay here for Madison, but there's no way of saying that without sounding as if every fiber in me wouldn't be screaming to help him.

As Kit unlocks the door, my gaze slides to Garrett. I see the first-aid book and remember that's what I'd been going for. It'll have to wait. I won't leave Madison's side—no matter what—but nor can I start leafing through a book while Kit is outside.

Kit closes the door.

"Don't lock it," I say.

"I wasn't going to," Jayla says.

"I meant don't let Kit lock it."

Kit lifts a hand, clearly hearing me. Once his back is turned away, Jayla eases the door open a half inch, and I'm sure not arguing with that. She needs to be ready in case anything happens.

Garrett sees Kit coming, as if spotting his reflection. His head swivels to watch. He says something I don't hear, and Kit replies.

Kit continues talking, something reassuring, as he very slowly approaches Garrett, tensed for trouble. When Garrett's head shoots up, Kit freezes and Jayla shoves the door open. But Garrett doesn't move. His gaze is fixed on something to his right. A figure on the deck stairs.

"Kit!" I shout.

Kit backpedals toward the door. Then he stops. The figure continues up the stairs, but I can't see more than a dim shape in the twilight. My brain insists that's wrong. There's a motion-detecting light that should be turning on and illuminating the figure. But that light stays off, and the figure keeps climbing.

"Laney?" Jayla says. "Are you seeing . . . ?"

She trails off, as if she can't bring herself to finish. I am seeing it. Sadie is at the top of the stairs. Except it's not broken Sadie, ruined Sadie. It's Sadie as she'd looked last night, in her perfectly clean sweatshirt and yoga pants, her blond hair swept back.

The figure stretches one hand toward Kit.

"Kit!" I shout.

Jayla reaches to yank Kit inside, but he's already dashing through. He grabs the door, slams it, and locks it.

Outside the window, the figure stays poised at the top of the deck stairs, on the edge, bedecked in shadows that seem to swirl around her. She's still reaching out, but now her hand is extended toward Garrett, who's on his feet.

Garrett is on his feet, one hand clenched to his stomach, holding in his intestines, the other outstretched to his sister. To this vision of his sister, whole and smiling and reaching for him.

"No!" I shout. "Garrett! It's not her!"

Kit bangs on the glass to get Garrett's attention. Jayla shouts for him to snap the fuck out of it, to see that it's obviously not Sadie.

The figure turns and heads back down the deck stairs. Garrett lurches after her. I run halfway to the door before stopping myself.

We all shout for Garrett. Jayla and Kit smack the window. Garrett doesn't hear us. He doesn't care.

There is nothing we can do.

No, strike that. Face the truth. The ugly truth. There is nothing we *will* do, and it isn't about Garrett or what he did to me or whether he'd help any of us. It is about Madison.

I will not open that door. I will not let Kit or Jayla risk their lives going out to stop Garrett, and I will not take a chance of letting something in this house with Madison. That door isn't opening again until help arrives.

I'm sorry, Garrett. I am truly sorry, and I only hope our daughter forgives us for what I am doing. I tried to help you. But you are going to follow that wraith of your sister wherever she leads, and it makes you an amazing brother, but it also means that I need to let you choose that path and not drag anyone along with you.

We keep shouting. Keep pounding. Keep cursing him. And he keeps walking, staggering now while he holds in his goddamn intestines.

Garrett reaches the first step, and nearly falls face-first, but he has the wherewithal to take a hand from his stomach and clasp the railing.

One step.

Two steps.

The figure of Sadie is gone now, but he's still moving down the stairs. He's almost to the bottom when his body jerks forward. I think he's lost his balance from the pain. Then I see he's tripped over a vine.

He yanks his foot up, impatient, but when he tries to move, the vine is still wrapped around his ankle. He pulls again. It's only a vine, after all. A thin strand of vegetation emerging from under the wooden deck, life taking root in the cracks between the rocks.

"Just stop, damn it," Jayla says. "Untangle the damn vine, and snap out of it."

That's all it might take. An irritation, that damnable vine, making him pause to pluck it from his ankle, giving his brain time to realize the figure wasn't Sadie, couldn't have been Sadie.

Garrett lifts his leg to swipe at the vine and . . .

Blood sprays from his ankle. I twitch, not comprehending what I'm seeing. Garrett screams. He lets go of his stomach, and his intestines tumble out.

"Oh God," Jayla says.

"The vine," Kit manages, stumbling over the words, as if unable to believe what he's seeing. "The vine . . ."

The vine is gone now. Disappeared into the flesh of Garrett's ankle like razor wire, and blood is spurting, and Garrett is screaming, and when he pulls—

Kit wheels, his hands going to my shoulders as he turns me away. It's too late. I already saw, and even if I didn't see, Garrett's screams would tell me what happened.

The vine cut through his ankle. Through flesh and bone, his foot falling free.

Through *bone*?

Not possible. That is not—

I glance back, and Garrett is on the ground, and vines are whipping over him, rising from the cracks between rocks and slicing into him and blood, oh God, the blood.

Kit turns me away, and I let him. Jayla has turned, too, doubled over, retching.

Outside, the screaming reaches a crescendo, an animal wail. I cram my hands into my ears. Then it stops, the wail cut off mid-note. I don't breathe. Can't breathe. I just wait. Wait until I am certain it has stopped.

Until I am certain Garrett is dead.

Kit guides me to a chair and lowers me into it. Then I dimly hear him talking to Jayla. I glance over to see them embracing. Then they both come farther into the room, studiously avoiding looking at the window.

I glance toward that window. I can't help myself. I don't see Garrett, though. We're too far into the great room, and his body is hidden at the base of the stairs.

"What just happened?" Jayla says. "What the *fuck* just happened?"

I shake my head.

"I saw the vine moving," Kit says. "Grabbing him. Cutting into . . . into him. Is that what you both saw?"

I nod, and Jayla mumbles something, as if she can't quite bring herself to say that she saw the same impossible thing.

"I need to look after Madison," I say, pushing up unsteadily. "I need the first-aid book. I need to take care of her."

My voice comes out in a monotone. Deadened by shock. The next thing I know, Kit is guiding me to the sofa bed and Jayla has the book open under a lamp.

"Tell me what to look for," she says, and I do.

THIRTY

We spend the next half hour tending to Madison while trying to forget that Garrett's mutilated corpse lies just below the deck. The first thing we discover is that my emergency-medicine book is a piece of shit when it comes to severe blood loss. What does it tell us to do? Get her to a hospital as soon as possible. I almost throw it across the room at that.

The answer, though, is that there is no first-aid solution for this. Madison and I share a blood type and Kit is O negative, a universal donor, so a transfusion is the obvious answer. Obvious if I were writing this scene in one of my novels, but in real life that is a last resort, because we have only the vaguest idea how to do it and my *Complete Book of Wilderness First Aid* isn't going to give DIY instructions for *that* to amateur hikers. We will do a transfusion if we have to—Kit goes to rummage up supplies—but we aren't at that point yet.

The book does tell us how to treat a neck wound, which is pretty much what we'd already done, with a few refinements. We peel off the bandages down to the last layer of gauze, confirm that the wound has closed, and then re-bandage it following the instructions.

I go into the kitchen next to make chicken broth and decarbonate a bottle of soda. Yes, I'm treating a serious neck wound like a case of the damned sniffles, but my brain insists that when Madison wakes, she's going to need sustenance. Salty broth and sugary flat soda. The fluids will be essential for helping with the blood loss. Give her that plus rest and warmth, and pray help comes soon.

Madison is resting more comfortably now. Am I worrying because she didn't stir when Garrett was screaming? Yes, but she'd been farther from the windows, and so I'll tell myself it hadn't been loud enough.

"Kit?" Jayla says when he comes back from gathering transfusion supplies. "Can I talk to you for a moment?"

I set down a cup of broth and a glass of soda. "If it's something you don't want me to hear, just say so."

"It's something—"

"Unless it's about Madison," I continue. "Then I'm not going anywhere. Whatever you have to say, whatever your concerns are, say them."

When Jayla hesitates, I lower myself beside Madison and smooth her hair. "It's about Madison then. Let me guess, you're concerned because of what Sadie became. You're worried whatever she has might be contagious. Sadie bit Madison. You're worried that could turn her into a zombie."

At my matter-of-fact tone, Jayla relaxes and sinks onto a chair. "Yes."

"Neither of those other victims was in any condition to bite Sadie," Kit says. "Whatever happened to her, that's not it."

I glance over, my look asking him not to get defensive. We can't do that, even when it's about Madison.

"Sadie bit her on the neck," Jayla says, almost apologetically.

"Raising the possibility of vampirism?" I resist the urge to shake my head. We must treat every suggestion seriously.

I brush back Madison's hair. "I didn't see any marks like that on Sadie or John Sinclair. I couldn't tell with Rachel Rossi. But it seemed to me that Sadie was just attacking in any way she could. She also bit Garrett's shoulder."

"And shoved you into a tree branch," Kit says.

"If we are concerned about Madison, we can restrain her," I say, my voice even. "I won't argue against that. If anyone suggests, though, that we put her outside—"

"No," Jayla says firmly. "Absolutely not. If she shows any sign of not being herself, then we should restrain her, and we should have things ready for that. But no matter what—even if she's like Sadie—we aren't putting her out. We will do whatever we can to keep her safe and calm until help arrives."

Is that possible? Jayla hasn't experienced how strong Sadie can be. If that happened to Madison . . .

If it happened to Madison, I would take her outside. I would protect Jayla and Kit, but I would stay with Madison, whatever that means for myself.

"Laney?" Kit says.

I look over, and it takes a moment to focus on him. Then I brace, as if I somehow voiced my plans aloud, but he only says, "We need to talk about what's happened. All of it. I know it's not like listing symptoms to figure out a disease. We're talking about something . . ." He spreads his hands. "Mystical? Paranormal? Supernatural? We need to make sure we're all on the same page, knowing what we've experienced and what we might expect."

I nod.

"So we all saw the fake Sadie, right?" Jayla says. "She came from the forest or the lake or whatever, and she looked fine. Some kind of illusion to lure Garrett away."

"Sadie saw the same last night," Kit says. "She claimed to have spotted me beneath her window, motioning for her to come with me, boat back to town. That's why she gathered up her things. Only I was in bed, sleeping . . . which I obviously can't prove."

"I saw your expression when Sadie said that," I say. "It wasn't you. I also saw you this afternoon. That's how I ended up on the bluff by the gazebo. I saw you heading that way, and I took off after you."

"Illusions," Jayla murmurs.

I nod. "There's lots of folklore about seeing someone you'd follow, which leads to your death. Here, in all three cases, the illusions didn't speak."

"They motioned and lured," Kit says. "So we need to make sure we hear something before we follow."

"Also be aware there might be more to it," I say. "Going after Kit on the bluff made sense, but for Sadie to honestly have thought Kit wanted her to run away with him seems a bit . . ."

"Delusional?" Jayla says. "And Garrett not questioning why Sadie was suddenly fine is definitely delusional. Seeing what they wanted to see, and some magic preventing them from questioning it."

"So there are illusions that will lead us away," Kit says. "Also the dead aren't dead. Was Sadie dead? Could anyone tell?"

"We saw her breathing near the end," I say. "I also caught a glimpse of her—the real her. She snapped back after attacking Madison, and she was horrified. That's why she ran."

"So something was possessing her when she attacked Madison?" Jayla asks.

"I think so," I say. "I saw it in the forest too, before Sadie threw me into that tree. She had a dislocated shoulder, yet she grabbed me hard enough to leave these." I show the bruises on both my fore-arms. "Then she threw me into a tree with enough force to embed a branch in my shoulder."

"Superhuman strength," Kit murmurs.

"It talked to me," I blurt.

Both Kit and Jayla's heads whip my way.

"I—I know I should have mentioned it," I say. "I thought it was Sadie speaking. Then after I found Sinclair and Rossi, I realized it might have been whatever . . . entity is doing this. I was going to say something, and then Garrett was here, and I . . . didn't need that."

"What did it say?" Kit asks.

"That I owed it. I'd made an oath and broken it. I knew if I said that in front of Garrett, he'd have . . ." I flail. "Thrown me out the door to appease it. He already thought someone summoned a demon. And before either of you asks—"

"You only summoned a tiny demon?" Jayla says. "In return for publishing your book?"

"If I'd made a blood oath for that, I'd have asked for a helluva lot bigger advance. But that's exactly the kind of thing Garrett would have thought—that I made a deal with the devil for literary fame and fortune. Or I summoned a demon to torment my ex-husband."

"I have been tormented," Kit says. "Company profits post-pandemic are down five percent. The shareholders are not happy."

Jayla shakes her head. "If Laney ordered demonic torture, it'd have been that every instrument you touch is out of tune forever. Or that your underwear is permanently itchy."

"True," Kit says. "Although, if she wanted me to pine for her eternally, that might explain a few things."

Jayla rolls her eyes. "That's just you, goof."

"No demon summoning or deals with the devil," I say. "In case that isn't perfectly obvious."

"It is," Jayla says. "You wouldn't do anything like that even if you believed it was possible. But what about other kinds of oaths or promises? To what seemed like an ordinary person? Or shouted into the universe, where some entity heard and took you up on the offer." She pauses and mutters, "I can't believe I just said that."

"I can say, with absolutely certainty, that I have not made any promises that might have landed in the ear of an evil entity."

"Wishes?" she asks.

"No wishes to a monkey's paw. No wishes to a djinn. I do wish on falling stars and birthday candles and wishing wells. And I have wished to be published, many times, but in the last few years . . ." My tone drops as I shrug. "All my wishes were for Anna, which obviously didn't come true."

Kit moves to sit beside me, and I lean against him.

Jayla shakes her head. "If falling-star and wishing-well and birthday-candle wishes could summon demons, I'd be one of the few people left alive. I don't believe in that shit."

"I've been racking my brain for hours," I say. "Even before I realized it wasn't Sadie talking to me. But it's not as if I randomly go around making rash promises to strangers or setting up hex circles in my basement."

"Oh!" Kit says, straightening. "What if it's not about Laney? It's about her house. This is her house, her island. Those idiots copied hex circles and other nonsense they found online. But it really did something, really did summon or wake something—and, yes, I also can't believe I'm saying this—but it summoned or woke some dark entity, and that entity thinks Laney is responsible."

"Because it's her property." Jayla looks at me. "You researched the stagings. The one on the crawlspace hatch was a real hex circle."

"Real in the sense they didn't make it up," I say. "It came from some old grimoire, but it was just meant to ward people away. Bad luck to those who trespass."

"Yeah, well, this is some seriously bad luck," Jayla mutters. "But that doesn't seem right. What about the rest?"

"The stuff in the boathouse was the same. An occult 'go away.' But I did find some other kind of symbol—rougher—on the bluff this morning."

"Plus the rat king," Kit says.

"And what about the bird-feather wind chimes?" Jayla asks.

"I never found anything online about that, though it was harder to search. I figured it was just generic creepiness."

"*That's* the answer," Jayla says, jabbing a finger at me. "Sinclair and Rossi found something, and they copied it. Whatever they summoned tried to imitate the wind chimes with parts of Rossi's body. That's the one it chose to copy, which means it's a message. Not a demonic wind chime obviously, but a configuration of materials Sinclair and Rossi used as a wind chime. Whatever that original configuration did, it made some kind of promise. An oath. It called this entity, who expects whatever was promised, and when it doesn't get it, it goes haywire, killing everyone in sight and leaving a similar configuration for you. It's saying you summoned it and reneged on the deal."

"So now what do we do?" Kit says. "Explain it's all a misunderstanding, shake hands with the spawn of evil and go our separate ways?"

"I know that sounds ridiculous," Jayla says. "But it *can* communicate. We just need to do that."

"Shout it from the rooftops? Hope it hears?"

"Do you have a better idea?" She looks from me to Kit. "Then the rooftop it is."

THIRTY-ONE

We don't actually go onto the rooftop. Kit doesn't want anyone leaving the house, and I agree. Jayla didn't mean it that literally anyway. I'm going to attempt to communicate via the sound system.

Yes, our off-the-grid summer house has a sound system. It lets me play a podcast while I garden or an audiobook while I cook or music while I entertain. It can also, apparently, broadcast. Or it can after Kit tinkers. And by "tinkers," I mean that he shows me how to record myself and then play it over the speakers.

Jayla helps me craft a message. I think she's worried I'll leave some loophole for the entity to exploit. We get it worked to her satisfaction, and I record it on my phone. Then Kit plays it over the speakers on a loop. We can hear it even inside. The night has gone eerily quiet, with storm clouds hovering as if waiting, just waiting.

How silly do I feel recording an apology and explanation for an evil entity terrorizing my island? Damn silly. But finally something makes sense, insomuch as anything involving "evil entities" can make sense.

John Sinclair and Rachel Rossi wanted to scare me. So like a couple of prankster teens, they googled "dark magic" and started staging hex circles on my island. Except they stumbled over something that summoned an actual entity and made a promise. That entity emerges on my island and decides that, as the owner, clearly I called it. When I don't fulfill the promise, it traps us all on the island and starts picking us off, one by one, until I give it what it wants.

What does it want? I cannot even begin to imagine, and I don't actually care because I didn't summon it. Does that matter? I'm not sure. Jayla's acting as if we can negotiate with this entity like a neighbor with a fence dispute. All I know is that it can communicate. It is sentient, and it can use Sadie to speak to us—use her physical body to speak and her brain to speak in a language we understand. If it has the mental capacity to demand payment on its debt, then presumably it also has the capacity to comprehend the situation Sinclair and Rossi placed us in. Or so we hope.

We're in the great room. Jayla sits cross-legged on a recliner. I'm on the sofa bed with Madison, who's still unconscious but seems to be resting comfortably. Kit gets a fire going in the woodstove to ward off the autumn chill as darkness falls outside. When he's done, Jayla rises for a bathroom break. Kit starts to say something, but she lifts a hand to stop him.

"Downstairs powder room only, because it's close by and doesn't have windows," she says.

She continues walking, and Kit perches on the arm of the sofa bed. I ease sideways to give him room, and he slides down beside me and puts an arm around my shoulders.

"Madison's going to be all right," he says. "We all are. If that message doesn't work, help will be on the way in a few hours. We'll get off this island, and we'll be fine."

I nod and lay my head against his shoulder.

He clears his throat. "Not to put the cart before the horse, but when this is over, can we try again?"

"Yes, please."

His arm tightens, and he goes to kiss the top of my head, but

I lift my face and meet his lips instead. He kisses me, tentative at first and then deeper, and I fall into that kiss, into the comfort and joy of it.

I will get through this. I will make damned sure I do, because here's what's waiting for me.

"And apparently I needed to take a longer bathroom break," Jayla says.

We separate. Not a guilty jumping apart, just a slow and regretful separation, with Kit's arm still around my shoulders.

"I have no idea how you two can make out with that." She gestures at the windows.

"An evil entity stalking the island?" I say.

"Nah, that's enough to get anyone's motor running. Near-death-experience sex. I mean *that*."

She points at my phone, hooked up to the sound system. Outside my voice continues its endless loop of apology and explanation.

When the wind picks up, Jayla says, "Even Mother Nature is trying to drown you out."

"Hey, as long as it works—"

A smack at the window has us all jumping. A dark shape swoops past. When we realize it's a crow, Jayla mutters, "Now you're driving the local wildlife to commit suicide."

I shake my head. "That's the problem with large windows. I've installed a few things that cut down on the fatalities but—"

Another crow flies at the window. This one swerves at the last second and then hovers there. The sight makes my skin creep. Can crows hover in flight? When it opens its beak and squawks, we all jump.

"Is it supposed to do that?" Jayla asks.

I hurry over to the phone and stop the recording. "It must be sending a weird frequency to birds."

My voice stops. There's a moment of complete silence. Then a sound outside the windows. A steady drumbeat. I start toward the windows.

I get three feet before Kit stops me. He nods toward the deck, and I remember Garrett and step back. Then something catches my eye—a black cloud heading for the house. My stomach plummets.

Please no more storms, nothing that will stop help from arriving.

It's not a cloud, though. It's inky black and undulating like a wave, that drumbeat drawing closer.

"Birds," Kit says beside me. "It's . . . birds."

He's right. A flock of crows is heading straight for the house. Again, my brain can only throw up questions. Do crows flock? I've never seen it like this—a huge undulating wave of birds flying over the—

The flock swoops toward the house. Kit yanks me back as the first birds hit the bank of windows. They smash into it hard enough that I think I've killed an entire flock of crows. Something in the broadcast frequency brought the birds crashing into our windows, breaking their necks.

But the crows don't break their necks. They hit the windows with their wings, smacking it as they hover there, a black mass covering the entire wall of windows. They smack the glass with their wings and claw with their talons and peck with their beaks.

"What the hell is happening?" Jayla whispers.

Nothing natural. That's obvious. At first, the birds peck and beat erratically but, like drummers finding a rhythm, within seconds every wing hits in sync. They stop clawing and pecking, and they hover there—impossibly hovering, their bodies still as only their wings move, striking the glass together, like a heartbeat that reverberates through the house.

Slap-slap-slap.

Jayla jams her hands against her ears. "Are they trying to break in?"

"Where can they get in?" Kit says quickly, turning to me. "Where do we have vulnerabilities?"

"Nowhere. Everything's sealed up."

That's partly for energy efficiency—critical with an off-the-grid house—but it's also for pest control—critical with a house surrounded by wilderness. Every spot I could get a fingertip through has been sealed or screened.

"They can't get inside," I say. "Not unless they break the glass, and they don't seem to be trying—"

The crows scream. In one voice, they let out a deafening sound like the scream of an eagle, getting louder and louder until we're running for Madison, hands jammed over our ears.

Then the lights go out. One second the house is ablaze, and we are running. Then it's pitch black. I hit something and go flying. Hands catch me. Kit's hands. A light appears, and I look over to see Jayla lifting her phone. I open my mouth to say something, but the screaming of the crows drowns me out.

I fumble past the table I'd tripped over, and I'm almost at Madison's side when the screaming stops. The beating stops. Everything stops.

I slowly turn toward the windows to see the crows in flight. Some land on the deck railing. The rest fly to trees or rocks and perch there. They all watch us. Dozens of black eyes stare at us, not a single feather fluttering, not a talon lifting to readjust its hold. They are perfectly, unnaturally still, black figures lit only by the barest wash of moonlight.

Silence falls. Complete silence, and darkness broken only by Jayla's flashlight.

"I thought you said we had enough power." She pauses and then snorts. "And that's a ridiculous thing to say, isn't it? We just had crows doing a synchronized drum dance against the windows. Obviously the power didn't coincidentally turn off."

"I can check the battery bank," Kit says, "but there are flashlights in the kitchen cup—"

He stops. I wonder why, and then I hear it. A *thump-thump-thump* against glass. Not the pound of crow wings but the muffled smack of what sounds like a fist.

I look at the front windows. The sound comes again, and we all turn, until we're facing the back hall.

Along the hall, we can see the patio doors. A dark shape blocks the moonlight.

Thump-thump-thump.

I look at Madison, still unconscious on the sofa.

"I'll stay with her." Jayla starts to hold out her phone, but Kit lifts his, flashlight on.

"Do you want to wait here?" Kit asks me.

I shake my head. Yes, I very much want to wait here with Madison. I want *all* of us to wait here and pretend we don't hear that knocking. Pretend it's just the wind hitting the door. But we need to see what it is, and I'm not letting Kit check by himself.

There's a reason Jayla didn't insist on going with him and letting me stay—whatever is out there blames me. It needs to speak to me.

Kit and I hold hands. Mine is clammy, but he only grips it tight. He tries to pass over his phone. I don't take it. I'll get mine later. For now, I just need to keep moving before I lose my nerve.

We reach the back hall. It's really too narrow for us to walk side by side, but we do it anyway, squeezing in together, hands clasped. We pass the powder room and approach the door to my office.

Thump-thump-thump.

That dark shape moves as it hits the glass. That's all I see, though. Motion and a huge dark shadow.

"I'm going to lift my flashlight," Kit says.

I brace and stop walking, my hand clutching his. His cell phone light rises, and I gasp, my free hand flying to my mouth.

The figure at the door is Garrett.

THIRTY-TWO

Garrett stands at the door. Stands there just as he did when he stormed back demanding to know why we were all inside and not out searching for Sadie. For a second, I'm sure it's a phantom doppelgänger. Then I see the blood. That's why I couldn't make out his pale face without the flashlight beam. It's awash in blood, streaked over his skin and soaking his clothing.

My gaze falls to his feet. I know I'd seen—

My gorge rises. I'd seen the vine sever his foot, and it is still severed. He's standing on bone, the flesh shredded and filthy with dirt. Intestines bulge from his torn stomach.

He lifts one hand to pound on the window. Where his other arm should be, there's ragged flesh and bone below the humerus.

His shirt is slashed open, as if vines had cut into his torso. His head cants to one side. His neck has been sliced, and his head tilts, the remaining muscles no longer enough to keep it upright.

Kit lets the flashlight beam fall back to the floor, and he grips my arm tighter as he forces us back a step.

"It's not him," he whispers. "Remember that. He's not alive. He—"

"Let me in," Garrett says, his voice gravelly and nearly indistinct, like he's talking from under a mountain of rocks.

Kit steers me back another step.

Garrett pounds the door hard enough to make us jump. "Let me in, you fuckers! You left me out here to die! You let me in this house *now*!"

"We didn't—"

I stop myself. Is this Garrett? Some part of him lingering? Or is it the entity, using his memories and his voice?

If it really were Garrett, I'd want to say something, to tell him how sorry I am that this happened. Whatever he's done, he did not deserve this. His family does not deserve this. But there isn't time to alleviate my own guilt. I didn't bring him here. I tried to warn him—over and over I tried to warn him.

"I want to talk to the other one," I say, my voice firming with each word. "Let me speak to it, please."

His lip curls. "What the fuck are you talking about, Laney?"

Kit says, "We need to speak to—"

Garrett pounds on the door. "You'll speak to me, asshole. Stop pretending I'm not here. Stop treating me like something you scraped off your fucking shoe. You think I don't see that? You and that dyke sister of yours act like you're so much better than me."

That is Garrett. Not some entity manipulating his voice. That ranting should harden my heart, but all I can think is that Garrett is in there, trapped in that mangled body.

Does he know what's happened to him? Is he even aware of it? From the way he's standing, the way he's pounding, I don't think he does. Like Sadie, he doesn't seem to register his injuries, and that is a blessing. It's horrible to witness, but it is a blessing.

"We need to speak to whoever is doing this," Kit says, his voice as calm as if he'd just waited through a spate of pleasantries. "We need—"

"Kit!" Jayla shouts.

Madison. Something must be happening with Madison.

I wheel to run back to the great room. Then I see what Jayla does. Sadie stands at the bank of great-room windows, and there's just enough moonlight for me to be sure it's her and not a vision of her. Dark avian shapes still dot the deck railing, silent and still and seeming to watch Sadie as she stands, equally silent and still at the window.

I take a few steps that way, and Sadie's head snaps up, an almost crow-like movement, unnaturally sharp. Jayla lifts her flashlight to shine on Sadie, and then drops the beam fast as she makes a noise of revulsion. I don't see Sadie's injuries, though. Oh, they're there—I can tell by the crooked outline of her form—but all I see is her eyes. Black gleaming eyes. Her head jerks from me to Jayla and then back, those birdlike movements, quick and darting.

Then her mouth opens, and the other voice comes out. The one that is somehow quiet and booming at the same time, like a whisper that pounds in my skull. The sound seems to come from everywhere, and when I turn around, Garrett has gone still, his eyes now black holes, his mouth open as he speaks the same words.

"You made an oath. You broke that oath."

"No," I say. "There's been a mistake. I didn't make any oath."

"This is your island."

"Yes, but I didn't make the oath, whatever it was."

Jayla's on her feet now. "Laney is not responsible for—"

"Silence!" The entire house shakes with the force of that single word. "I am not speaking to you."

Those bird eyes turn my way again. "You *are* responsible for what they did because you made the oath."

"I didn't make any—"

"Who are you?" Kit says. "What are you?"

Those eyes swing his way, mouth opening, but he lifts his hands.

"Yes, you aren't talking to me," he says. "But I'm not arguing. I'm trying to clarify. Laney can't understand what's happening if she doesn't know what you are."

"I am me," Sadie and Garrett snarl together. "I am *me*."

"But what—"

"Do you want pretty words? I could say them in a dozen languages long forgotten." The voice spits a stream of indecipherable words. "Does that help? All of them are me, and none of them are me. I am *me*. I am not a word."

"Did someone bring you here?" I ask.

A sound between a snort and a snarl. "Bring me here? To myself? *I* am here. *This* is me."

"This isn't getting us—" Jayla mutters, but at a look from Kit, she stops.

I replay the words, how they were said, the emphasis.

I *am* here?

No.

I am *here*.

No.

I am here.

This is me.

A sick feeling settles into my gut.

"Now you remember," the voice says. "You remember the oath."

Jayla turns my way. Kit only gives me a sidelong glance, as if a straight-on look might seem like an accusation.

Before I can speak, the thing continues, speaking through Garrett and Sadie together in that reverberating voice that is everywhere and nowhere at once. "Did you not wonder why no one has stayed on this island since before you were born?"

"It was bought by a company," I say. "They couldn't find a buyer."

The thing gives its mocking snarl of a laugh. "For all that time?"

"It's a remote island. People—"

"You are not the first to live on this island," it says. "It has been here forever. I have been here forever. People have come since you humans first emerged, toddling infants barely able to communicate. They came, and if I wished, they stayed. I would sleep, and I would have peace until they were gone, their firefly lives snuffed out. Then more would come, and I would say no. No, you are not right. No, you may not stay. No, you may not have my island. There are many ways to stop humans. To send them away gibbering in terror, or to make sure they never return, their bodies never found . . . or if they are found . . ."

A thump from both sides of the house as Garrett and Sadie slam into the glass as if they are puppets. As if they are props, making a point.

The entity continues, "Fear is the most powerful weapon I have against invasion. The fears whispered from mother to child, brother to brother. *Do not set foot on that island. There's something wrong with that island. Stay away from that island.* That is why there was no one here. People came. I said no."

"You frightened them off," I whisper. "No one told us that. They made up explanations and excuses for why no one lived here."

"Of course they did. I have been here for an eternity, and I have watched you humans. I have slid into your bodies, into your thoughts. Someone sold you a dream. That is the word, yes? Sold it to you? An exchange of goods? One must never let a silly superstition stand in the way of the exchange of goods, whether it is animal furs or shining coins."

"Why didn't you frighten us off, when we visited?"

"Because you brought him."

"Brought . . ." I think back. "Nate?"

Kit nods. "Nate brought us out the first time to show us around. I knew his family once owned the property, and so I asked to talk to him— Well, I was trying to talk to his father but ended up speaking to Nate. He met with us and brought us out."

"Yes."

That's all the thing says. Yes. The word sets my mind racing as Kit continues.

"*I* bought the island," Kit says. "This is on me."

"It is hers, is it not?" The entity doesn't let him answer. "It has always been hers. A dream bought for her, and an oath made by her."

Now Kit turns to me, and in his eyes, there's no accusation, just understanding. "The construction problems. We came out to investigate . . . and then it stopped."

"Wait," Jayla says. "What construction problems?"

"Accidents and issues," I say. "Tools disappeared. Wood caught on fire. A worker nearly drowned. It was endless. Workers started joking about curses. Then they weren't joking—they were threatening to quit. Kit and I came out to see what we could do. While he was talking to the crew, I wandered around the island and . . ."

"Spoke to me," the entity says.

"It wasn't like—" I cut myself off. "I was wandering around and . . . I already loved this island. I was thinking we might not be able to build here after all and grieving for that dream. I had favorite places, and I was going to all of them and just . . ."

"Reaching out to me," the entity says.

I throw up my arms. "Not like that. It wasn't as if I thought there was something here to communicate with. I just felt . . ." My cheeks heat at the memory. "I started to feel like the island was angry, rightfully so. We'd invaded a pristine wilderness and started building, and that felt wrong, but at the same time . . ." Another flail. "I wanted to be here, if she'd allow it. I wasn't thinking that there was actually someone—some*thing*—here. Just a general sense of nature. That we were intruding on her territory, and I recognized that and the responsibility that came with it."

"You made an oath," the entity says.

"It wasn't like—" Anger rises in me. "It wasn't as if I knelt and made a blood oath to the island. It was a whim."

"Not a whim."

"Fine, it was a promise to myself. A promise that I wouldn't forget my responsibilities. That I would respect the nature of this island and intrude as little as possible."

"That you would care for it. Be its guardian."

"I guess? If that's how you interpreted it."

"You *lied*."

"What?" Kit says. "Laney did *not* lie. I remember this now. Laney joked that the island didn't like the intrusion. Joking and not joking. I agreed. We wanted to do right. Laney made changes to the construction plans. Working with the land. Intruding as little as possible. Raising buildings that didn't permanently change the island. Laney hasn't planted a single flower that isn't indigenous to this island. She *kept* her promise."

"She did not."

"The renters," I whisper. "I let others on this island. They did things to it. Disrespected it."

"So?" Jayla says. "What the hell does that have to do with you?"

"She made an oath!" the entity shouts, and there is a boom, like an explosion. Kit pushes me down. Something hits my cheek. Hot blood wells up, and I lift my hand, and sharp pain flashes as my finger touches something embedded in my cheek. I yank it out and stare down at a shard of glass.

"Kit!" Jayla shouts.

My head whips up. Glass everywhere, shards of it all around us, scattered over the floor. I scramble up and wheel toward the wall of windows. Wind blows through it. The glass is gone.

All the glass is gone.

"Madison!" I run for her, Kit at my heels.

A shriek sounds at my ear. A crow dives. A wing smacks my face. I duck and keep running.

Jayla is already at Madison's side, scooping her up. Caws and shrieks fill the air. The crows swoop and swarm around us, but I bat them off as if they're blackflies.

What matters is Madison. What always matters is Madison.

Kit takes her from Jayla.

"The crawlspace!" I shout to be heard over the cacophony. "Get her to the crawlspace!"

"Open it for me!" Kit calls back.

A crow pecks at my face. I slam it hard enough to send it smacking into others.

"It's not locked!" I say.

"Yes, it is. Madison was worried."

Shit! The hatch has a combination lock, a complicated one after a renter's bored kids got the last one open.

And why the hell do you have renters, Laney? That's what this is all about. You abdicated your responsibility. You let strangers onto the island.

Let them? It wasn't like I got greedy.

Yes, it was. I wanted to keep this island. I wanted it so bad. The one thing I wanted to keep.

I have given up so much in my life, and for once, I saw the chance to fight back.

I lost my friends, and I told myself it was my fault. I lost my husband, and I told myself I didn't deserve him. I lost my baby—

Tears sting.

My baby.

I've said that I never once regretted giving Madison to Anna, and that is true. I loved my sister, and I wanted her to be happy.

And me? What about me?

I'd felt as if I'd "let myself" get pregnant. I'd gone to a party with a boy when I knew I shouldn't. I drank when I knew I shouldn't. I couldn't even be one hundred percent certain that I hadn't—in a drugged stupor—consented to sex.

I could not keep my baby. I already wasn't a good mother. Anna would be. Anna was.

That was the start. *I don't deserve Madison. I'm not good enough for Madison.* Then Sadie and Jayla. Then Kit.

I didn't deserve any of that, however much I wanted it. So I would have this. My island. No one would take it from me.

Was that wrong?

Was it really wrong?

It doesn't matter anymore. All that matters is Madison and Kit and Jayla.

And you? that little voice whispers. *What about you?*

I don't answer. I just keep fighting my way through the birds, heading for the hatch in the laundry room. A crow grabs my hair, and I barely notice until it yanks hard enough to make the tears in my eyes spill out. Then I wheel and beat at it, all my anger exploding.

The crow shrieks, and I stop as I see blood on my hand.

"I'm sorry," I whisper. "I'm sorry."

I'm apologizing to a crow. To a damn bird.

Because that bird is real. It's not some puppet. It's a real creature that has been drawn into this, and it doesn't deserve to be hurt, because that isn't fair.

I give a shit, even about a bird that's attacking me. I have paid attention to this island. I've live-trapped invading mice and released them. I've fed a fox that was too injured to hunt. I haven't fed anything that I shouldn't because that is as wrong as letting the fox starve.

I promised to look after this island, and I did it to the best of my ability, and this is not fair.

It is *not* fair!

None of that matters. I'm not facing a person. I'm not even facing an evil entity. I know that. Whatever this spirit is, it goes beyond good or evil. It is *above* good and evil. It is nature, and its justice is blind. I broke my word, and this is my punishment.

I fumble with the lock as the crows beat and peck at me. Blood drips from my scalp and my face and my hands and my arms.

Keep going.

Just get the hatch—

A hand grabs my upper arm.

"Almost done!" I say. "I'm almost—"

The hand wrenches me off my feet. I twist to see who has me, and it isn't Kit. It isn't Jayla.

It's Garrett.

Garrett has me in his grip, his face lowered to mine. His eyes aren't black anymore. They're blue. Garrett's eyes.

"You did this to me," he says, his face twisted with rage. "You brought me here."

"The fuck I did," I snap.

I'm dimly aware of the horror of his ravaged body. Of his sliced neck, his severed arm. But I don't care. I no longer give a fuck about Garrett. I am no longer afraid of Garrett. He might be holding me so tight I could gasp with the pain, but he is dead, and I am sorry for that but I am *not* afraid of him anymore.

"You ruined my life," he says, his voice that gravelly distant sound, as if that's all he can manage with his torn neck. "All for one night. Less than a fucking hour. My girlfriend dumped me. My dad disowned me. He took away my college money, and I had to drop out. For what? For *what*? No one made you get in my car. You chose to get in, and you chose to go to that party."

"Because I thought it would be fun," I say. "I was fifteen, and a college boy—a boy I trusted—was inviting me to a party, and I wanted to have fun."

"And you did. I helped you relax, and I gave you what you wanted. A little fun."

A little fun?

Seventeen years of tamped-down rage erupts in a single howl, and I lash out with both hands, pummeling him with everything I have. One fist hits his jaw. His head snaps sideways, and there's a terrible ripping sound. The sound of flesh tearing.

I don't see what I've done. I don't care. I only care that his hand releases me, and I shove and kick at his mangled body until I am free of it. Then I drop to the crawlspace, spin the lock one more time, and throw open the hatch. When someone nudges my shoulder, I start to swing. Then I see Kit with Madison.

Kit's gaze drops to Garrett's body. It's on the floor, twisting and contorting. Kit yanks his gaze away and prods me into the crawl-space. I jump down and take Madison, lowering her to the bottom as gently as I can.

When Kit scrambles in and starts to close the door, I shout, "Where's Jayla?"

He goes still. So completely still. Then his gaze swings past me, into the inky darkness of the crawlspace.

"She was right behind you," he says. "I was getting Madison, and she ran to help you and—"

He doesn't finish. He's already shoving open the hatch to leave. "Stay here. Whatever happens, stay—"

A scream. An earsplitting scream of pain and rage that could come from only one person.

Jayla.

THIRTY-THREE

I scramble out of the hatch. Then I remember Madison. Two excruciating seconds tick past. I need to stay with Madison, to protect
Madison. And Jayla? Let Kit fight whatever is attacking Jayla while
I huddle in the crawlspace? No, Garrett is taken care of. Madison is
safe here . . . at least until I know what's going on.

I glance back to be sure Madison is safely in the crawlspace. Then
I slam the hatch shut.

Kit's already running into the great room. I follow, and absolute
black envelops me. I can't see Kit's cell phone light. I can't see moonlight through the broken windows. I am plunged into a darkness so
complete that animal terror explodes from me.

I'm blind. I've been blinded.

"Laney!"

Kit's voice, sharp with panic, then his hand paws at my arm, as if
trying to find me in equal darkness. I catch it and grip his hand, and
he squeezes so tight I gasp. He doesn't hear me. *I* don't hear me.

"Jayla!" Kit shouts. We're barreling through the complete darkness
toward a noise, but the noise isn't Jayla screaming. I can't tell if she *is*
still screaming. All I hear is the roar of wings flapping. We're heading
that way because Jayla is there. She must be.

Something takes form in the darkness. Black against black, visible only as a whirling blur of motion. The crows. They're a funnel-cloud mass, swarming, and in their midst, I catch flickers of something pale. Kit's light-gray hoodie. My gut seizes. No, I'm holding Kit's hand.

Am I sure it's Kit's hand?

I try to wrench loose, but he only tightens his grip and my brain says this is Kit. Really and truly Kit. Then I remember earlier, Jayla shivering and Kit giving her his hoodie.

Jayla. That is what is at the locus of that whirling mass of crows. Jayla. Except . . .

Except something is wrong, because she is not fighting. Jayla would be fighting like a demon, snarling and thrashing and punching. Grabbing crows and crushing them in her bare hands.

Once, I'd snuck into a courtroom to see Jayla. I'd hidden at the back, and I'd watched her argue her case with such brilliant ferocity that I'd wanted to cry with grief and something like pride.

That's my Jayla.

My Jayla would be in that maelstrom fighting. But her arms hang down, her shoulders slumped forward, as if she's given up.

Jayla never gives up. Never, never, never. I'm the one who gives up. I surrender. I am afraid, and I do not fight for what I want. She always fights, and if she is not . . .

The darkness lifts, just a fraction, my eyes adjusting until I can see more than that hoodie. I see Jayla, and she isn't standing there, defeated. She is being held aloft in that swirling mass of crows. She is unconscious.

Unconscious or . . .

I remember that scream. That bloodcurdling scream. Kit must too, because he drives himself forward, only a few feet remaining until we reach Jayla. He's dragging me, as if no longer aware he's still holding my hand.

We're almost there. Almost to those crows. Almost to Jayla.

Except we don't seem to get any closer. Kit lets out a snarl of frustration. Then I realize what's happening. The crows are carrying Jayla toward the empty windowpanes.

I try to run faster. So much faster. We need to get to her. Need to stop them.

Through the darkness, I can make out that hoodie but nothing more. The only sound is the relentless flap of wings, moving in eerie syncopation.

They fly through the window, and then they're swooping her up, Jayla's figure nearly lost in that swirling mass as I try to track it.

Jayla. Get to Jayla.

How?

It doesn't matter. We'll figure it out. We have to. This is Jayla. *Jayla.* I will let nothing happen to her.

The clouds part and the moon shines. Kit and I are charging toward the broken windows, and the crows are hovering. They stop there, and then the mass begins to separate, crows winging off, leaving Jayla suspended by only a few.

Suspended twenty feet over the rocks.

"No!" I shout, my scream mingling with Kit's as we run.

Jayla hangs there, bent backward. There is a boom, a crack, a sound that I can't even understand. Something dark sprays against the night, a nimbus of blood around her. Then her body plummets to the rock.

Kit drops my hand, running as he screams, as we both scream. We finally reach the broken windows. Something hits me, like a tidal wave of air, smacking the oxygen from my lungs and hurling me backward.

I hit the floor. My hands slapping down on broken glass. Kit is beside me, scrambling up and running for the windows before I can even start to rise. The force hits him again, and he hurtles past me, hitting the recliner and knocking it over. When he doesn't spring up, I race over.

Kit lies on his back, arms sprawled, eyes closed.

I can't breathe. I can't breathe. For a moment, it is as if the floor opens, darkness spewing up to swallow me whole. Then I drop to my knees and shake him so hard his head lolls to one side. But his chest is rising and falling.

He's okay. Unconscious but alive.

I turn back toward the window. In my mind, I see Jayla again. See the explosion of blood. See her plummeting to the rock. Then I hear a voice, rising from the past. Jayla's voice with the pitch of childhood.

"So you're Laney."

"Your new study buddy," I say brightly. *"I—"*

"I don't need a buddy. I just need to study. Talk while I'm doing that, and I will duct-tape your mouth shut. Got it?"

My knees wobble, and I want to fall to the floor and sob.

I can't see anything. The room swirls into memories, all our firsts popping like fireworks. That first time we met. The first time I saw her smile. The first time I made her laugh. The first time I balled up the courage to ask her to a movie and she shrugged and said, "Sure, whatever," in that too-cool Jayla way. The first time I dared call her my friend, feeling like I'd somehow managed to snatch a rare gem from under the oblivious eyes of our classmates.

My Jayla is gone.

My Jayla.

Except she's not only mine. She has a girlfriend who might have been "the one." She has parents who adore her. And then there's Kit, and there is no way in hell he is going to wake up to hear me say that I did not go after his sister.

Don't give up. Don't walk away. Don't abandon her, even if it's too late.

I make it three steps before a small voice behind me rasps, "Laney?"

I turn, and there is enough light for me to see a figure in the back hall. Madison's figure. She's moving slowly, hand to her throat, and behind her, Garrett's arm is outstretched on the floor. That arm twitches, and I race to Madison. I yank her away from Garrett's body. His arm twitches once more, and then falls.

"Laney?" Madison rasps.

I guide her into the great room. She's moving slowly, as if in a trance, not having seen Garrett, not seeing Kit as I steer her around his unconscious form. I take her to the sofa bed, and I lay her down. Her eyelids flutter shut.

I glance toward the window, remembering Jayla. I need to go after her. For Kit, I need to go after her.

But I can't leave Madison. Earlier, I did. I ran to Jayla and let Madison stay in the crawlspace because I recognized who needed me more in that moment, and part of me screams that Jayla needs me— *what if she's still alive?*—but it is that small, infantile piece that only reacts, cannot reason, can only feel. I saw what happened. I know she is gone. The pain of that has me doubling over in excruciating agony, but I know what I need to do.

Who needs me now? Madison.

"Mads?" I say. "I have to check on Kit—"

Her eyes fly open, and they are dark as night. I stagger backward, smacking into the coffee table. Madison's head twists my way, those bird eyes fixed on mine.

I see those eyes—see that thing in her—and rage roils in me. Impotent rage, because I want to grab that thing and shake it and do whatever I can do to it . . . and I can do nothing, because it is in Madison. In my *daughter.*

This thing murdered Jayla. *Jayla,* who'd done nothing wrong.

"Why her?" I rasp, barely able to speak through my rage. "Why *her?*"

"You broke your oath. There is a price to pay."

That rage turns the world red. "Jayla was not a *price.* She was a *person.*"

"You promised me peace. Then you brought strangers. You let them poke and prod at me, rip out plants, chop living trees for fires, torment foxes, kill rabbits for sport, pull fish from the lake and let them die, gasping on the rocks. Like I did to your friend."

That is not the same thing! I want to scream the words, but I clamp them back because it has a hostage, the most precious hostage of all.

"I am sorry," I say, as evenly as I can. "I will leave this island—"

"Oh, no, you will not. You are the guardian. You made an oath."

"You killed my friend—my *friends*—and you think I will stay—"

"You think me cruel? I would have forgiven you for waking me with the cries of the island. I would have acknowledged the mistake and accepted penance. But it was not enough. You let *them*"—it spits the word—"on the island. Let them try to summon *darkness* here. They kept coming back, and you did nothing. Then they killed him."

"Killed . . . ?" My heart seizes, and I whisper, "Nate."

I remember what it said earlier.

"You said you let us stay because of Nate," I say. "Because we came with him."

"That was why I did not chase you off. Why I gave you a chance."

"His family had this island before the company bought—"

"*Stole,*" it snarls, Madison's lips curling. "His family took care of me. They had been coming here so long that I was part of them, and they were part of me, and those people stole it from them when they could not say no."

I remember what Nate said about the sale of the island paying for his grandmother's cancer treatments when she was young.

The entity continues, "The boy's mother would still come, sneaking over to visit me, drawn back by her blood to this place. Then she would bring him, and she showed him how to care for me, how to talk to me and let me sleep in peace."

"Then he brought us, and you took that as a sign that we would be acceptable guardians. When we were not—when we began to build—you thought we'd tricked him. Then I made my oath and I changed the building plans, and Nate kept coming, kept visiting, and you knew all was well."

"All was well. Until they came. He caught them—that man and

woman. He saw them doing their evil. He ran. He ran to *me*. But I was sleeping, and I could not wake in time to save him. They hit him with his own shovel. Killed him. Oh, they were horrified . . . for a heartbeat. Then they cut off his hand. Desecrated his corpse and stuffed his body into the crevice."

"I'm—"

"The boy *died!*" the thing snarls at me. "He was *mine*. My guardian. The last of my family. The last of my *blood*. And you let those people on this island to kill him. That requires a price."

Grief washes over me in a wave that pulls me under for a moment, the world going dark before I rise, gasping, my lungs burning. I want to channel that grief and pain into rage, but it's as if every ounce of energy I have is gone. Sapped by the realization that this isn't about fairness or justice in any sense I understand. It's her justice. *Her,* because that is what I felt before and I feel now, as hard as I try to think of this as a "thing."

She is a spirit. She is the island. And I have wronged her and paid a price through Jayla. If I could fight for Jayla, I would. If I could offer myself instead, I would. But it's too late—for her and Sadie and Garrett. They all paid a price for Nate's death, which the spirit blames me for.

"You can rest now," I say, fighting for calm. "It's over, and you can rest."

"It is not over. I'm not done. The price is not paid."

My head whips up.

Madison's lips move, the spirit speaking through her. "This girl."

My brain stutters. Long heartbeats pass as it struggles to comprehend. Then it does, and I lunge forward, grabbing for Madison, but the spirit yanks her back and something smacks me to the floor.

"This is the final piece of the price," it says. "Your child for mine."

"No," says a hoarse voice, before I can form words. Kit pushes up from the floor and wobbles toward us. "No."

He pauses midstep, something pulling his gaze toward the window. The grief that passes over his face steals my breath, and I start to rise, but he's swung his attention resolutely back to us as he continues our way.

"It is the price," the entity says. "The girl—"

"Laney's child for yours," Kit says. "I understand that. But if you kill Madison, Laney will never stay. She'll leave and not look back. She'll leave you to anyone who wants you."

"Then I will kill every human who comes after her. Innocent or guilty. Grown or child. I will slaughter them the way I killed the others. Dead but not dead. Left to rot in their husks."

"Laney won't care."

"She will. She will hate me, but she will care."

"Not if you kill her daughter. Anyone but her daughter."

I go still, my gaze rising to his, but he's moving toward Madison, looking only at the thing in her, talking only to it.

"I did this," he says, his voice low.

"No!" I say. "You . . ."

I keep talking, keep arguing, but Kit drowns me out. "I bought the island. I gave it to her. A bribe so she'd see what life with me would be like. All her dreams come true." His mouth twists. "I tried to trap her with this island, but it wasn't enough, and I left her with a dream she couldn't afford. The only way she could keep that dream alive was to let others come here. I gave her no choice."

"He didn't trap me," I say. "I had a choice. I always had a choice."

But Kit doesn't hear me, and she doesn't either. She only hears him.

When I grab for Kit, Madison's hand flicks up, almost casually, and that force throws me back.

"Don't you dare!" I scream. "Kill either of them, and I will leave you and I won't care who dies."

"You will care . . . if one of them still lives. If I hold their lives in my hand. But I only need one."

"Take me," Kit says.

I scream with everything I have. Scream to drown him out as I fight the force that holds me from him. That force slams into my mouth, stealing my air, making me choke, unable to speak, to scream, to shout.

"Take me," Kit says. "I'll pay the rest of the price."

There is a pause. One terrible heartbeat of a pause, the room utterly silent, as I fight so hard I black out and surge back. And then the entity says, "Done."

Kit turns to look at me. His face is twisted with sadness as he struggles for something like a smile. "I love—"

The entity doesn't let him finish. She hits him with that force, and he sails across the room, slamming into the wall, his head snapping back. He crumples to the floor as I inwardly scream, still unable to make a sound, to move a muscle. Then a figure appears, hobbling down the hall.

Sadie.

She bends before Kit's unconscious form, wraps her fingers in his short curls, and heaves. I try to scream again, and the world goes black with my trying. The last thing I see is Sadie dragging Kit through the broken window, dragging him away into the darkness.

THIRTY-FOUR

The moment Kit and Sadie disappear into the night, whatever force holds me down evaporates. I shoot to my feet and race to the window, expecting at any moment that the force will shove me back. It doesn't. The entity is focused on Kit. On her prize. She has him, and nothing I can do will change it.

Oh, we will see about that. He is alive, and I am going to—

"Laney?"

I stop, skidding on the broken glass. I turn slowly, almost reluctantly, because I know what I will see. The one thing that could stop me.

Madison is on her feet, wobbling, her hand to the bandages over her throat.

"Get in the crawlspace," I say as I race back to her. "I'll lock you in there."

"No."

"Yes! That thing has Kit, and—"

"I know, and I am going with you." She takes my arm, her grip weak but firm, and starts for the door.

★ ★ ★

We are outside, and I struggle to focus, feeling as if I'm being wrenched apart by two colossuses booming in my head.

What the hell are you doing taking Madison out here?

Move faster! That thing took Kit! It has Kit.

The second one wins out. It should be an easier fight. Not only does Madison insist on coming with me, but she's hardly safe in the house. Still, every instinct I've tried so hard to bury—constantly reminding myself I'm not her mother—has sprung to life, screaming at me to get my child back in the damn house.

Back in a house with no windows? Without me? With Garrett lying on the floor, still alive in some way, still conscious enough that he might attack Madison in his final fury?

No. She is with me, and she will stay with me.

She is where she wants to be, and that is enough.

As we run across the deck, I catch sight of blood below, of blood spatter on the rocks. I remember Jayla, and I almost body-slam Madison in another direction, so she won't see her.

"I know what happened," she says, her voice a rasp, as we move. "To Jayla. I . . . I was in there. I heard what that thing said." Her voice catches. "I'm sorry, Laney. I'm so sorry."

Don't be sorry for me. Be sorry for Jayla.

I know what she means, though, and my eyes fill. Madison is not a child. She has said that again and again, and only now am I starting to see it—to see the woman she is becoming.

She will be the best of me. Certainly the best of Garrett. That is what I am protecting. Madison might insist she can look after herself, and maybe she can, but I'm protecting that precious seedling of infinite promise in her. I'm protecting her future.

We run to the side steps. Before we race down, I stop and peer into the night. I'd seen Sadie drag Kit to the right, but there's no sign of them. There isn't even a damn crow left. I hadn't noticed that, but now when I look for them, I see nothing but the moonlit night.

"There!" Madison rasps, jabbing a finger at the forest beyond, and I catch a glimpse of Sadie's blond hair.

Madison is already galloping down the stairs, and I have to fight the urge to tell her to go slower. She's lost so much blood. But if she can run, then we must run.

I race after her and grab her hand. I expect her to resist, and there's a flash of memory, of me taking her to the zoo and reaching for her hand and having her shove it into her pocket. Oh, even at eight, she'd been discreet, not wanting to offend me, but I'd understood. She was too old to hold hands with her auntie, and from that day forward, she would always be too old. Today, though, when I reach for her hand, she takes mine and holds it tight as we run across the rocks.

We lose sight of Sadie during that run. Madison had spotted her from the deck, but now we're down in the low stretch with the beach on our left. With Jayla's body on our left.

Don't think of that. Don't look and don't think.

The rocks climb toward the forest, and when we are in that dip, we can't see Sadie. Can't track her pale hair. We run as fast as Madison can manage, steadying each other when we slip or stumble. Then we are scrabbling up the rock to the forest's edge.

"Do you see her?" Madison says.

"No, but we know which way she went. And she's dragging Kit. That's going to leave a trail."

We run faster, bearing down, both of us focused on the spot where we last saw Sadie. My heart gives a little leap of satisfaction. We're moving so much faster than Sadie. Wherever she's going, wherever she's taking Kit, wherever the entity intends to kill him, Sadie will not get him there before us.

We reach the spot. I know it's the right one because the downed tree I'd snuck around earlier is right in front of us.

Still holding hands, we search, our ears attuned for any sound.

"We should be able to see something, right?" Madison says. "She's *dragging* him."

"She is."

She was.

What else could she do? Carry him?

She could, with the entity's strength.

"You look at the bushes," I say. "I'll look at the ground. It's still damp from the storm."

"Sadie's only wearing one shoe," Madison says quickly. "I noticed that. She lost a shoe."

That's something. Even if she is carrying Kit, the weight will press her bare footprints into the soft ground.

"Where would that thing take him?" Madison says as we scour the bushes and ground. "It didn't kill him at the house. It wants him someplace. Where?"

"I don't—"

I stop as everything in me screams an answer. I almost brush it off. Find a trail. Be certain.

There is no time for certain.

"The tree," I say. "The oath. I made the oath—"

"—at the oak tree."

Madison veers that way, and I resist the urge to stop her, to insist on finding the trail and doing this logically.

I'm not dealing with a creature of logic. I'm dealing with an ancient and unknowable sense of justice.

I made the oath at the tree. I did it there because to me that tree was the beating heart of the island. The tree is the tangible symbol of this thing, this entity, the spirit of the island, and even if I hadn't comprehended that, I'd sensed it every time I was drawn to that tree.

My oath wasn't spoken words. It wasn't even a mental promise. I'd reached out with my heart and my fervent determination to do right by this island. I was an intruder, but I hoped I could be more.

I hoped I could be an intruder that the island might accept. One who came with respect, who came to protect, not destroy.

Madison and I run for the tree. We run through the forest and along the stream, sloshing in the water, knowing it will take us to the tree.

The heart of the island.

Finally, I see the tree, the gnarled and terrible beauty of it rising from its clearing. I see it . . . and I do not see Kit.

"There!" Madison says, lifting our joined hands to jab.

Something is moving in the forest. Coming from our left. It's Sadie, still dragging Kit by his hair. Seeing that, I snarl in rage and launch myself—

Madison holds me back. I twist toward her, but she's looking to the right. Another figure is lurching through the forest. Another human figure.

Garrett?

The other figure passes through moonlight, and my heart stops, my knees weakening.

"Jayla," I whisper.

It is Jayla. Or what remains of Jayla. The husk of her broken body. She's dragging herself from tree to tree, bracing against each as if those trunks are all that's holding her up. She still wears Kit's hoodie, and it's red with blood.

Jayla is heading toward Kit and Sadie.

I let out a string of curses. This goddamn entity knows exactly how to stop me from saving Kit. She doesn't need invisible forces to slam me back. Just wake Madison in hopes I'll stay in the house. If that fails, bring Jayla. I would attack Sadie to get Kit back, but how much will I dare do that to Jayla?

No, I have to. Remember it's not Jayla. Remember—

"Put him down," Jayla rasps.

She's still moving toward Sadie and Kit. Dragging herself from tree to tree.

"Put my fucking brother down," she says, "or I will grab *you* by the hair and drag you from one end of this fucking forest to the other."

"Jayla?" I whisper.

Madison's hand squeezes mine. "It's a trick, Laney. That thing is using Jayla to trick you."

Jayla's face swings our way. Her face is a mask of blood.

"Hey, kid," she croaks. "How'd you get so smart?"

My knees weaken.

"You really think I'm that easy to kill?" she says. "And do you think I'm going to let that thing kill my little brother?"

"Will you duct-tape me to a tree if I try to help?" I say.

"Nah, this time, I actually *could* use a buddy."

My eyes fill, and I say, "Jayla is the most amazing person ever, and I'm so lucky to be her friend."

"See? You do remember the magic words."

I let out a sob, as Madison and I run for Jayla. She doesn't stop moving toward Kit. When she's near him, she lunges, and it is not a smooth or elegant lunge. It is a broken lurch, but she throws herself into it and hits Sadie square in the chest, sending her flying backward.

I run toward them, Madison keeping up.

"Be careful!" I shout. "That thing can—"

Sadie bucks, throwing Jayla off her with incredible force. I scream. Madison lets go of my hand and runs to Jayla. I stop before I do the same, and I force myself to block Sadie instead, as her ravaged body rises, grotesquely pulled up by invisible strings.

"Stop!" I say.

Sadie's eyes go black, her mouth opening. The open flap of her cheek has torn all the way to her mouth now, and my gorge rises as her jaws open, torn lips and cheek quivering.

"We have had this conversation," the entity says. "I will not have it again. There is a price. He offered to pay it. The woman is still alive. Take that as my show of mercy."

"Yeah," Jayla rasps from the ground. "You failed to kill me, and now you're calling it mercy."

"I failed nothing. I made a statement, and then I let you live. If you took that for a sign that I might show mercy again, I can correct that mistake before you draw another breath."

"I made you a promise," I say. "I made it here. In this spot. I meant it, and you know that I meant it or you'd drive me off this island. But you don't want me gone. I might have done a half-assed job, but you would still rather have me—properly motivated—than leave the island unguarded." I pause. "Is that right?"

"Yes, you can have your island," she says. "But I must have my price."

"Okay then. Just clearing that up. You want me. You need me. Got it."

I wheel and run in the other direction.

"Laney!" Madison shouts.

Madison comes after me, and I don't try to stop her. I run twenty paces north, to the edge of the pond. There, I trample down the warning sign as I wade in to get what I need.

At a shriek behind me, I turn to see Sadie's broken body flying toward me. I lunge out of the way and lift the dripping leaves so the entity can see them. Then I stuff one of the roots in my mouth.

Madison screams. "Laney, no!"

Madison runs for me, but Sadie knocks her aside and charges.

I dodge Sadie and spit out the root. Sadie stops, eyes black as the entity watches me.

I lift another root from the bunch clutched in my hand.

"Water hemlock," I say. "The island is named after it. The most poisonous plant in North America. One of these roots will be enough to kill me." I meet those black eyes. "How badly do you want me alive?"

The thing snarls, and I don't see Sadie in that face anymore. I don't see anything remotely human.

"I have a deal for you," I say. "You are going to hear me out or I will stuff these roots in my mouth and swallow them before you can stop me." I meet her eyes again. "You know I will."

The spirit gnashes Sadie's teeth and jerks her head with those bird-like movements, but that black-eyed gaze doesn't leave mine.

"You want me as the island's guardian," I say. "You can only have me if you let Kit live. Let him live, let Jayla live, let Madison live. It's too late for Sadie, I know that, but the others must live, and in return, I will give you what you want."

"You will give me what I want *after* you pay the price," it says. "You will give it to me knowing that if you do not, I will *take* the others."

"So you'll force me into being your protector? *Blackmail* me into it? Would it not be better to have my compliance willingly? To have my promise—my *oath*—willingly? Because that is the only way I'm giving it. You threatened to kill everyone else who sets foot here." I shrug and lift a root of hemlock. "That can't bother me if I'm not here to see it."

"Oh, I can make sure you are here to see it. Even if your body is dead."

"That's a chance I'm willing to take. Because I will not look after this island for a spirit that murdered my child or my husband or my best friend."

Sadie's shoulders twitch, an odd movement, almost like a bird trying to flap wings it doesn't have.

"You stay," she says finally.

"Yes, I'll stay here every summer, and no one will come unless I'm here to watch over—"

"No, you stay. *Here.* On our island. Forever."

Fear licks through me, a looming vision of being trapped on this island. I love it. I love it so much. But I have a life elsewhere. Madison has a life elsewhere. Kit has a life elsewhere. If I am here—always here—I will lose them.

Except I won't, will I? They will still be alive and that's all I wanted two minutes ago.

I open my mouth to agree.

"No," Jayla's voice rasps as she appears, dragging herself from tree to tree. "She can't. Literally, she cannot do that."

Sadie's body turns on Jayla.

Jayla lifts her hands. "I'm pointing out facts. We're in the middle of Lake fucking Superior. You said you've seen people come and go on this island. How many of them survived a winter? Oh, maybe at one time, when humans knew how to do that, but we've adapted to a different life. Laney isn't a survivalist. She teaches children."

I jump in. "She's right. I won't let Kit die because I'm too afraid to stay here. But I wouldn't survive more than a winter or two. I can be here in the summer—all summer—and make sure no one else comes—"

"You can only be sure of that if you are here. No one comes in the winter. The lake does not freeze enough to cross. From spring equinox to winter solstice though, you must be here."

"I can't boat over when the lake's partly frozen."

"Then you will fly. I know what is possible. I have seen it. First thaw to full freeze, and you will not set foot on the mainland during that time. Not for a day. Not for an hour."

I swallow. This isn't summers on the island, a dream I'd once held.

Someday, I will be able to write full-time, and I'll spend the entire summer writing on the island, and it will be glorious.

This is a perversion of that dream, as if I did indeed find a monkey's paw.

Be careful what you wish for . . .

I wouldn't be holed up here of my own free will. I'd be chained, like Persephone in hell. Except this was supposed to be my paradise.

Be careful what you wish for . . .

I don't turn and try to see Kit through the trees. I don't need to, because there is no doubt what I will do.

I made an oath, whether I intended to or not, whether this is fair or not, whether this is justice or not.

I made an oath.

I will pay the price.

I turn to the entity in Sadie's body. "Make your vow," I say. "And I will make mine."

EPILOGUE

It's been a week since that night when I agreed to the entity's bargain, and I am locked into it, unable to leave until December twenty-second. Then I'll be able to go home for three months before I must return, and if I do not, anyone who sets foot on this island will die horribly.

Kit and Jayla's parents showed up that next morning, as expected. They'd even brought a doctor, and I have never been more grateful for parental paranoia.

Kit was fine, just bruises and contusions. Jayla was . . . Well, Jayla had fallen twenty feet onto rock, and maybe the entity cushioned the blow enough for her to survive, but she'd still broken a half dozen bones. That "spray of blood" may have been mostly an illusion, but she'd needed stitches and a blood transfusion. So did Madison.

Madison and Jayla had been airlifted from the island. Madison fought that. It had taken a while for her to comprehend what I'd been forced to agree to, and when she did, she broke down in such panic and fear that I can only be glad she didn't fully understand before I agreed.

Kit promised Madison that she could come back to Hemlock Island until I can leave. Screw school. We'll worry about that later. She can be with me from March until December if that's what she wants, or she can go back and forth, if *that's* what she wants. Because it must always be what *she* wants.

That might be the hardest part of this. I will not say I've lost Madison. I came so close to actually losing her that if I ever even think those words, I'll mentally slap myself so hard I see stars.

I have done what I set out to do: protected her future. And if I might not be as big a part of that future as I dreamed? I finally got my daughter back . . . and then lost her? She comes first. Her choices come first, and my mission is to ensure that if she doesn't want to spend summers here with me, then she will never, *ever,* feel pressured to do so. This is the best gift I can give my daughter. Freedom.

After Madison and Jayla were airlifted to the hospital, there was the unavoidable police investigation. We couldn't cover up what happened here. That is to say, *we* couldn't. The entity who did all this, though? She absolutely could cover it up, and it was in her best interests not to have her guardian dragged off to prison, so that is what she did.

Sadie's and Garrett's bodies were found a few days later, washed up onshore with the remains of the boat. We explained to the police that there'd been an argument Saturday night. Sadie had wanted me to tell Madison the truth—that Sadie was her aunt—and I hadn't thought it was the right time. Sadie had already been angry with Kit for running to his ex-wife's rescue. After we went to bed, Sadie and Garrett must have left on my boat and had a horrific accident, given the damage to the boat and to them.

As for John Sinclair and Rachel Rossi, no trace of them remains on the island. They are literally gone, the earth of the island having opened to take them in.

I won't mourn them. I won't even dwell on the horror of their deaths. The spirit of this island might hold me responsible for what happened, but that is bullshit. Here I will finally find the confidence to say something was not my fault.

If the spirit's issue was that we were wrong to build here, I'd have agreed, but that is not her grievance, and so I do not take responsibility. Nate came to the island because it was part of him, and I am furious that his family lost it to pay for critical medical care, but I did not steal it from them and he never, in any way, made me feel as if I had. I did not force him to come here either. I did not kill him. John Sinclair and Rachel Rossi did, and they have paid the price.

Like his killers', Nate's body is gone. Taken down into the island, where he will never be found, and I *will* mourn that. I will never stop mourning the boy who loved this island and who'd been nothing but good and kind—to me, to Madison, to the island itself. I will mourn Sadie, too, but the biggest tragedy here is the death that came at the hands of ordinary people with ordinary greed.

The police investigation has already moved on. There was a storm. Garrett and Sadie were caught in it on the lake and died in a horrible boat crash. Jayla and Madison were caught in that storm here and were badly injured. No one is to blame except nature itself, and that is truer than the authorities will ever realize.

Kit and I have spent the past week here together, alone and coping, reunited and planning. Kit's planning. Endless planning, almost frenetic, as he filled page after page with ideas and solutions. I will spend three-quarters of my life on this island, and he can't do anything about that, but he can make it easier for me, and so he will.

Part of me wants to tell him to step back and breathe. I put myself into this situation, and I will figure it out. But he wants to do it, and if that alleviates any of his own misplaced guilt over what happened, then I will not stand in his way.

Kit has covered every contingency in a three-page list of actionable items. Buy a satellite phone. Get satellite internet. Get our ham radio licenses as a backup. Replace all the watercraft. Buy a second small motorboat for backup. Buy a floatplane so he can come and go easily. Get his pilot's license. Increase the solar array. Build a storage unit to hold enough food for months, just in case. Also a greenhouse.

Also a backup water-filtration system. Oh, and a dog. As soon as Madison is up to it, she's going with Kit to get me a poodle puppy.

The list goes on, and I love Kit for it. I love him even more for all the promises he makes to me. He'll move in and work remotely when he can, boating or flying back when he can't. Whenever Madison needs—or wants—to be on the mainland, he'll act as her guardian— she'll be off to college soon enough.

We will work it out. That's his mantra. We will work this out, and we will be together.

Is he right? Can we make a marriage work under these circumstances? Oh, I know he's not going to be able to run the company as remotely as he hopes. That's fine. The pandemic taught us that being together endlessly—just the two of us—doesn't work, however much we love each other's company.

Beyond that, though, can we make it work? I hope so, but I also hope that, if it doesn't, I will have the strength to do what I vow to do with Madison: set him free. Never make either of them feel obligated to share my prison cell.

And I need to do something else, which is what I'm working on this morning.

I can't see Hemlock Island as a prison cell.

I must recapture my love for this island, despite what happened here. I must move past my anger and grief and forgive the entity. Forgive the island.

I am the guardian of Hemlock Island, in a way I don't yet truly comprehend. I have made a sacrifice I don't yet truly comprehend. There will be moments—days—weeks—when I will rage against my fate. When I will curse this island and want to storm from its shores and say to hell with the strangers who set foot here after me. But I won't, because I made a vow. A real and cognizant vow this time, and I must come to terms with it.

No, I must come to *relish* it. To see this not as a sentence but an opportunity. I have spent half my life giving things up, convinced I don't deserve them. I could see this as giving up my hopes and dreams . . . or I can see it as seizing new ones.

I have Madison. I have Kit. I have Jayla. I have my island. I won them all back, and if Madison or Kit or Jayla ever drifts, I will be grateful for the time I had with them. And I will always have my island. Hemlock Island and I are tied together in a bond I must cherish as much as I cherish the others.

I dreamed of the day I would be able to write full-time. I dreamed of a life where I spent my summers holed up on this island, lost in my words and my worlds. I have that now, and if it is not how I wanted it? Well, I have spent my life remolding my dreams to suit my reality, and this one should be easier than most. Don't focus on what I've lost but on what I've gained.

As I circle the island, the sun beating down, time seems to shift and sway, and I see myself walking this path in ten years, holding Kit's hand. Is it just us? Is there a child or two? Is such a thing even possible under these circumstances? That remains to be seen, but for now, I see us, growing older and growing closer as we walk this path for the thousandth time.

Ten more years pass, and I'm walking it with Madison, older than I am now. Is someone with her? Someone as dear to her as Kit is to me? Perhaps, if that is her dream.

Ten more years, and I'm with Jayla as she visits. We're two friends approaching their twilight years, walking this path together as she tells me everything new in her life and I revel in her happiness.

Ten more years, and then ten more, and I am an old woman walking this path alone, a dog or two snuffling in the woods alongside me. Are there loved ones in the background? Kit at the house, making lunch for children and grandchildren as I walk? Maybe that's too much to hope for. But in that vision, I see something that makes me smile. I see a crone picking her way along that path. The wise old crone of the island? Or the wicked witch of the north, a figure main-landers use to scare their children into steering clear? Either suits me fine. *Both* suit me fine.

I will be the wise crone, and I will be the terrible crone. I will be what the island needs me to be, and I will be what I need myself to be, and most of all, I will be happy.

It won't be easy, but I *will* be happy. This place deserves that. *I* deserve that.

As I pass the old oak, I bend and pick up an acorn. Then I press my fingers to the ground, and when I close my eyes, I swear I feel the spirit of the island peacefully sleeping. I take another acorn, and I walk to where Sadie fell for the last time. I bend and dig a small hole and I put in the acorn. Then I plant the other beside the huge oak for Nate, forever bound to the spirit of this island.

I put the acorns in, cover them up, and take a moment to reflect before I rise and continue along the path, seeing what my island needs from me today.

ACKNOWLEDGMENTS

While I've been writing short fiction horror all my life, it's never been the right time to try a full-length horror novel . . . and I've been waiting.

So first, a huge thanks to my agent, Lucienne Diver, who knew I'd been waiting and mentioned that if I wanted to write that horror novel, 2021 was a good time to do it.

Thanks to both Lucienne and my longtime writing buddy, Melissa Marr, for helping me mold a pitch into shape.

Next, thanks to Michael Homler at St. Martin's Press, who saw promise in my pitch and bought it.

Finally, thanks again to Michael, for his editorial advice, and also to Lucienne, for hers. Thanks, too, to writing group member and fellow author Christine Rees, who read an early draft and provided excellent suggestions. You all made this book so much better.

ABOUT THE AUTHOR

Kelley Armstrong graduated with a degree in psychology and then studied computer programming. Now she is a full-time writer and parent, and she lives with her husband and three children in rural Ontario, Canada. She is the author of the Rockton mystery series, featuring Detective Casey Duncan, which begins with *City of the Lost*, and the novel *Wherever She Goes*. She is the editor of the young adult anthology *Life Is Short and Then You Die*.